I0785217

STEPHANIE PAIGE KING

ii

FRAZZLED MOMS PLAY MATCHMAKER

Stephanie Paige King

For the real Zola, who was kind, lovely, and the very best
Granny there ever was.

Chapter 1

Dana

For Dana Harding, plotting fake crimes came easy, but managing her actual life was harder than getting away with murder. She clicked between two browser pages—"meal prepping for picky eaters" and "makeshift weapons one might find in a library." A search to keep her family alive, another to kill her characters. The dryer beeped, demanding she pause her research and roll back into reality.

She pushed away from the desk in her leather office chair, prized for its highly sought-after lumbar support, and swiveled to reach a laundry basket. After years spent using the breakfast bar as her workspace, her husband, Will, transformed half of the utility room into her official writing nook. As official as a room shared with dryer lint and large appliances could be, anyway.

To reach her new desk, she had to sidestep a pile of her sons' gym clothes, but this writing haven had something she'd never had before—a door. Unfortunately, closing it trapped her in the only humid spot in Lubbock, Texas, with poor ventilation and the constant rumble of machines. Still, it was progress.

"Mom, can I use your credit card to buy this swimsuit?" Leah, the recent high school graduate, leaned against the doorjamb, her eyes glued to her phone.

"I already bought you one at the beginning of summer, remember?" Dana transferred an armful of warm towels from the dryer into the basket.

"You bought me a boring one-piece for camp. I can't wear that thing to the pool at college. Everyone will think I'm in a religious cult."

"Modesty is always in style, sweetie," said Dana.

"Real world modesty and church camp swimwear aren't even in the same league."

Dana shook a towel out of the basket and folded it. "A second new swimsuit would fall under nonessential expenses, which we agreed you would use your graduation money for."

Leah finally looked up from her device and shifted into debate mode, the same tone that would serve her well someday in a courtroom cross-examination. "Based on my previously stated reason for needing a new one, technically, it would count as a *school expense,* which you and Dad already agreed to cover."

This argument could spiral into a full afternoon of Teen Rationalization Decathlon, and Dana's manuscript was waiting. "Before I even consider paying for it, I want the price and a picture."

"It's right here." Leah turned her phone around as if presenting evidence to a jury. The bikini on the screen left very little to the imagination but somehow covered a lot of financial ground with its steep price tag.

Dana flinched. "Absolutely not. You'd have more modest swimwear if you wore the Caraway triplets' outgrown training underwear."

The Caraways, Hunter and Josie, lived across the cul-de-sac with a trio of four-year-olds in their pants-optional phase.

"I'm an adult now and moving out in a week. I can wear whatever I want."

"Funny," Dana said. "Adults usually pay for their own stuff. They also don't have to ask to borrow their moms' credit cards."

"This is so unfair," Leah stomped away, no doubt rolling her eyes.

Leah's moods changed faster than a pop star's costume mid-concert, and ever since the Texas Tech acceptance packet arrived, Dana had been dragged along for the show. One moment, she was teary-eyed, convinced her oldest had only learned to talk last week. The next, Leah's sass and sharp opinions had Dana counting the days until real life knocked her down a peg and maybe, just maybe, taught her some gratitude for the parents who'd worked so hard to give her a good life.

She'd barely returned to her desk when another Harding child interrupted her train of thought. "Hey, Mom. What's for dinner?"

Nate, fifteen, was in the throes of the world's longest growth spurt. Between that and daily football camp, his insatiable appetite threatened to put the family in the poorhouse.

"I made your lunch an hour ago. Are you starving already?"

"No, I'm just mentally preparing."

Here was a wild thought—someone else could plan dinner for a change. "I promise I'll let you know what we're having as soon as I know myself, but I need a solid hour to work, okay?"

"After that, can we get in some driving practice?"

Dana's eye twitched. Nate's lead foot turned every driving lesson into an exercise in survival rather than anything remotely educational. His refusal—or inability—to keep a two-second following distance was especially distressing. Had public schools abandoned the "one Mississippi, two Mississippi" method of counting seconds? Only through God's grace and Dana's well-timed screams had he avoided rear-ending someone so far.

Still, more hours behind the wheel lowered the odds of a novice mistake once Nate got his license. So, despite her terror, Dana agreed to ride along. "Sure, but first entertain your brother so I can get a little writing done."

As if on cue, Adam yelled from the kitchen. "Mo-om. Didn't you say I had an orthodontist appointment?"

"It's not until—" Dana glanced at her phone and smacked

her forehead. Time was not on her side today. "Good call, buddy. We've gotta get a move on, or we'll be late."

"Do we still get to go driving?" asked Nate.

"I'll do my best, but it'll depend on how long the appointment takes."

Nate huffed. "You always make time for Adam and Leah, but I'm the forgotten middle child."

She tipped her head to the side, brow creased. "I'm sorry, what was your name again?"

"Hilarious, Mom."

"Look, there are only so many hours in a day, and this one's getting away from me. But I'll do everything in my power to squeeze in time for you to drive before it's over."

Dana stepped around Harvey, the hundred-pound Bernese Mountain Dog sprawled on the tile, and grabbed her purse off the kitchen counter. "Don't let me get in your way, Harv." She followed Adam to the garage and climbed into the driver's seat of the family's well-worn Tahoe.

Adam buckled his seatbelt. "I think we need to get a puppy to make Harvey more active again."

"He has the three of you and Patch Johnson to entertain him." Her father's mutt was the only dog Dana had ever known who went by his first and last name.

"At least *think* about it. With Leah going off to college, the house is going to be quiet and lonely." Adam looked up at her through his lashes.

"Nice try, but we're not replacing your sister with a puppy. Besides, she's only moving across town. We'll see her all the time." Would they? A knot formed in Dana's stomach. Again.

The campus was only fifteen minutes away, which meant Leah would probably come home to wash clothes after the first time an inconsiderate fellow resident yanked her wet load from a washer and dumped it on the floor. But if college kids had developed into kinder humans since Dana's era, Leah might not resurface until her dining account ran dry.

"How do you think Harvey's going to feel when Leah leaves?" Adam asked.

Dana shrugged. "Like he can finally stretch out and have the entire bed to himself, probably." No way was she taking the bait. A new puppy was the last thing they needed. She steered the conversation in a safer direction. "Are you looking forward to getting braces?"

Adam's eyebrows sank as if she'd asked if he enjoyed weekend homework. "Of course," he deadpanned. "Who wouldn't be excited about a mouthful of metal?"

She let his sarcasm fall unanswered but made a mental note to start praying for his future wife. "When I was your age, those of us who didn't get to have braces would straighten out paper clips and wear them on our teeth to look like we had retainers," Dana said.

The look he gave was one of pure adolescent horror.

"You know, if you keep it up, your face is going to stick that way."

"Why would you fake having a retainer?"

"To fit in, I guess." Why *did* she do that? Dental hardware couldn't have been that cool.

Adam squinted at her like he was studying a museum exhibit. "Retainers in the nineteen hundreds were metal instead of clear plastic? That's weird."

The weird thing was how he talked about her childhood as if it had happened a hundred years ago. Her phone rang over the car's Bluetooth, and her dad's name appeared on the screen.

"Hey, Dad. Please inform your grandson I'm not as ancient as he thinks I am."

Edward Johnson cleared his throat. "I'm not stepping in the middle of that. I called because I'm baking a cake for Leah's going-away dinner, and I don't remember what her favorite flavor is."

Why would an elderly man who didn't cook plan to bake a cake?

"Hey, Pops," said Adam. "She likes red Velvet with cream cheese frosting."

"Thanks, kiddo."

Dana shot Adam a grateful smile. "Since when do you bake, Dad?"

He grunted. "Maggie enrolled me in a class at the senior center. Turns out, it's not that hard to make a simple bundt." He pronounced the T so heavily Dana was sure he spit a little. "I made a chocolate one in class."

"Bundts, huh?" Her dad had a primary care physician, a cardiologist, and a neurologist. They all agreed that lowering his triglycerides and limiting his sugar were in his best interest. The last thing he needed was to eat an entire cake by himself.

"What did you do with the first one? You know you're not supposed to have that much sugar."

"I'm not a toddler, and I know how to take care of my health. Sent it home with Maggie."

Dana pulled onto the main thoroughfare, relieved he hadn't turned it into his primary source of nutrition for the week. "Why did your housekeeper sign you up for a baking class in the first place?"

"Something about cognitive and sensory stimulation. She's pushy. Makes me play Scrabble with her too. I don't pay her for that."

Maggie had been cleaning for Dana's dad for over a year, but she was more than simply an excellent housekeeper. She was a godsend who forced Edward to keep his mind and body active beyond what Patch Johnson did. And she didn't take no for an answer the way Dana often had to when her dad was stubborn and uncooperative.

"I'm impressed. I guess you're enjoying the class if you're going to give baking another go on your own," Dana said.

"Anything for my grandkids."

"No fair," said Adam. "You didn't make my birthday cake."

"Two months ago, I hadn't learned how to bake yet. And you had that elaborate video game cake. Kind of hard to decorate a bundt with controllers."

"I don't even know what that means." Adam shrugged. "I thought 'bundt' was a baseball thing."

Dana snorted. "It's okay, son. Words are hard. Listen Dad, if there's nothing else, we're about to pull into the orthodontist's office. I can call you back later."

"No, that was it. Adam, your mouth is gonna be sore when you're through. What kind of ice cream do you want me to bring you?"

"All of them!"

Chapter 2

Josie

With a practiced flick of her highlighting comb, Josie Caraway folded the last foil on her client's head.

"Do you think this will make me look ten years younger?" Mrs. Pierce asked.

"Absolutely. Although you're plenty young and fabulous already." Josie steered her toward the dryers, set a timer, and whispered a silent prayer that the bleach and toner would behave. She had exactly forty-six minutes to finish Mrs. Pierce's makeover, clean up, and sprint out the door. The pre-K open house began at six sharp, and if Josie was late, her kids would never let her hear the end of it. At the ripe old age of four, the triplets had already mastered the dramatics of tiny soap opera stars.

There was also the matter of her mother. Marie Saldana had been watching the kids this summer while Josie worked part-time at the salon, growing her clientele as a new hairdresser. Or "beauty operator," as her mother insisted on calling it. Marie let the triplets get away with everything short of arson, but when it came to Josie's schedule, she was a drill sergeant with a French tip manicure. More than once this summer, she'd read Josie the riot act over being late.

"I'll be back to check on you soon." Josie handed her client a magazine and dashed out to get a jump on cleaning up her station. She narrowly avoided crashing headlong into a boy running in the hall. She caught him by the shoulders just before he collided with a rolling cart of dye bottles. "Slow down there, Beckett."

He flashed her an impish smile. "Sorry, Miss Josie."

Zola, the salon owner, juggled single motherhood and spotty childcare, which often left her seven-year-old son, Beckett, to wreak havoc while she conducted business. His antics were the one blemish on Josie's enjoyable experience working here. What the kid needed was consistency and structure. And more outside time.

No way, though, was Josie willing to risk everything to point out Zola's parenting weaknesses. She'd worked too hard to get her cosmetology license as a mother of toddler triplets, and she'd just settled into her booth at the chic salon.

Besides, after this week, Beckett would be back in school, and Sanctuary Salon would no longer be under siege by a loosely supervised, pint-sized ruffian. Whispered gossip and the sacred ritual of women trading life crises for blunt cuts and bangs could continue to the peaceful hum of blow dryers without threat of Nerf guns being fired around every corner.

Elisa, the stylist in the next booth, poked her head around the partition. "Don't you have to go?"

"I've got loads of time." Josie brushed a strand of hair from her forehead with her wrist. "It'll be fine."

Elisa pointed to the brown streak of hair color marring the sleeve of Josie's shirt—the only spot her smock hadn't protected. "Not enough to run home and change first."

"When did that happen?" A great first impression Josie would make, meeting her kids' new teachers while wearing dirty clothes. And worse, her mother's disapproval would stain the memory of open house for the rest of her natural life.

"Don't worry. I keep an extra in my car for just such emergencies." Elisa patted the partition and disappeared, presumably to save the day.

At six feet, Josie towered over her neighboring stylist by several inches. The only way the backup shirt had a chance of fitting was if it were a tunic on Elisa.

With her booth now tidy, Josie said a prayer that her chatty client with a penchant for lingering wouldn't be offended by being shuffled out the door in a hurry. Because short of a natural disaster and regardless of a dye stain, Josie would meet her family at the elementary school on time.

Elisa breezed back in, holding out an emerald green lump of fabric. "Try this."

"Thanks. To be on the safe side, I better wait until I finish before I change." Josie draped the shirt over the back of the lone side chair and checked the timer. She stepped into the shampoo room, lifted the dryer, and peeled back a layer of foil on her client's head, exhaling in relief. The hair underneath gleamed a pale yellow. Time for toner.

"Let's get you to the sink." Josie fought the urge to scrub that scalp fast and furiously.

"I wish my son's wife were more like you. She's short and frumpy. Doesn't pay her appearance a bit of mind."

Josie pointed out the stain on her sleeve. "I'm not sure aspiring to be like me is all it's cracked up to be."

"My son works hard all day, and when he gets home,

the house is a disaster, and he must make dinner for the kids while she goes off to class. It's unbelievable. Ouch. Careful, dear."

"Sorry." Josie lightened her grip on the comb. Mrs. Pierce's criticisms of her daughter-in-law tracked closely with Josie's own life. "It can be tough raising kids and trying to better yourself at the same time. I know there are days I work my tail off to keep the house clean, but my three have it destroyed faster than I can blink." Why did she feel the need to defend a stranger she'd never met?

"Oh, I know you work hard, but my son's wife is just spoiled and lazy."

Josie cringed and bit her tongue to keep from saying more.

The Lord himself must've been rooting for her to be on time because Mrs. Pierce's chic bob only needed a quick trim and blow dry.

Afterward, as the client dug through her purse to locate her wallet—still ranting about her daughter-in-law—Elisa came to Josie's rescue once again. "Hand me your broom, and get going or you'll be late."

Mrs. Pierce snapped to attention. "Are you in a hurry?"

"I, uh…" Josie's response would mean the difference between a satisfied, returning client and a complaint to Zola. The truth was her only option. "My triplets have an open house at their new school."

"Hm." Mrs. Pierce handed over her credit card with a grimace full of judgment. "I'm surprised you would schedule appointments this late, knowing you had somewhere to be."

Whatever Josie said would land wrong, so she let it go.

"Would you like to get on the books for your next appointment?"

"I'll be in touch." Mrs. Pierce lifted her chin and swept out of the booth without a backward glance.

Elisa leaned around the partition as if confirming the client's departure. "She's something else."

Josie grabbed the shirt off the chair. "Yeah, but she's not wrong. About my time management, anyway." Mrs. Pierce made too many negative comments about her daughter-in-law for all of them to be true.

"I should've blocked off more time for my kids' sakes." Josie darted into the restroom, swapping out her marred professional blouse, chosen specifically to meet teachers in, for the rumpled, green tee. She inspected herself in the mirror. "So much for a tunic." The hem barely met the waistband of her dark wash jeans. She'd have to keep her arms pinned to her sides or risk exposing her midriff.

Elisa was putting away the broom and dustpan when Josie returned to grab her keys and purse.

"Thanks for the shirt. I'll return it as soon as I wash it."

On days she worked, Josie left her minivan for her mother, Marie, to cart the triplets around town. Three booster seats wouldn't fit across the back of Marie's beige Camry, and even if they could, *both* vehicles shouldn't have to be littered with smashed Goldfish crackers and stray socks.

Josie folded herself into the Camry's driver's seat and sped toward Llano Elementary. Her mother had already thrown a fit about enrolling the triplets in pre-K, insisting it was too soon, and being late would only reinforce her argument.

"If you can't even get yourself here on time," Marie

would say, "how do you expect morning drop-off to go every day?" The kids had turned four last week, and in her eyes, her *nietos* were still babies. She'd argued with Josie and her husband about it several times over the summer. "You should wait until they're older. Lots of kids with August birthdays don't start kindergarten until six, and they're better off for it."

Nobody else had brought up kindergarten. They had plenty of time before that milestone came around. Besides, what rule said the kids had to promote if they weren't emotionally ready? But the two-day-a-week Parents' Day Out program no longer cut it with Josie's work schedule. She was also certain the director had sighed with relief at the news that the triplets were moving on to public preschool.

Josie eased the Camry into the only available parking space, sandwiched between two large SUVs. She'd catch an earful from her mother for parking too close, but that was a problem for later. She killed the engine and speed-walked into the foyer.

The triplets spotted her before she'd even had time to get her bearings.

"Momma!" Connor plowed into her first, wrapping his arms around her hips.

Josie staggered backward as Ben and Olivia piled on as well. "Hey, guys. How was your day with Abuelita?"

"She bet Daddy you would be late," said Olivia. "Are you late?"

"Nope." Josie checked her watch. "Six o'clock on the dot." She shot a glare at her mother. Hopefully, the wager had been something good, like a homemade casserole or dessert.

Her husband, Hunter, dropped a peck on her cheek. "Who's ready to go see their classes?"

The triplets released Josie from their iron grips and jumped with hands in the air. "Meee."

"Cutting it close, aren't you, *mija*? And what are you wearing?" The repulsion on her mother's face was a reaction more appropriate to seeing a sequined bra in church. "You look like you just rolled out of bed."

Josie clamped her lips between her teeth. "A dye mishap. It was this or a blouse with a suspicious brown streak. Would you rather me be wrinkled or walk around with what looks like poop on my shirt?"

Her mother shook her head. "You really should wear a smock over your clothes, so these things don't happen."

Josie let the dig slide without defending herself. She pulled three postcards from her purse, each listing a child's new teacher and classroom number.

In Parents' Day Out, the triplets were always in the same class. But now, Connor and Olivia were assigned to one preschool room, and Ben was across the hall.

Josie had worried about them being split up, but Hunter reassured her. "It'll be easier on the teachers than putting the boys together. And since Connor's the one most likely to incite chaos, we can get a full report from Livvie every day."

The pre-K hallway buzzed with nervous parents and high-pitched kid energy. Olivia slipped her hand into Josie's, Ben wandered off toward a wall covered in bright shapes, and Connor trailed a pack of older kids heading toward the intermediate wing. Hunter weaved through the crowd to catch him.

"Wrong way, bud." He steered Connor back as Marie's

face shouted her tacit disapproval.

Josie balled her free hand into a fist. Which kid was her mom keeping tabs on? As if she could read her thoughts, Marie sidled next to Ben.

"I are-dee know all this. That's a green circle. Purple square…" Ben identified each shape and color for his grandmother while Josie and Hunter fell in line behind other families waiting to be greeted by Miss Piper, the cheery teacher sporting a sunflower lanyard, who couldn't have been a day over twenty-three.

"This is my first year teaching, and I can't wait to get started," she said to the family ahead of them.

Hunter nodded toward Connor and whispered, "He's going to eat her alive."

Josie shushed him with a grimace, but he was probably right.

The line moved forward, and it was their turn to go in.

"You must be Connor and Olivia." Miss Piper bent to their level. "I was excited to see I had twins on my roster."

"Triplets, actually." Hunter pointed at Ben and Marie, who were still at the bulletin board.

The teacher's mouth twitched, and the color drained from her face. "Oh." Her voice came out tight and high.

"Ben's in the class across the hall," Josie quickly added before the new teacher suffered her first stroke.

"Ah." Miss Piper's face remained placid, but her shoulders eased, as though relieved at not having a sibling group of three to incite mutiny in her class. "Take a look around and locate your desks and cubbies."

Olivia clung to her mom while Connor pushed past the other families to get to a bin of dinosaurs, grabbed as many as his hands could hold, and plopped onto the carpet.

Hunter gave Josie's shoulder a gentle squeeze and made his way to the manipulatives play center. "Buddy. Let's go see where you're going to hang your backpack next week."

Connor kept his eyes on the toys in front of him. "No, Dad. I'm busy."

"Livvie, can you find the desk with your name on it?" Josie pressed a guiding hand to Olivia's back.

"Are you going to leave?" Her little voice wavered.

"No. We're just visiting today, remember? We also still have to go see Ben's classroom." Together, they located Olivia's desk, her name laminated on red cardstock. "This is where you'll sit." Josie pointed out the storage compartment underneath. "You can put your crayons and pencils in here."

Hunter pried the dinosaurs out of Connor's fingers and put them away. "It's not playtime."

"I'm not done with this T-Rex." Connor tried to liberate the plastic reptiles all over again, while Josie led Olivia to her cubby.

"Lemme go," Connor wailed.

Josie caught Hunter's eye and gave a quick nod toward the door. With Olivia's hand in hers, she scurried out, leaving Hunter to wrangle their velociraptor on his own.

Outside the room, Olivia tugged on her grandmother's arm. "Wanna meet my teacher?"

"Of course, *preciosa.*" Marie followed Olivia to Miss Piper's door as Connor's tantrum drew both knowing and appalled stares.

"I'll meet Ben's teacher another time." Hunter hoisted Connor over his shoulder and made a hasty retreat.

The hallway crowd thinned as families trickled out—

off to visit older siblings' classes or whisk their well-behaved preschoolers home for dinner. Josie envied them.

"Your turn, Ben. Let's go meet Mrs. Tyson." She gave him a gentle nudge toward the open doorway, where a rotund, seasoned teacher greeted him with a broad grin and an enveloping hug and a firm handshake for Josie.

Her warmth didn't fool Josie. Mrs. Tyson emanated no-nonsense energy. Her classroom procedures were posted on a photo chart next to the door, each step color-coded, laminated, and designed for efficiency.

"On Monday, we encourage parents to drop off at the door and not linger. The quicker they get going, the less time there is for crying or clinging," said Mrs. Tyson.

Ben took a cautious step into the room.

"You wouldn't be interested in trading Caraway boys with the teacher across the hall, would you?" Josie's question came out more plea than joke.

Mrs. Tyson's brow lifted. "You've got twins?"

"Triplets. But I'm worried Ben's brother might be... a lot for Miss Piper."

The teacher gave a reassuring smile. "Don't you worry about that. The first few weeks are a learning curve for everyone, but your boy and Miss Piper will settle in just fine." She leaned in, lowering her voice like they were co-conspirators. "And if they don't, we'll talk."

Josie nodded gratefully and scanned the space to find Ben. "Oh, geez."

He stood proudly atop a wooden shelving unit stocked with neatly organized, clear toy bins. "Benjamin!"

Rather than heeding his mother's call, he swan-dove off the furniture and landed in a bean bag chair below.

"No, sir." Mrs. Tyson marched across the room and helped him to his feet. "Come with me."

Josie held her breath and watched without interfering.

The teacher took Ben to the window and pointed toward the playground outside. "See all those toys out there? The swings and the slide?"

He nodded.

"You can climb on those and jump around all you like at recess. But *not* in Mrs. Tyson's class. Got it?" She looked him square in the eye and waited.

Ben nodded again.

"Can you say, 'Yes, ma'am?'"

"Yes, ma'am."

Josie placed a hand on Ben's shoulder. "I'm so sorry. I don't know what's gotten into him tonight. My kids aren't usually such heathens." She pursed her lips. That last part was definitely a lie.

Chapter 3

With the triplets finally tucked into bed, Josie collapsed onto the sofa and rubbed her eyes.

Hunter slumped beside her with a groan. "Remember when the kids were babies, and we thought we were going to die? I miss when they couldn't fight, talk back, or run away from us."

"Mm. I call those the good old days."

"Weren't they supposed to get easier as they got older?"

She rested her head on his shoulder. "At least they feed themselves now, and we're not elbow-deep in eighteen diapers a day. Not getting sprayed by the boys is a win."

He expelled a heavy sigh. "Yeah, well, tell that to their teachers. When they call about the tantrums and base jumping in the reading center, we'll say, 'Three years ago, they'd have peed on you too'."

Josie sat up straight and turned to face him. "Was my mom right? Should we have waited longer to put them in a real preschool program?"

"It's only a half day. Lots of young kids go longer than that," he said. "It'll be good for them."

"Olivia was so timid, and both boys acted like they've never been inside a building before. They're feral cats."

"They'll adjust." Hunter's placating tone only frustrated Josie more.

"Before or after Miss Piper and Mrs. Tyson have total breakdowns?"

"Jos, it'll work out. But let's not worry about it anymore tonight." He wrapped his arm around her. "Tell me about your day."

She closed her eyes. "It was fine. Except for getting dye on my shirt and having to face Mom in a borrowed tee fished out of Elisa's trunk."

He chuckled. "You know Marie. She'd have found something to nitpick either way."

"True." It wasn't about the shirt. Josie had been falling short of her mother's impossible standard for thirty-nine years. "I can't wait for Monday though. Zola's son was a next-level terror today. I was ready to throttle him when he nearly tripped an old lady on a cane. But after how our boys acted tonight, I feel bad for all my hostile thoughts. It's not Beckett's fault he's cooped up instead of running around outside."

"Why doesn't Zola put him in daycare or hire a sitter?"

"She tries, but the sitters are high school and college girls and not always reliable."

Hunter ran a hand over his face. "Makes me thankful for Leah."

Josie's chest tightened. Leah, who was never late because she lived right across the cul-de-sac. Leah, who could get the kids to listen better than Josie could. She would be moving into her dorm next week with a full course load and no obligation to drive across town to babysit a trio of preschoolers. Would she still come when they needed her, or would another family with less noise and better snacks steal her away?

Josie tugged a blanket over her lap, even though she wasn't really cold. "Yeah," she murmured. "Me too."

Hunter's phone hummed in his pocket. He pulled it out, glanced at the screen, and answered. "Hey, Ma."

Josie leaned toward him and said, "Hi, Em."

After a beat, he reported, "Mom says 'hi' back."

She pushed the blanket aside, gave Hunter's leg a quick pat, and headed down the hall to get ready for bed. Josie had a great relationship with her in-laws. After all, they'd paid her way through cosmetology school, but Hunter deserved a little privacy.

Josie washed her face and dabbed on the fancy eye cream the Sephora employee had recommended last summer. Back then, the triplets were transitioning from cribs to toddler beds, and their all-night ragers gave Josie the hollowed-out look of a thousand-year-old vampire. Thankfully, that toddler phase was short-lived, even if her perpetual exhaustion and under-eye bags weren't. Maybe Hunter was right, and the kids would settle into their new school routines soon enough.

She was brushing her teeth when his heavy footsteps halted in the bathroom doorway. "How are the Okies?" she asked through a mouth full of toothpaste.

Peter and Emmaline Caraway had moved from Lubbock to Oklahoma to care for her parents after Hunter's grandmother suffered a stroke months before the triplets arrived.

"They're fine. Grandpa's recovering well from his cataract surgery, so Mom and Dad want to take a mini vacation and make up for missing the triplets' birthday. They asked if we would meet them in Dallas for Labor Day weekend."

"But wh—" Toothpaste dribbled down Josie's chin. She spat and rinsed. "What about Grandma and Grandpa? Wasn't the whole reason your parents couldn't make it for the party because Grandpa wouldn't be able to care for Grandma while he was recovering?"

"Mom said Stephen volunteered to help. He kind of owes them anyway after living there rent-free for so long."

Hunter's older brother moved home after a career setback a few years ago and had only flown the nest again last fall.

"Good for him. Dallas, huh?" Josie gathered her long red hair and twisted it into a high bun. Road-tripping with little kids wasn't exactly a vacation, but they'd done worse. At least now the triplets could talk instead of screaming for three hundred miles straight. "What exactly did they have in mind for us to do there?" Josie aimed for a casual tone, even as the idea of leaving town on short notice turned her stomach. Only a week to rearrange her work schedule, pack for three kids, and pretend this was all totally manageable.

"She mentioned the zoo, possibly an indoor water park, or a Rangers game. Oh, and a tea party in a doll store for Olivia." Hunter shook his head as if the thought made no sense. "Is that even a real thing?"

It was real, alright, and those dolls cost more than some computers. "I'll spare you the details. I guess it would be wrong to deny your parents and the kids a weekend together, and it's not like we already have other plans."

"So, it's okay if I tell Mom we're in?" Hunter held his phone with his thumb poised over the screen.

Josie gave him a quick kiss on his mouth as she slipped past him. "Sure, but you get to go with Em and Livvie to the creepy doll store."

The bed shook. Josie snapped awake, heart racing. She'd never felt an elusive West Texas earthquake herself, but the news reported them with growing frequency. Except this activity wasn't seismic.

Ben and Olivia catapulted onto the mattress like caffeinated capuchin monkeys. Olivia yanked off the covers with a triumphant, "Time to go to school!"

Josie opened one eye. "You don't start until Monday. What is today?"

She nudged Hunter with her foot. He had a pillow over his head and was either faking being asleep or blessed with the ability to snooze through natural disasters, including the kind they'd created together.

Ben shouted directly into her ear, "Monday!"

In one movement, Josie sat up and scooted him to his dad's side of the bed. "It's Friday. After you guys go to the science museum with Abuelita, we're shopping for school supplies."

Ben wrinkled his nose. "What's school supplies?"

"Crayons, pencils, backpacks. Things you use at school."

"I don't need that. I'm just gonna play on the slide and

swings."

Josie planted her feet on the floor and stretched.

From under the pillow, Hunter groaned and rolled over. "No, you're going to listen to your teacher and do what she tells you."

At least Josie didn't have to worry about the house collapsing on his unconscious body while she rescued the kids on her own in an emergency. "Where's your brother?" An unsupervised Connor was at least as worrisome and probably more destructive than an earthquake.

Olivia shrugged.

Josie stretched and trudged into the hall. She poked her head into the boys' bedroom, which once served as a guestroom for visiting grandparents. No Connor.

A chair screeched across tile in the kitchen. Never a good sign. Josie made her way across the house and found the missing triplet standing on the chair to reach the counter where bread, lunch meat, and cheese packages were laid out in front of him.

She came up behind him and tousled his hair. "What are you doing?"

"I making my lunch for school."

Last year, the triplets assisted—a term Josie used loosely—in packing their lunches for Parents' Day Out. Sure enough, Connor's insulated *Bluey* lunchbox sat under his collection of ingredients. Hadn't Josie stashed the lunchboxes in the cabinet above the dryer when school let out for summer vacation? One glance at the open dryer and cabinet door above it in the mudroom answered that. He could remember vague storage locations hypothetically out of reach, but he couldn't find his shoes five minutes after kicking them off.

She scooped up the sandwich fixings and returned them to the fridge and bread box. "First, this is science and shopping day. No school. And second, pre-K is only in the mornings. You'll eat lunch at home."

"Ah, man." Connor's shoulders slumped.

Josie hoisted him under the arms and set him on the floor. "And another thing, mister. Climbing the dryer is dangerous. Don't do it again."

"Why?" He blinked with genuine confusion. "I do it all the time and never get hurt."

How could she argue with that logic? "Because I said not to." She recoiled at hearing her mother come out of her mouth. "Please put this chair back where it goes."

Hunter shuffled into the kitchen, yawning and scratching his head. The other two early birds danced around his feet.

"We get to play in the water at the science museum. It's *so* fun." Olivia hopped and pumped her fists.

The science museum wouldn't even open for four more hours. Harnessing their excitement until Abuelita arrived and Josie left for work would take everything in her.

"How about you draw a picture of all the things you're going to do today while I have some coffee and make breakfast?" Josie suggested.

No matter how hard she and Hunter tried to get the triplets to sleep in, they awoke by 6:15, like clockwork. Keeping them up later at night only stole from their parents' time to decompress together and did nothing to push back the morning wake-up call.

"I want coffee," Connor announced.

"No." Josie and Hunter said in unison.

Connor rebounded to his next idea without missing a beat. "Ben, Let's go play ball." He bolted toward the back door.

Hunter jogged around the counter and scooped him up before he could get the lock undone. "You know the rule. No going outside before the sun's up." A decree they'd put in place after the next-door neighbors complained about the predawn noise. Not so much complained as called the police, believing the screams of one of the Caraway children in the backyard to be a sign of abuse. In actuality, Ben had snuck out while his parents were still asleep and encountered a possum hiding in the kids' wooden play fort. Thus, the reason for the newly installed security alarms on the doors and windows.

Hunter deposited him in the hall with the order, "Go to the playroom until we call you for breakfast."

Josie pulled a carton of eggs and a jug of milk from the fridge and bumped it closed with her hip. "Did you wake up on the wrong side of the bed?" Another phrase her mother had used often.

"You got in my head, and I didn't sleep well, even before our very rude awakening."

She tossed a glance over her shoulder as she readied the skillet on the stove. "How did I do that?"

"Your question about the kids starting pre-K so young." He filled a mug with coffee and set it at Josie's elbow. "I got to thinking about how the boys acted last night, and then I laid there wondering if we're doing the right thing."

"Ah, babe. Why didn't you say something?"

He poured a cup for himself and leaned against the

counter. "We can't both spiral, and you called being worried first. So, I tried to blow it off, but it didn't work."

Josie turned from the stove and wrapped her arms around him. "Thank you."

"For what?" he asked into the top of her head.

"For having the same fearful thoughts as me, but also for putting on a brave face for my benefit. You don't have to, you know."

"I'm not doing it just for you." He nodded down the hall. "They can smell weakness."

Josie's mom knocked but let herself in without waiting for someone to answer the door. "Good morning," she sang. "Who's ready for the science museum?"

"Me!"

"Me!"

"Me!"

Josie threaded a gold hoop through her earlobe. "Morning, Mom. They're a little wild today, so good luck."

Marie set her purse on the coffee table. "I'm surprised the boys have any energy left after last night's show."

"I know. I was so embarrassed." Josie scooped a few stray toys off the floor and tossed them into a basket.

"Look on the bright side. At least they distracted everyone from judging your messy appearance."

Josie bristled. "And on that happy note, I'm out of here." She hugged each triplet, thanked her mother for watching the kids, and beelined it to the Camry before her mom could find something else to analyze.

Last summer, when her mother announced she was retiring and moving to Lubbock, Josie panicked and faked a camping trip with the neighbors to keep her away. The plan backfired, and a bout of appendicitis forced Josie to confess. Somehow though, Marie still ended up nearby. Six months in, having her around was a huge help…most of the time. Josie's standards of housekeeping, parenting, and her appearance were forever under Marie Saldana's microscope.

The constant scrutiny chipped away at Josie's confidence. No matter how long she scrubbed her kitchen or fought Olivia to style her hair, nothing was ever quite right. At least at work, she only had paying customers watching her every move.

Josie waved to another stylist working on a blowout as she walked to her booth. Sanctuary Salon bustled with activity as Friday was always its busiest day of the week. Josie opened her cabinet and bent to stow her purse.

"We need to talk."

Josie jumped at the stern declaration and hit her head in her haste to turn around.

Zola stood with her arms crossed and her stance wide. "Sorry for startling you, but did you send Raina Pierce home yesterday with wet hair because you didn't have time to style it?"

Josie's eyes grew round. "Of course not. Did she say that?"

"More or less. Said you practically shooed her out the door because you were late getting to another function."

Raina Pierce had cycled through half the stylists at the salon thanks to her reputation as a difficult client. Before Josie started working there, the owner herself had taken on

Mrs. Pierce until she conveniently reassigned her to Josie, claiming the need to trim her client list to focus on managing the business. The only thing Zola had trimmed was her tolerance for the pushy woman, who never stopped badmouthing her poor daughter-in-law.

Josie rushed to explain about the open house but assured Zola she'd treated her client with the utmost professionalism. "I only nudged her toward the door *after* the cape was off and the credit card was back in her hand. Elisa was here. She'll vouch for me."

"That's what I figured. I know Mrs. Pierce can be difficult, but my reputation rides on my staff, so I had to check." Zola turned on her heel without so much as an apology.

Josie stood frozen, jaw slack in the owner's wake. *Staff,* as if Josie weren't an independent operator paying rent like everyone else. The only actual employees were two part-time receptionists who mainly existed to answer phones and misplace appointments.

Beckett rolled by on his retractable skate wheels, arms full of towels. A second later, a crash echoed from the hallway, followed by swearing.

Josie would have given anything to be on her way to the science museum with her own unruly children right now, critical mother and all. Anywhere but here.

Chapter 4

Dana

Dana took a sip of her now-tepid latte and tucked one foot beneath the other leg. Her writing group had been so deep in edits this morning, she hadn't looked up from the manuscript in her hand long enough to enjoy the drink while it was still hot.

Across the table, Carlos Ruiz dropped his reading glasses with a clatter and rubbed his forehead.

"What's wrong?" Dana grabbed a pink highlighter and marked a passage. While most writers in the digital age edited on screens, their group did their best work the old-fashioned way—killing trees over pricey coffeehouse beverages.

"Bev, I think your love story here is a little far-fetched." Carlos stabbed a finger at the offending page. "I liked it better when you were writing speculative fiction."

She gave him a cool look and reached for her coffee. "As much as I appreciate your vote of confidence, I couldn't get the speculative published. Which part do you think is a stretch?"

"No one really rekindles a romance with their ex and lives happily ever after."

"Readers like a happy ending," said Dana. "The H-E-A never gets old."

The older lady flashed her an appreciative grin.

"That's not what I mean." Carlos's mouth twisted into a grimace. "The male lead always glosses over the fact that the woman humiliated him and broke his heart, and he takes her back because he's been pining for her all this time."

"It's the second-chance romance trope. Very popular. And judging by the number of my old classmates who have ended up with their high school sweethearts later in life, I'd say it's not going anywhere." Romance novels weren't Dana's thing either, but she couldn't let Carlos railroad Beverly like that. Their group had been together for a couple of years now, and regardless of their personal tastes, they made each other better writers.

"It's silly, and I'm not a fan." He shook his head.

Beverly folded her hands and tilted her head. "Something else eating you today? You're not usually so cynical about romance."

"Everything's fine." Carlos reached for his glasses but stopped short of putting them on. Instead, he pointed the earpiece at the chapter in front of him. "If people are rekindling old flames, it's probably because the dating pool is nothing but a festering pond full of snapping turtles. Maybe it's easier to return to the devil you know...or whatever that saying is."

Beverly clucked her tongue. "Well, don't you paint a pretty picture."

"Yeah, well. My ex-wife just got engaged."

"Oh, sweetie. Were you hoping to get back with her?" Bev reached over and patted Carlos's arm.

"Nooo." He shook his head as if clearing away the very thought. "We're better co-parents apart than we ever were married. But I'll admit. I'm a little envious she found someone before I did."

Dana capped her highlighter and set it aside. "Have you tried a dating app? There are all kinds now."

Thank goodness she'd met Will back in the pre-swipe era. A librarian who rarely left the house after work, she'd only landed a hot, broke, aspiring chef because he came to the library to use the computers for free. Dating online now? She shuddered.

Carlos stared at her, lips pressed into a thin line. "The last woman I met on an app brought her emotional support ferret on our date."

Beverly snickered. "That's not so bad. Everyone in your generation has an emotional crutch of some kind, don't they?"

He blinked. "A *ferret,* Bev. In her purse. So, I'm wondering how my ex, who is a remarkably difficult person, met her soulmate, and I can't find a single woman I'd want to see twice, let alone spend my life with."

"Maybe your standards are too high," Dana said.

Carlos threw his hands up. "Forgive me for not wanting to marry someone whose plus-one is a purse otter with abandonment issues."

"Easy there, Romeo." Bev hefted her oversized tote onto her lap and began stuffing papers into it. "I hate to bail when you've got more feelings to unpack, but I've got a doctor's appointment." She paused, giving Carlos a meaningful look. "Don't give up on love. There are still fish in that snapping turtle pond you mentioned, and they can't all be weirdos."

Carlos handed her the copy of her chapters he'd been editing. "I'm done unpacking."

She stood and slung the tote over her shoulder. "Somewhere out there, a perfectly wonderful woman is waiting for a suspense writer to sweep her off her feet. Just you wait."

"Thanks." The corner of his mouth creased, not quite pulling into a smile.

Bev waved as she made her way to the door.

"I should get going, too." Dana gathered her supplies into a neat stack. "Despite months of collecting dorm necessities, we somehow still need one more shopping trip to stock Leah's one hundred ninety square feet of shared space."

"How are you handling your little girl leaving home?"

"Depends on the moment. When she's in a bad mood, I'm ready to help her pack, but then she turns sweet again, and I think about how I'm about to be alone in a house of boys. It's driving me to stress eating."

"She'll be home for Christmas break before you know it."

Carlos's words were of little comfort. Dana had returned home from her first semester of quasi-adulthood, hostile to curfews and her parents' boundaries. Now the curse of "what goes around comes around" would return to bite her.

"Yes, I'm sure by December I'll be ready for my little

birdie to be back in the nest." And probably ready to set her free again by January.

He followed her out. "Continue working on that novel. Nobody writes criminal masterminds like you do, and they'll keep you too distracted to show up at Leah's dorm unannounced or track her twenty-four-seven on a locator app."

Dana loved writing methodical killers. They had to be meticulous to avoid detection. While she had no desire to inflict harm in real life, she envied her characters' abilities to keep their misdeeds efficient and orderly. If only her own brain could manage the same.

A stack of boxes threatened to topple in the corner of Leah's room. Dana set another one containing an air purifier atop a Keurig box. "Remind me why you *had* to have a coffeemaker when you don't drink coffee."

The teen rolled her eyes. "I drink decaf tea and hot cocoa. How else am I going to make them?"

"By heating water in the microwave or going downstairs to the cafeteria."

"Mom, this is easier, and it saves money over buying from the cafeteria or campus Starbucks."

Dana cocked an eyebrow. Saving money hadn't been Leah's MO even once in the last eighteen years. She scanned the piles stashed in every available space. "Do you really think all this and Skylar's belongings will fit in your dorm room?"

Leah shrugged. "If not, I'll bring some of it back here.

Or return it. No big deal."

Oh, to be carefree and eighteen again. Dana would trade almost anything for one day where the only person she had to keep alive was herself. Not three kids. Not a husband who operated under the illusion their laundry hamper had mystical powers—that if his dirty clothes landed anywhere near it, they'd reappear clean, folded, and stacked neatly on his dresser. And especially not her father, whose daily antics could keep a Navy SEAL team on its toes.

"Have you and Skylar talked about who's bringing what, so you don't both show up with a vacuum, a Keurig, and matching air purifiers?"

"Mom, it's not that deep."

Dana pinched the bridge of her nose. *Not that deep.* Why couldn't the kids say, "not that serious," like normal people? "I don't appreciate the backtalk. And with the small fortune we just spent outfitting your dorm room, I'd think you would show a little more gratitude."

"For months, you've been reminding me how expensive college is. But guess what?" Leah threw a hand in Dana's direction. "You're the one who's been pushing me to go in the first place. Either you want me to be an adult, or you want to control me, but you can't have it both ways."

Dana pressed her lips together. Legally, sure, Leah was an adult. But anyone who had to text her mom for her own social security number and email password shouldn't be left unsupervised overnight.

She drew a slow, steady breath and willed herself not to rise to the bait. "All I'm saying is maybe it would've been smart to wait until after move-in day to see what you actually need."

Even though over half of Leah's graduating class was attending Texas Tech University, Leah opted to room with a stranger chosen in roommate roulette. She and Skylar from San Antonio had been texting for months, planning their aesthetic and ordering matching bedding sets.

"We have it figured out already." Leah flopped onto the bed and held her phone for Dana to see. "We have a shared mood board, and yes, we're keeping track of what each of us is bringing." Her face turned sullen, and a whine crept into her tone. "I'm more responsible than you give me credit for."

Josie and Hunter Caraway had trusted Leah to keep their triplets alive countless times over the last four years, so maybe Dana wasn't giving her daughter enough credit.

"You're right, and I'm proud of the responsible young adult you're becoming." She reached out to envelop Leah in a hug, but the teen drew back to avoid the embrace as if Dana carried the plague.

"Why can't you just say you're proud of me as the adult I am? Why do you have to qualify it with *young* and *becoming*? It's so rude."

Dana stiffened. "And we're done." She stepped into the hall, ignoring Leah's demand that she close the door behind her.

Nate and Adam's shouts over a bitter video game competition filtered down from the second floor. She needed a real grown-up to talk to. One besides her dad, who would laugh about how the tides had turned and how Dana was finally getting that payback her own mother had wished on her. And not Will, who would say Leah was her spitting image. She pulled out her phone and texted her neighbor Josie.

You busy?

Josie: Nope wanna come over?

Dana didn't bother with a response. She bolted out the front door and crossed the cul-de-sac.

"Door's open," Josie called.

Dana let herself into the quiet, clean living room. She might've thought she'd walked into the wrong house except for Josie's six-foot frame leaning in the doorway to the kitchen. "Where are your kids?"

Josie chuckled. "Why do you ask? Did you stop by for a playdate?"

"It's so tidy, and there's no noise." Dana peered down the hall. "I'm worried about whether they're safe and, you know, still living here."

"My mom took them to see a movie. Their last hoorah before school starts." She motioned for Dana to follow her into the kitchen. "Tea?"

"Yes, please."

Three cartoon-themed backpacks lined the counter. Dana ran her fingers over the applique details of one. A wave of nostalgia fluttered in her gut. In the Harding home, the excitement of the first day and fresh supplies was long gone, replaced with grumbling, a handful of pencils, and a homework planner that would never see the light of day outside of a backpack.

"Marie's going to miss being with them every day, isn't she?"

"She'll still pick them up on Fridays." Josie plinked ice cubes into two glasses, poured tea into them, and held one out to Dana. "It's my biggest money-making day, and leaving by noon would cost me too many clients. Let's go relax before the chaos crew gets back." She carried her glass to the living room, sank into the sofa, and propped her feet on the coffee table. "Today was rough between nonstop clients and Zola trying to take my head off. If this keeps up, I'm going to need a vice. Something with more of a kick to it than sweet tea."

"I can't picture Zola chewing you out," said Dana. The petite stylist with the edgy pixie cut reminded her of Tinker Bell—more sparkle than intimidation.

"Then you should've seen her today." Josie took a sip. "She treated me like a bad employee when I'm an independent operator. It was demoralizing."

Dana winced. "I'm sorry. I hope you don't blame me for introducing you to her." She'd given up her appointment with Zola so Josie could get her hair done for her first night out after the triplets were born.

"Not at all. It's still a great place to work. Or at least it will be when Zola's rambunctious kid goes back to school next week." Josie waved away her own complaint. "Enough of my griping. What's going on with you?"

"An easier question would've been 'what isn't going on with you?' We have the first meeting of the Wednesday moms' group next week. Then on Thursday, Nate has his first JV scrimmage right after we move Leah into the dorm. People complain about how hectic December and May are, but the end of August is every bit as awful."

Josie nodded and raised her drink in solidarity. "Here, here. Back-to-school is way worse because the whole household shifts schedules after months of vacation."

"Absolutely and buying Christmas gifts and decorating the house are child's play compared to making teenagers go to bed at a decent hour and then waking them up early."

"Maybe, but I can't wait to find out firsthand. It's been four years since I've gotten to sleep late. Which means Hunter and I must keep the same bedtime as the average first grader to be rested enough to wrangle our kids before the sun even rises."

Dana never minded her toddlers crawling into her bed early in the morning. When Leah was still an only child, Will would plop her between them with a bowl of dry cereal and turn on cartoons. They could squeeze in another half hour of sleep before she got bored and ground smashed Cheerios into the sheets.

"The only event next week I'm looking forward to is MOMS," said Dana. "Between my dad and the kids, I haven't had time to connect with Serena or any of the other ladies all summer."

Serena was their pastor's wife and the mastermind behind MOMS—Moms on Mission. They met once a week to talk about the blessings and woes of family life and to support one another. They'd also become Dana's biggest fan base for her two crime novels.

"Me too." Josie took a drink. "I mean, now that I'm working, the desperate need for social interaction has gone away, but I've grown to love those women, especially Anita Steen. She's become like a second mom to me. A non-critical mom, which is something I haven't had before."

"You should invite Zola to the group. Maybe she needs friends to help her find her happy heart again." Dana smiled, proud of herself for thinking to suggest it.

"Or she'll be a bummer and ruin Wednesday nights for me." Josie set her tea on the coffee table and folded her legs onto the sofa. "At this point though, I'm willing to try anything."

"It's been a busy summer, and I'm ready to get back to a routine and only buy groceries for my three kids instead of for all their friends, too."

Josie cocked her head. "But you won't be buying groceries for three kids once Leah moves out."

Dana's lungs deflated like a punctured pool float. Leah would be gone in a few days. So much of her day-to-day life revolved around caring for three kids. How many gallons of milk would she even need to buy for only two?

Chapter 5
Josie

Monday morning, Josie's phone buzzed on her nightstand half an hour before her alarm was set to go off. Her mother's name lit up the screen.

"Mom? What's wrong?"

"Nothing's wrong. Why would you assume that?"

"You've never called this early before."

Her mother cleared her throat. "I figured you'd be up by now getting ready for the first day of school. Thought maybe you could use a hand."

Beside her, Hunter rolled over. "What's going on?"

Josie gave a quick shake of her head to let him know everything was fine. He grunted, punched the pillow into submission, and settled back in.

"We've got it under control, Mom."

"I see." Marie's disappointment traveled through the airwaves.

"But if things go south this morning, we may hit you up for some help tomorrow."

"It's fine, Josefina."

The only thing worse than dealing with Marie Saldana's criticism was hurting her feelings. How was Josie to know she wanted to be included in the kids' first day of school? She should have expected it, though. Her mom had been taking care of the kids most weekdays since Josie started working at the salon. Being their Abuelita was her reason for existing, and they wouldn't need her as much anymore.

Connor barreled into Llano Elementary like he'd been there a million times instead of just once at meet-the-teacher night, while Olivia clung to Josie's side. Hunter walked next to Ben with his hand on his shoulder. "You're going to mind your teacher and do everything she tells you to."

"If she tells me to hit, I won't do that."

Hunter shot Josie a worried look. She responded with a giggle. Leave it to Ben to find a loophole in any argument.

At the preschool hall, Josie hugged Ben and reminded him she would pick him up at noon. His inquiry floated after her as she guided Connor and Olivia across the hall. "Is it time to play outside now?"

She said a quick prayer for Mrs. Tyson. At least she only had to contend with one Caraway boy in her class.

Josie helped the kids put away their supplies and settle into coloring the pages on their desks. Connor scribbled and made conversation with the boy across from him.

Olivia put her hand on Josie's arm. "Mama, will you stay with me?" she asked, barely above a whisper.

Heat burned behind Josie's eyes, and she looked away. "Moms can't stay at school. But I promise to come and get you soon, okay?"

Olivia nodded slightly. Josie kissed the top of her head and made a hasty retreat before she lost it.

Hunter met her in the hall. "I think Ben's—" He reached for Josie's hand. "You okay?"

She shook her head. A sob loitered in the back of her throat, waiting to choke out her words. Hunter put his hand on her back, guiding her out of the building. He opened the passenger door of their Honda Odyssey and held it for Josie to climb in, then slid behind the wheel. He took a route that led them farther from their neighborhood.

"Where are we going?"

One corner of Hunter's mouth teased a sly grin. "You'll see." They drove in silence until they reached the edge of town. He pulled into the gravel lot of the little diner they used to haunt back in their pre-triplet days.

Josie gazed at the neon sign. "Are we even allowed back in here?"

The last time they came, toddler Connor had smeared syrupy hands across a senior woman's freshly set curls in the booth behind them, earning them a lifetime ban, or at least a warning not to return until their children learned how to behave in public. So, same thing. That had been two years ago.

Hunter leaned across the console and brushed a kiss on her cheek. "I'm sure it'll be fine. Without the triplets, no one from before will even remember us." He opened his door to get out. "This is the perfect place to celebrate our babies starting big-kid school."

Josie's stomach growled. She unbuckled, already tasting the buttery banana pancakes she hadn't had since the incident. "I barely got out of there without bawling. I'm not celebrating."

He draped an arm over her as they walked to the entrance. "With the kids in school, we can come here more often, and that's worth celebrating."

The hostess seated them right away, and the heaviness of the morning slipped from Josie's shoulders as she scanned the familiar menu.

"I forgot how much I missed this place." She checked to make sure banana pancakes were still on the menu and set it aside. "What were you saying about Ben when we were leaving?"

"Oh. I think his teacher is going to get on her knees and thank Jesus she only has one of our boys and not both. He marched up to her as soon as he walked in the door and asked when they were going to the playground."

She started to tell him she'd had the same thought about Miss Piper, but their phones pinged. No news might be good news, but simultaneous texts usually meant something awful. She glanced at her screen. A group text sent by her mother.

How did it go?

Josie didn't blame her mom for asking. Of course, she'd have wanted to be included in such a momentous occasion.

Josie: Everything went great. No tears.

That was mostly true. Her own tears didn't count, and she'd kept them in until after drop-off. Three dots pulsed on the thread for way too long as her mother presumably typed her response.

"We both know her next question is whether they were late, so what's taking her so long?" Hunter asked.

Josie stared at the phone until her mother's message

appeared.

Did you give yourself enough time before the tardy bell?

Hunter shook his head. "Your mother has no faith in us."

"Shh. Don't get us kicked out again."

He shoved his phone back in his pocket. "Let's enjoy our breakfast date and not think about your mom or the children, okay?"

Easier said than done, but she tucked her own phone under her leg and vowed to try. When the server set the plate of fluffy pancakes and crispy bacon in front of her, Josie forgot everything except her own name. Her eyes rolled back as the first bite hit her tongue. "I bet this is what they serve at God's banquet table in Heaven." She stabbed a second bite with her fork.

"If I'd known four and a half years ago I would have to choose between eating here or having kids, I would've thought seriously about my answer before committing to triplets," said Hunter.

Josie kicked him under the table.

"Ow, I was kidding."

Hunter bent to rub his shin when their pastor and his wife approached.

"Hey guys, where are the kids?" asked Serena, the leader of their Wednesday moms' group. As usual, she exuded the well-rested, polished look of an empty nester.

Josie flashed them her biggest smile. "First day of school."

Serena tipped her head to the side. "Aw, I remember those days. Feels like last week when our girls were that age." She nudged her husband with her shoulder. "Doesn't it, babe?"

Pastor Gray gave a noncommittal grunt, eyes locked on Hunter's plate. "This place has the most addictive breakfast in town, doesn't it?"

Hunter nodded, finishing a bite. "We've been banned for two years, so I wouldn't say we're addicted."

Josie crossed her ankles to keep from kicking him again. "It's hard to go places when we're always outnumbered," she said, aiming a warning look his way.

"I'm so glad I ran into you, Josie." Serena placed a manicured hand on her arm. "I actually wanted to talk to you about an idea I had for Moms on Mission."

"Oh?" Josie clenched her fists in her lap. Whatever Serena was going to ask of her, it would likely require more time than Josie had to give.

"We're partnering with an organization that supports women coming out of tough situations, helping them rebuild with job coaching, a clothes closet, that kind of thing." Serena's smile widened. "They reached out to see if we could offer free haircuts. You know, to help the women feel more confident and professional heading into interviews."

Josie dabbed her mouth with her napkin, stalling. It wasn't that she didn't want to help, but her schedule was already stretched thin. How much time would Serena expect her to commit to this project? Guilt needled her. If not for the generosity of her in-laws in funding her cosmetology schooling, she wouldn't be where she was now. Didn't she owe it to them to pay their kindness forward?

"That sounds amazing," she said finally. "I'm sure some of the other stylists at the salon would also love to help."

Even as the words left her mouth, an additional weight settled in. Dana had floated the idea of inviting Zola to MOMS, and this kind of outreach would be the perfect inroad. But the thought of sharing her safe space with the salon's high-maintenance owner made Josie's stomach churn.

Still, one rookie stylist with triplets wouldn't be enough to pull off Serena's project. If this was going to work, she'd have to bring Zola in, whether she liked it or not.

Chapter 6
Dana

Dana eased into the driveway, stealing a look at her sons, one scrolling through his phone beside her, the other half-asleep in the back seat. The boys, who used to chatter non-stop all the way home, offered nothing about their first day of school other than two "fines" and one "someone pulled the fire alarm in fifth period." The rest of the ride was silent, save for the intermittent chorus of complaints about their hunger status and groans over her so-called oldies music. Since when had Aerosmith become oldies? That kind of disrespect should earn them groundings.

They sprang back to life the moment they walked into the house.

"I have to stay late for football tryouts the rest of the week," Adam said as he dropped his backpack in the middle of the walkway on his way to the pantry. "And I have to get a particular mouthguard that fits around braces."

"Mom, don't forget. My first game is on Thursday. Technically, it's just a scrimmage, but it's still a big deal." Nate poked his head out of the fridge. "I can't leave beforehand, so you'll have to bring me food at the field house."

"Got it." Dana set her purse on the counter and eyed her vulturous spawn. Last year, between Nate's freshman football and Leah's soccer schedules, high school sports almost killed her. There weren't enough hours in the day to cook a decent meal, hit her writing deadline, and cheer from multiple bleachers. Would it be wrong to pray Adam didn't make the team?

She shook away the thought. Her youngest child deserved the same opportunity to play and see his family yell for him from the stands as his older siblings. "I'll do my best, but it's also dorm move-in day."

Nate left the fridge door wide open as he poured a glass of milk. "This family revolves around her. It's always 'Leah this' and 'Leah that.'"

Not this again. As if his middle-child grumblings summoned her, Leah sauntered into the kitchen. "Close the fridge, doofus. Don't you know how much energy it takes to cool the interior back down after you let all the heat in?"

"You're the doofus," said Adam. "It would be letting the cold air out."

Leah rolled her eyes. "Take a physics class and get back to me."

Why had Dana lamented reticent children? Silent siblings didn't insult one another. "Stop arguing. Nate, close that door unless you want to help pay the electric bill."

He pushed it with more force than necessary. "Sorry, Mom."

"Leah, don't call your brother names. You know better." Dana waited for her mumbled apology before addressing the third kid. "Adam—"

Under his breath, he muttered, "Sorry."

"She's right though. Cold is the absence of heat." Dana crossed the room to her office. "And on that pleasant note, I'm going to work on my manuscript."

"But Mom." Nate wiped his milk moustache with the neck of his shirt. "You have to take me driving. I still need twenty-two more hours of practice to get my license."

"Your birthday's not for three more months, and it's not like you're going to pass the driver's test, anyway." Leave it to Leah to interject uplifting commentary.

"Whatever," Nate shot back. "It can't be that hard to pass if they let *you* get a license."

"I passed on the first try, genius."

"Your test examiner must've been blind since you backed into a fire hydrant the next day."

"Shut up, stupid," Leah said. "I'm still a better driver than you'll ever be."

Nate opened his mouth, but Dana cut him off. "That's enough out of both of you. I warned you once to stop arguing, but since you didn't, you're going to work together on a project."

Blank stares.

"It'll help you learn to appreciate one another." Or at least bond over mutual suffering. Now she just needed to devise a task to teach them a lesson and buy her some peace.

Adam pulled her head to his and whispered in her ear. Dana grinned. "That tub of LEGO bricks upstairs needs to be sorted by color and size before we donate it to the women's shelter. When you're finished, Nate, I'll take you driving."

His shoulders sagged while Leah sneered.

"And if you're thinking, young lady, that you can

punish your brother by dragging your feet or not helping, here's the twist. I'll be holding your phones as collateral until the work is complete."

Leah's face fell. "That's not fair. Besides, I'm not a kid anymore. You can't just take my stuff."

"Watch me." Dana set her most threatening mom face and loomed over Leah. No easy feat since her daughter was an inch taller than she was. "According to the name on the bill, it's *my* phone, and I can do with it as I please." Dana held out her hand. "We can do this the easy way, or I'll turn off all your apps through my parental controls."

Leah's jaw flexed as she begrudgingly set her phone on the counter and stormed up the stairs.

Nate trudged after her. "Why do the LEGOs have to be sorted, anyway? Can't the kids at the shelter play with a mixed-up bin like Adam and I always have?"

"I don't want to dump our junk on someone else in a jumbled mess. Organizing it first is more like giving a new toy, and don't you want other kids to get that experience?" Dana asked.

"Not if it means I have to cooperate with Leah to do it."

Dana shook her head, choosing not to entertain his gripe. As the older kids headed to their shared misery, she turned to Adam. "That was quick thinking with the LEGO sorting. But didn't I ask you to do that last week?"

"You said to get *started* on it. Which I did, but then I built a robot and a city for it to destroy. I don't even know that I still want to donate them. But I'll wait to decide until after all the pieces are separated."

Dana snorted, not quite sure what to make of Adam's scheme. "Tell me more about football. What position are you trying out for?"

"Well, I was hoping for defensive line," he said through a mouthful of Cheetos Puffs. "They get to plow into the other team's offense."

Dana winced. Size-wise, Adam was a perfectly average twelve-year-old but not exactly built to plow into anyone. He would get injured on the line for sure.

"But I'm fast," he added with a shrug. "So, Coach has me at running back. I blame you and Dad for making me run laps around the cul-de-sac every time I got in trouble."

Her gut twisted. Being a smaller kid on the defensive line was one thing. Being the one they were all chasing down? Even worse.

"Why'd you run so fast?" she asked. "Kind of feels like you created your own problem."

"Yeah, but you and Dad always tell us to do our best. Besides, if I run faster than everyone else, I'll make first string."

She wrapped her arm around him and pecked his cheek before he squirmed away. "I'm proud of you. You're such a hard worker and always have a good attitude."

He nodded, his attention on the tablet in front of him.

Dana ducked into the laundry room/office to hang out with her imaginary friends before the driving lesson or starting dinner, whichever came first. Her fingers flew across the keys, and time blurred as the real world faded into the one she created with words. A soft knock on the doorframe pulled her back.

"It's never this quiet. Where is everyone?" Will asked.

She spun her chair to face him and stole a glance at her watch. An hour had passed since she first sat down. "I didn't even hear you come in."

He leaned down and kissed her. "How was the first day of school?"

"Your guess is as good as mine. The boys hardly talked about their days. Nate and Leah were at each other's throats within five minutes of walking in the door, so I sent them upstairs to do busywork." She followed Will out of the laundry room and through the kitchen. They found Adam sound asleep on the living room sofa. "He still looks like a little boy when he's sleeping."

Will wrinkled his nose. "Smells like a teenager, though."

She folded her arms and stared down at her baby, the eternal optimist who used to talk way too loudly. If she blinked, he'd be leaving for college too. "Did he tell you he's trying out for running back?"

Will's face lit with a proud, fatherly grin. "Yeah. How cool would it be if both our boys got to play football this year?"

Cool? She could think of plenty of things it would be other than cool. "Yeah, great. I'll start dinner and you wake our little running back or else he won't sleep tonight."

"How about we order in? I'll go get your dad, and we'll have a combined celebration of the first day of school and Leah's going away."

"You know we're having her farewell *tomorrow*."

He scratched the back of his head. "Yeah, about that…"

Dana sighed. "You have to work, don't you?" Their last family meal before Leah moved into the dorm, and he was bailing?

He pulled her into a hug. "No, I'm not working

tomorrow night." He tipped her face to his. "Listen, I don't want you to get mad, but Leah made plans to go out with her friends tomorrow night, so I thought we could move our family gathering up."

"When did she talk to you about this?"

"Couple of hours ago." He took her by the hand and led her to their room. "It's understandable. Her friend Kaitlyn is going off to Oklahoma State, and the other Kate is moving to…somewhere else."

"Texas A&M."

"Right. So, she wants to spend time with her friends before they leave." He sat on the edge of the bed and motioned for her to join him. "Are you okay with having dinner together tonight instead of tomorrow?"

"Fine." Dana might've been angry the two of them had made plans that affected the whole family if her feelings weren't so hurt Leah called Will instead of her. "I can't believe you didn't give me a heads-up before now."

"I'm sorry. It's been a hectic afternoon. And I didn't think it would be a big deal."

It would've been one if she'd already made other plans. And what about that cake Dad was making? Had Will or Leah even considered how their secret curveball would affect him? "Why would she ask you when I was home with her all day?"

"Hon, don't make it a thing. You two haven't exactly been getting along lately, and she was afraid you'd get mad."

"What do you mean we haven't been getting along? I take her shopping. I make all her meals. She's the summer princess who keeps reminding me how grown up she is, and I keep on taking care of her like a little girl."

Will shook his finger. "See, I think that's the thing she was trying to avoid by not talking to you. You can't deny there's been tension."

Heat crept up Dana's neck. If she were a cartoon character, smoke would've shot out of her ears. "You're calling me the problem and Daddy's perfect little girl hasn't been acting snotty and entitled."

"I'm not taking sides, but you have to realize how scared she is to be on her own." He rested his hand on her thigh. "She's acting out, but you need to give her grace because you're wiser and more mature."

If being wise and mature meant letting her daughter treat her like a doormat with a grocery list, then sure, she was basically Yoda in yoga pants. "Grace is one thing, but you're condoning her bad behavior."

"Let's try to have a good night together. She leaves in less than three days. Do you really want to spend them bitter and angry?" He tried to put his arm around her, but she shrugged him off and stood.

"Tell you what, I'll pick up Dad, and you and Leah figure out dinner." She left him sitting on the bed and hollered from the base of the stairs, "Nate, let's get some driving in."

He bounded down, jumping from the second step. "Great timing. We just finished."

"Can I get my phone back now?" Leah called.

"Sure, it's in the kitchen." Dana kept her tone even, but her molars ground together. "Why didn't you tell me you made plans for tomorrow and wanted to move your going away dinner up?"

"Because you practically bit my head off yesterday

about organizing my dorm purchases, and I knew you'd be upset."

Dana fisted her hands on her hips. "And you thought keeping it from me was a better alternative." She didn't wait for a reply.

Nate already had the keys in hand and one foot out the garage door. She trailed him to the Tahoe without a backward glance.

Dana's knuckles whitened on the door handle as Nate pulled away from Pops's house. His driving could've been worse, but not by much. The concept of easing onto a pedal hadn't quite clicked yet. Her seatbelt had locked three separate times on the way there, nearly cutting off her airflow and eliciting a full-blown claustrophobic spiral. But there was no way she dared unbuckling to loosen the tension with him behind the wheel.

Hopefully, the ride back would be smoother, for her dad's sake. Stress could trigger another decline that could send him to an assisted-living facility. Letting Nate drive was a huge mistake. She was about to suggest they swap seats when Pops spoke up.

"Nate, I'd like to get this red velvet cake to your house in one piece, so let's work on gentle braking and accelerating. Okay?"

"Yes, sir." Nate sat up straighter and adjusted his grip at ten and two.

Dana kept her attention on him and the road as she addressed her dad. "How did you know to bake it early for the dinner that was supposed to be tomorrow?"

"This is only my second bundt." He tapped the lid of Dana's mom's ancient Tupperware carrier. "I figured I better give it a go this morning, so I'd have a day to start over if it didn't turn out well. Pure luck that I had it ready when Will called."

Between bouts of mini whiplash, Dana spent the rest of the ride vowing to lighten up and enjoy her time with Leah, conflict-free. Right up until they pulled into the driveway and found conflict staring back at them like a deer in headlights.

Chapter 7

Dana glared at Leah through the windshield. Her daughter stood at the curb, arms looped loosely around a guy's neck. He leaned against a sleek black Camaro, his hands resting on her waist a little too cozily. Their posture screamed, "more than friends, " and Dana was not amused.

The teens sprang apart at the sight of the Tahoe. Leah fidgeted with the hem of her shirt, and the guy shoved his hands in his pockets. They each studied their feet intently.

"Who is that?" Nate asked.

"Not sure, but I'm about to find out." Dana unbuckled her seatbelt. "Don't bother pulling into the garage until we take Pops back home." She took the cake carrier from her dad. Less of a chance she would go to jail for throttling Leah or the guy if her hands were full.

Neither teen had bothered to look up from examining their shoes or whatever they found so fascinating on the ground.

"Leah, aren't you going to introduce us to your friend?" Dana shifted the bundt onto her hip and extended her hand to the boy who moments ago couldn't keep his off her little girl. "I'm Mrs. Harding, Leah's mom."

"Jordan Hirschfield." He shook Dana's hand.

"We met at church camp, remember?" Leah stood on her toes to hug her grandfather. "Hi, Pops. Thanks for the cake."

Leah had spent the last month going to the movies and the mall with a Jordan, never once letting on she was hanging out with a boy. "You told me I could invite him to my going-away dinner, remember?" She threaded her fingers with his and pressed herself to his side.

Dana tacked on a welcoming smile. "Of course." She'd okayed inviting Jordan when she'd assumed the new friend from camp was female, not a handsy, sports-car-driving guy.

Dana's dad grasped her elbow and hissed, "Be nice."

"Let's all go in and eat." Dana nodded toward the front door. Inside, she deposited the cake on the counter and cornered Will in the kitchen. "Did you know Jordan was a boy?"

Will pulled takeout containers from a bag. "Who's Jordan?" How he was so oblivious was beyond Dana's comprehension.

"Go into the living room and see for yourself." She nudged him forward and took over plating salad, pasta, and garlic knots. She passed the dishes to Nate and Adam, who set them at each spot on the table.

"You must be Jordan," Will trilled with a touch too much enthusiasm. "Welcome." He urged everyone to the dining table and took drink requests. "I hope you're hungry. We've got enough chicken alfredo here to feed an army. It's Leah's favorite."

The boy cleared his throat and rubbed his hands together. "Actually, I'm a vegetarian."

Will's face blanched. His eyes widened, and he looked

to Dana as though she might make a vegetarian meal materialize out of thin air. "I, uh…no one told me."

No one had told Dana either. She didn't even know about this relationship until five minutes ago, and so far, she wasn't a fan.

Leah laughed. "He's messing with you, Dad."

Jordan raised his shoulders and flashed a full-tooth grin, the kind people gave after popping bubblegum in church—guilty, unbothered, and skating through life on an extra helping of charm.

Will chuckled. "Good one. You got me there. And just for that, how about you offer grace for us, Big J?"

If looks could kill, Will would've dropped right there on the tile, and Dana would've been called to testify against her firstborn.

"Dad, are you kidding me right now?"

Jordan took Leah's hand. "It's okay. I've said grace before."

The whole family bowed their heads, but Dana kept one eye trained on Jordan as he offered a short, respectable blessing.

The second he said "amen," Adam and Nate tore into their pasta. Dana cast another furtive look at the interloper as he traced a finger along the back of Leah's hand. Clean-cut with no visible piercings or tattoos. Maybe she should give him the benefit of the doubt. After all, he hadn't blessed the meal with the Pledge of Allegiance or a poem, and Leah *had* met him at church camp. His raising couldn't be that far removed from the Hardings' own family values.

She cleared her throat. "So, Jordan, where did you go to school?"

He named a small town right outside of Lubbock.

"And what are your plans for the fall?" Harmless question, in Dana's opinion. Leah clearly disagreed. She delivered a warning nudge with her foot under the table and a death glare above it.

"I'm working on my uncle's ranch," Jordan said.

Dana nodded slowly. She had the good sense to know college wasn't for everyone. Plenty of hardworking folks made great livings without a degree. Still, *her* daughter dating a ranch hand? That one was going to take some internal reframing.

"A cowboy, eh?" Pops twirled noodles onto his fork. "Thought you fellas all drove pickups."

Jordan dipped his head. "Yes, sir. My truck's caked in mud and sporting a fresh dent, thanks to my cousin letting go of the gate in the wind. Mom figured I'd make a better first impression driving her car tonight."

Great first impression indeed. Dana fidgeted with her napkin as her self-righteousness fizzled in thin air. She'd pegged the kid all wrong. Mostly wrong, anyway. He'd still had his hand on Leah's hips in full view of the entire neighborhood, as if her reputation meant nothing. Nonetheless, her chicken alfredo now had a distinct aftertaste of crow.

"So, how did you two meet?" Pops asked.

Leah groaned and dropped her face into her hands. Jordan shoved a garlic knot into his mouth.

"I hit him with a paddleboard oar," Leah mumbled.

Nate and Adam exchanged knowing glances, like they'd been on the receiving end of their sister's wrath and understood.

Will chuckled. "Well, that's a new one."

"She thought I was a snake," Jordan added, rubbing Leah's shoulder.

An easy mistake. Jordan might be more slimy than reptilian, but Dana wouldn't be surprised to learn he slept under a heat lamp at night.

"It wasn't my fault." Leah sat up straighter. "A snake slithered into the reeds right by the ramp where we were getting paddleboard lessons." She jabbed her thumb at Jordan. "And this guy wasn't watching where he set down his stuff. The strap of his life vest brushed my foot, and I freaked. Thought the snake came back."

"So, she clocked me," Jordan confirmed.

Nate held up his tea glass in salute. "Blunt force trauma on the first date. Nice."

Dana made a mental note to investigate buying an oar. Next time she caught teenagers being a little too lovey-dovey, she'd feign a snake sighting of her own.

Conversation drifted to safer ground as the boys grilled Jordan about ranch life, and he promised to take them out to ride horses sometime.

"You're welcome to come too, Mrs. Harding," Jordan said. "We've got a sweet old mare who's real gentle."

A sweet old mare? Dana's lips flattened into a tight line no one would mistake for a smile.

Before she could say something she'd have to pray about later, her dad came to the rescue. "Dana grew up riding. Took lessons every week."

"No way," Nate said. The other kids mirrored his amazement. And incredulity.

"It's true." Pops took a long sip of his tea. "She was

jumping fences before she could ride a bike, right, sweetheart?"

Dana gave a modest nod. The last time she'd been on a horse was during the Clinton administration, but the kids didn't need to know that part. Or that she'd swapped reins for shopping bags and boy crushes sometime around age fifteen. Maybe there was a way to work that preoccupation in reverse. If Leah spent a little time at that ranch, she might fall in love with horses instead of the cowboy.

By the end of the meal, Dana's uncertainty about Jordan had only grown. The guys, on the other hand, were more than ready to welcome him into the family. In fact, when he invited Pops to go fishing in the stock pond at the ranch, there was no going back. The entire clan—minus Dana—had been indoctrinated into the Jordan Hirschfield Fan Club.

Chapter 8
Josie

Despite a full morning of preschool, the triplets came home bouncing with energy and flat-out refused to nap. In a desperate bid to wear them out, Josie took them to the park and even invited her mother along. Much to her dismay though, even after dinner and baths, the only people dragging in the Caraway house were the adults. The kids, meanwhile, were wired, chatty, and ready for anything except bedtime.

"I drawed a picture of a ginger-bed man," Connor announced.

Olivia, busy lining up her stuffed animals in their highly specific sleep formation, looked up. "I did that, too."

"That's great," Josie said, gently herding Connor and Ben out of their sister's room. "But it's ginger*bread* man."

Connor shook his head with conviction. "Nope. He's a cookie. Not bread. And the people chase him. We read the book."

"Yeah," Olivia chimed in. "We get to make a real one tomorrow."

Josie tried to picture Miss Piper and fifteen four-year-olds baking together and shuddered. She'd be keeping that poor woman on her prayer list until summer break.

Hunter hoisted Ben onto his shoulders. "What about you, buddy? Did you draw a gingerbread man today too?"

He clung to Hunter's head like a koala. "Let me think. Yes, I did. Mine had blood on his leg. I drawed him falling off the swing."

Ben's playground fixation was getting out of hand. At least he did his assignment, even if his mind was outside. That was progress, right?

The next morning, Olivia hid behind Josie as they hung her backpack in her cubby. Her bottom lip quivered when Josie kissed her goodbye at her desk.

"What's the matter, Livvie? You're going to get to decorate that gingerbread man today, remember?"

The little girl nodded. "Then you're coming back to get me, okay?"

"Just like yesterday." Josie prayed it wasn't a lie. She had a mid-morning client who couldn't commit to a side part, much less a haircut. Her indecision had a way of dragging one-hour appointments into two. "If I can't get here in time, Abuelita will."

Olivia's eyes grew round. "You can't come?"

"Sweetie, I—"

A shriek rang out from across the room.

"That's mine." A little boy fought to keep a grip on the dinosaur toy Connor was actively trying to rip out of his hands.

Josie gave Olivia a quick squeeze and rushed to break it

up, but Miss Piper beat her there.

The teacher touched Josie's arm. "I've got this. It's okay for you to go now." Her voice was soft, but the look in her eyes said leaving was not a suggestion.

Miss Piper knelt between the boys as Josie backed away. "It is not center time."

Josie stalled, waiting to see if Connor obeyed or gave Miss Piper trouble, but Ben tugged at her shirttail. He'd been patient long enough and was ready to be dropped off.

It was just as well. Gentle parenting wasn't Josie's strong suit, so the last thing she needed was a note home about how traumatized the other child was from her attempt at disciplining Connor. She'd definitely have to leave the salon on time because if her mother caught wind of this little skirmish, it would only reinforce her belief that the kids were too young for pre-K.

It could only have been through divine intervention that the lady, who usually dithered about every slight change to her coif, handed Josie a photo with a decisive nod. "Do it before I change my mind."

The client left happy, and Josie had an hour to kill before picking up the triplets. She could treat herself to a smoothie without wasting money on the kids—one who would inevitably stab a straw through the Styrofoam cup while the other two would take two sips and let the rest melt. She reached for her purse but stopped short when the salon owner appeared in her doorway.

"Hey Jos, you got a sec?" Zola hooked her thumb

through the belt loop of leather pants so tight they could've been painted on.

Internally, Josie braced for confrontation as she plastered on a cheery smile. "Sure, what's up?"

Zola raised her phone. "Watch this video." She pressed play on a woman claiming to be both a psychologist and a forensic profiler, detailing the attributes of narcissists and how to cleanse your life of their negative energy.

Afterward, Zola slipped her phone into her pocket. "What do you think?"

What was Josie *supposed* to think? Was Zola suggesting Josie fit the characteristics, or was she merely looking for validation that she herself couldn't possibly be a narcissist?

Josie said the only thing that wouldn't stir up trouble. "Why don't *you* tell *me* what you think about it?"

"Did the lady's description remind you of me?"

"I…" Josie offered up a silent prayer for the right words. Zola tended to be self-centered and difficult, but she could also be kind and generous. "Everyone is selfish at times. I wouldn't think that makes them narcissists. Why?"

"Beckett's dad said I'm the most narcissistic person he's ever met," Zola said. "And that he's worried about how our son will turn out under my influence." Her mouth twitched, like she was fighting tears. "We've always had shared custody, but if he really believes that, he might try to take Beck away from me."

Josie reached out and gave Zola's shoulder a clumsy pat. "That won't happen."

Zola turned, one brow arched. "Really? Would *you* let your kids stay with the person the video described?"

Even with the most selfless husband on the planet, the

idea of only seeing her kids half of the time made Josie nauseous. "When's your next client?"

Zola glanced down. "I'm done until two."

"Come on." Josie reached for her purse and led Zola out of the booth. "Let's drown our sorrows in a smoothie, and you can tell me more."

Josie kept quiet until they pulled away from the salon. "Are you and your ex having issues?"

Zola sat hunched, eyes fixed on the window. She looked small, nothing like the fireball who'd scolded Josie last week for rushing a customer.

"Today he asked to switch weekends, which is *so* last minute, and I said no."

Tuesday hardly counted as last minute, but Josie kept her thoughts to herself and simply nodded.

"He expects everyone to rearrange their lives for him but never returns the favor. Yet *I'm* the narcissist." She turned to Josie, her eyes sharp. "Last month, I had to drive my grandma to her sister's funeral in Corsicana. He wouldn't take Beck, even knowing the kid gets carsick. So, I ended up hauling vomit bags, a queasy child, and an eighty-year-old with limited mobility across Texas."

"Did he have a good excuse?" Josie asked.

"Work. Same reason this time. But he could call his mom or a sitter like I have to."

If only Zola had been using sitters all summer instead of letting Beckett run wild in the shop. "And why can't you trade with him Friday?"

She gave Josie a sheepish grin. "I have a date, and he doesn't know I'm a mom. With Beck at his dad's, I won't have to explain or introduce them when he picks me up."

Josie shifted in her seat but kept her gaze forward.

"I saw that." Zola wagged her finger. "You're thinking it won't end well for me to go out with someone I can't be honest with."

"It's none of my business."

"You don't know what it's like out there. I haven't had a decent relationship since the divorce. As soon as a guy finds out about Beck, he dashes like I'm handing him a bag of scorpions. I just want a chance to see where we might be headed before this one finds out about my baggage."

Josie hit her blinker and turned left into the smoothie shop parking lot. "You shouldn't call your child baggage."

"Don't judge me. You know every single man out there thinks that. I'm never going to find love again if someone can't get to know me without worrying he's expected to become an instant stepfather. It's hard enough to keep a man's attention once he finds out I'm a business owner. My being a boss babe already intimidates them, but the kid thing sends them running for the hills." She paused as if waiting for Josie to say something.

The more Zola talked, the easier it was to see why her ex called her a narcissist. Josie was the last person to pass judgement on someone else's parenting or about whether they chose to disclose their parenthood status. She hesitated every time someone asked how many kids she had. At the mention they were all the same age, eyes widened, and the phrase "bless your heart" came out.

Zola unbuckled her seatbelt and did a quick check in the visor mirror. "I even looked into dating apps for instant families, but dudes with stepdaddy dreams are a red flag all their own."

Josie winced. Maybe she hadn't gone out with anyone else in almost twenty years, but when did finding a mate become so complicated? Wait, twenty couldn't be right. She and Hunter weren't that old. Quick math confirmed they *were* in fact that old after all.

"Maybe instead of concealing the biggest part of your life to get a guy to like you, what you really need are friends who understand what you're going through." She told Zola about the Wednesday moms' group as they made their way inside.

They ordered and stood next to the counter to wait.

Josie picked up where the conversation had left off. "You should come tomorrow night and check it out. I've made some of my closest friends there." Who didn't weigh in on her questionable parenting choices because they all had their own issues. "Oh, and our group is partnering with a women's shelter this year, so it would be a good chance to get out of your own head by helping others who are much worse off." She left out the part about free haircuts for now.

"I'm not making any promises, but I'll think about it."

"Good enough." Maybe if Zola's confidence grew from surrounding herself with caring women who built her up and understood her, she would find a man to love her and Beckett the way they deserved. "And for the record, I don't think your ex would really try to get sole custody, but it wouldn't hurt to help him out of a jam. I can babysit Beckett while you go on your date."

An employee in a neon apron set two smoothies on the counter.

Zola picked up the bright orange one and took a slow swig. "You'd really do that for me?"

"Sure. What's one more when I already have a houseful?" She bit the inside of her cheek. Between the triplets and the seven-year-old wrecking ball in rolling sneakers, Josie was pretty sure "one more" would be just the right amount to level her entire house to its foundation.

Chapter 9
Dana

Dana all but sprinted into Moms on Mission Wednesday night. Here, she was more than a snack machine and a human lost-and-found. She burst in and scanned the room, ready to hug every woman in sight. It still amazed her that one awkward run-in with Serena on a brutal night over three years ago had snowballed into this crew of unlikely superheroes. Since then, they'd renovated a school playground, helped a dad race to his daughter's birth, and last year, they built seven wheelchair ramps for people in the community. Who knew what they'd pull off this year?

Dana locked eyes with Anita Steen, and a smile spread across her face.

The older mom, who acted as a mentor for Dana and Josie, enfolded her in a hug. "I haven't seen you in ages. How was your summer?"

Dana shrugged. "The usual frenzy of trips to the pool, sports, and camps. Add to it driving lessons, boys from camp, and getting Leah ready to go off to college, and it was one for the books."

"What's this now? Does Leah have a boyfriend? Is he also going to Texas Tech?"

"Yes, to the first. Or at least as far as I can tell. Until two days ago, I thought her new friend, Jordan, was a girl. Leah may be hiding a husband and three kids from me for all I know. And no to your second question. He's not going to college."

Anita's deadpan expression said Dana was being dramatic. "Bless your heart. When does she move into her dorm?"

"Tomorrow." She held up a finger. "Which, incidentally, is the same day as Nate's first game."

"Oh my. You might need a different kind of support group to get you through this semester." Anita shook her head and laughed. "I don't miss those days one bit."

A hand squeezed Dana's shoulder.

She turned to see Kathy, another veteran mom in their group standing behind her. "You're back." Dana leaned into Kathy's open arms. "How was San Francisco?"

Kathy was a few years younger than Dana but had a grown daughter already out of college and a son a year behind Nate. She'd bailed Dana out of several jams over the last few years, and they'd become close friends.

"Ridiculously cold. We had to buy fleeces from a street vendor. *Fleeces* in *August*. Can you believe it?"

How could any Texan gripe about jacket weather while it was still get-branded-by-your-seatbelt-buckle season here?

Dana tipped her chin to Josie as she snagged a cookie off the snack table. "Are you surviving the first week of school better than I am?"

"Depends, how's it going for you?" Josie sank into a chair and let her purse slide off her shoulder and drop to the floor.

"Let's see, I have to clone myself between now and tomorrow afternoon to be there for the boys while also moving Leah into her dorm. Oh, and she has a new guy that she's been seeing for over a month without my knowledge."

Josie's eyes lit up. "Does he drive that sweet Camaro I saw the other night?"

Dana grunted in reply. "How's preschool going?"

"I think this was all a huge mistake." Josie scratched her eyebrow.

Anita rested a gentle hand on Josie's arm. "What happened, dear?"

Josie exhaled. "Yesterday the triplets decorated gingerbread men and watched the cafeteria manager put them in the oven. While they were back in the classroom waiting for them to bake, the gingerbread men 'escaped,' and the kids had to search the school to find them."

Dana smiled, a little wistfully. Not so long ago, Leah had come home bubbling with excitement about her own gingerbread hunt. Her kindergarten class found their runaway cookie hiding in the principal's office.

"The point of the hunt is to help the kids get familiar with places they'll go during the year—the nurse's office, gym, computer lab." Josie brushed a crumb from her lap. "Well, Connor took it upon himself to search everywhere his teacher *wasn't* showing them. And he got lost. His teacher said they had a lovely morning exploring the campus. Didn't mention losing my son at all. But when we got home, Olivia filled in all the missing details."

Anita's hand flew to her mouth. Dana couldn't tell if she was trying to smother a laugh or a gasp. "Where'd they find him?"

"In a third-grade art class."

"At least he didn't leave the building," Anita said.

"True, but this afternoon Hunter and I had a conference with the teacher and vice principal to discuss why we weren't notified when one of our children went missing. It was awkward for everyone, and now the Caraways are probably getting a mark in our file branding our entire clan as challenging." Josie suddenly stood and waved at someone across the room. "Zola, you came."

The salon owner weaved her way to their table and slipped into the open seat beside Josie. "This church is enormous. I got lost twice between dropping off Beck and here."

"I'm sorry," Josie said. "If I'd known you were coming, I'd have met you at the door."

"I thought about what you said. I could always stand to have a few more friends." Zola smiled at Dana. "I didn't know you'd be here. It's good to see you."

Josie made quick introductions. "This is Zola. She owns Sanctuary Salon. Dana connected us back when the triplets were babies." She pointed at Anita. "Mrs. Steen is our resident parenting guru, and Kathy had her second kid when the first was ten, so she basically birthed her own live-in nanny."

Kathy reached across the table to shake Zola's hand. "I don't recommend it. Best to have your kids back-to-back before you get a taste of the light at the end of the tunnel."

Dana chuckled. "What flavor would that light be?"

"Oh, you know what I mean." Kathy dismissed her own mixed metaphor with a flick of her wrist. "I'd already sold every bit of baby gear and sworn I was one and done before I met my husband, and our son surprised us. It's a pricey way to do motherhood."

Zola let out a breathy sigh. "Yeah, I'm pretty sure my son Beckett is destined to be my only. His dad and I split two years ago, and the closest I've come to romance lately is the barista remembering my name and drawing a happy face on my cup every morning.

Josie perked up. "What about the guy you're going out with this weekend?"

After a long pause, Zola shrugged. "I told him about Beckett, and it wasn't meant to be."

Josie gave a solemn nod.

Dana glanced between them, trying to decode their unspoken exchange. Zola's dating lament echoed her writing buddy Carlos's. Her knee bounced as an idea took shape. Reckless, premature, and possibly brilliant. She'd have to run it by Josie later when the eyes of the county's best prayer warriors weren't trained on them.

"Mom, wipe your face. Your mascara is running so much you look like you just got dumped," Leah hissed.

Dana, Will, and Leah stood shoulder-to-shoulder in the sweltering dorm elevator, arms loaded with heavy-duty moving bags.

Dana tried to raise her arm to wipe her face against her shoulder. "I can't help it. It's two thousand degrees in here, and I'm a mom leaving her first child at college. I'm allowed to have wet eyes."

Will cocked his head and gave her a sympathetic smile. "You're beautiful, hon, even as a raccoon."

"Pull yourself together." Leah ground her teeth. "My roommate can*not* meet my parents like this. You're so embarrassing."

The elevator chimed, and the doors opened on the fourth floor.

Dana staggered under the weight of two moving bags. She dropped them in the hall and rubbed under her eyes with her ring finger. She lifted her face for Leah's inspection. "Better?"

"Fine. Come on." Leah stomped down the hall, dragging one bag and wearing another like a backpack.

Will hefted two bags of his own with one hand and reached for one of Dana's with the other. "How is all this going to fit in that tiny room?"

"We're not allowed to question the decisions of the supreme overlord," Dana whispered out the side of her mouth. "She'll bite our heads off if she hears us."

Leah whipped her head back. "Hurry up!"

"Too late." Will chuckled under his breath.

Leah's dorm room was empty, save for the built-in furniture. Skylar, the roommate, wasn't there, probably berating her own parents in the parking lot. Will and Dana left Leah to put away her clothes and made another trip to the car to retrieve a Tahoe's worth of items.

"Was everything we just carried up *just* her wardrobe?" Will pressed the button on the back hatch.

"No, but more of it was than you want to know."

He pulled out a laundry basket holding shoes, a lamp, a fan, and Leah's heavy coat. "It's August. She knows she only has to drive across town to get her winter clothes when she actually needs them, right?"

Dana shook her head. "Rational thought left when she bought a mini-ironing board. In eighteen years, that child has not once ironed a single thing, but when I reminded her of that, she accused me of stifling her becoming a functioning adult." She swept her hand over the coffeemaker box. "Case in point. Four full-service coffee shops right on campus and access to multiple dining halls, but the kid who vehemently opposes putting caffeine in her body *had* to have a coffeemaker."

"Dana, it's your job to give her guidance on these things." Will's admonition came off a bit too patronizing.

She bristled. Why was it solely *her* job? "You're the one who defended her when she went out with friends the night we were supposed to have her family dinner because of the 'tension' between us." She threw his own word back at him with air quotes. "How much tension do you think there is when I try to weigh in on what she should or shouldn't bring with her to Tech?"

"You're right. I'm sorry. Let's not turn on each other." He gave her a quick peck.

Leah stood at the side entrance waiting to let her parents back in. She circled her arm in a motion meant to rush them along. "It's hot out here."

Of course, there was no elevator on the side of the building. They would have to haul this load upstairs while sweat blinded them.

Dana checked her watch and tucked the coffee maker under her arm. "We do need to get a move on, or else we'll miss Nate's kickoff."

Will sucked air between his teeth. "We forgot to pick up Adam and take food to Nate."

"You may have, but I packed Nate extra food this morning and arranged for another mom to bring Adam home." She snagged the hot pink shower caddy, laden with toiletries and a new loofah.

Will cast a furtive look at Leah and stuffed the puffy coat back in the Tahoe's cargo bay along with a pair of fur-lined boots. "I'm doing her a favor. She won't even miss these."

Maybe. But if she did go looking for them, Dana would be the parent Leah blamed for their absence.

"What's taking y'all so long?" Leah called.

Back in Leah's room, Dana hid her wheezing from the three–flight climb by busying herself with the bedsheets. Skylar and her parents never appeared, which was just as well. Dana, Will, and Leah kept bumping into each other in the shoebox-sized space as they hung photos and put away Leah's belongings.

At last, Dana put her hands on her hips and assessed the room. "What else can we do?"

"I dunno." Leah shrugged.

"Okay, then I guess we're going to head to Nate's scrimmage. Want to join us?"

Leah shook her head but said nothing. The look in her eye, similar to the one she wore when she was about to lash out at Dana, held fear rather than anger.

A lump rose in Dana's throat. She wrapped Leah in a hug, although the teen's arms hung limp for two solid seconds before she reciprocated the embrace. "I love you so much. Call me if you need anything. And you can come home anytime you need a home-cooked meal, clean laundry, or a break from your roommate." She let go and sniffled. "Or even just to hang out."

"Love you, too." Leah looked away quickly, stifling a sniffle of her own.

Will grabbed Leah and planted a kiss on the top of her head. "Don't forget about us, kiddo. I love you."

They left through the side stairwell. Less traffic reduced the chance someone would catch Dana weeping. Heaven forbid if word of her emotional outburst got back to Leah.

As they walked out, a guy shouldering moving bags like Leah's called from several yards away. "Hold the door, would ya?"

"Sure thing." Will swung it wide and waited until the kid walked through before letting it close. He laced his fingers through Dana's as they headed to the car. "Should I have asked that kid why he was walking into a girls' dorm on his own?"

"He's probably helping his sister or girlfriend move in. What else would he be hauling?" Those bags were large enough to transport a body and waterproof. She gulped. Where had that thought come from?

"I'm not a fan of boys coming and going as they please in our daughter's dorm," Will said.

Great. One more thing for Dana to worry about. At orientation, they'd been assured of the highest security measures on campus, but now all she could think about were dangerous what ifs—kids sneaking contraband up the stairs while the RAs were none the wiser, overnight guests of the opposite sex lurking in the bathrooms, lost keycards in the hands of someone with bad intentions.

They were quiet as they snaked their way through campus traffic.

Finally, Will flashed her a small smile. "She's going to be fine."

"I know. It's weird. Our little girl is gone, and nothing is ever going to be the same."

"That's okay. Once all three of them move out, you and I can travel and start a new chapter in our lives." Even as he reassured her, Will's own eyes were ringed in red.

"Maybe instead of looking forward to our kids growing up and abandoning us, we can take this one step at a time."

"Step one, JV football."

Chapter 10
Josie

Josie climbed out of the passenger seat and stretched, the gas station pavement radiating heat through her sandals. They'd barely made it fifty miles out of Lubbock, and she was already questioning every life choice that had led to this holiday weekend road trip to Dallas.

From the middle row, Olivia shrieked, "Get me out or I'm gonna potty in my seat!"

"We might as well take everyone while we're here," Josie sighed, pressing the button to slide open the van door. "Boys, why don't you come with us so we don't have to stop again for a while?"

Hunter glanced at his watch and grumbled. "Connor, Ben, do either of you even need to go?"

The boys shook their heads.

"Leave them in the car with me. It'd be great if we didn't hit the metroplex at rush hour."

At any other time, Hunter was the laid back, fun parent. But put him behind the wheel for more than an hour, and he morphed into an obsessive drill sergeant.

Inside the dim, questionably mopped gas station bathroom, Josie coached Olivia through her business, then washed both their hands with the tiniest drip of soap left in the dispenser.

By the time they made it back to the van, Hunter was drumming an agitated rhythm on the steering wheel. "Are we all set?" He backed out of the parking space without waiting for Josie to buckle herself.

They drove another twenty miles in relative peace until Ben announced, "Dad, I need to go potty."

"Me, too. Really bad," said Connor.

Some emergency if he didn't even think of it until his brother brought it up first.

Hunter groaned and rubbed his forehead. "This is ridiculous. You two can hold it."

Josie fixed her gaze on the faded white stripe along the shoulder of the highway, her own frustration mounting right along with Hunter's. Getting caught in five o'clock traffic wasn't her idea of a good time either, but refusing bathroom breaks for tiny bladders guaranteed disaster. "Maybe they can, but if not, we'll be at a laundromat with urine-soaked car seat covers and miss dinner with your parents. Are you willing to take that risk?"

In a huff, Hunter turned onto a dirt road and pulled over next to a pumpjack. Then came the fearful wails of two little boys afraid to get out of the car next to the scary metal monster emitting a high-pitched moan.

"That's just the pipe squeaking as it pumps oil out of the ground." Hunter lifted Ben out of his seat. "If you can't potty in front of the oil well, you clearly don't have to go that bad."

Josie's delusional belief that road trips would be better with four-year-olds than with toddlers flew out the window before they'd even gone a hundred miles.

Hunter was in a snit after catching a slowdown on the LBJ Freeway and had declared no one could drink anything for the rest of the weekend. By the time they reached the hotel, they'd stopped no fewer than five times.

While he headed inside to check them in, Josie stayed in the van with the kids and texted her mother-in-law to let her know they'd just pulled up. She hadn't even pressed SEND before Emmaline Caraway burst through the hotel's front doors and charged the Honda Odyssey.

"You're here!" She pulled Olivia, who was closest to the door, out of her seat and into a bear hug. "My sweet Livvie. I've missed you so much." She patted Josie's shoulder in the passenger seat. "I'm glad all of you are here."

Josie got out and unloaded luggage from the back of the van.

"Gramma, gimme out of here," Connor demanded from his seat in the third row.

"Yes, sir." She lowered Olivia to the ground and climbed in to free the boys.

"My teacher says 'sir.'" Ben locked his arms around his grandmother's neck. "She says, 'No, sir. Get down from there and find your seat."

Poor Mrs. Tyson. Maybe before the school year was over, she'd get to put a "yes" in front of that "sir."

"She sounds very polite." Emmaline kissed him, set him next to Olivia, and scooted her way to the third row. "What about you, Connor? Do you like your new school?"

"Yes, but I don't want to go every day."

Josie snickered. She could say the same about her job.

Connor gave Emmaline a quick hug and practically dove for the open van door. Josie reached in to give her mother-in-law a hand getting out of the van. They embraced.

"Man, that's a workout. No wonder you stay in such great shape," said Emmaline.

Josie beamed. So many of her friends complained about how their mother-in-laws treated them. Or maybe it was mothers-in-law? Either way, Josie had the best one ever who made her feel beautiful, safe, and loved. Emmaline had never once criticized her for her mediocre housekeeping or bronze-medal parenting. If only her own mom were as kindhearted.

"Any day now I expect them to be able to unbuckle themselves so my days of hitting my head on the doorway and straining my back will be over."

Hunter returned as the boys were scuffling over which small rolling suitcase covered with cartoon characters belonged to whom. "Mom and Dad got a room with two beds and a fold-out sofa for them and the kids and a room with a king bed for the two of us." He leaned in and whispered, "And they're not even adjoining."

Josie turned to Emmaline. "You sure y'all don't want to switch?"

Emmaline shut her down with swipe of her wrist. "Absolutely not. We want as much time as we can get with our grandbabies, and you two could probably use a break."

Ben thumped his chest. "I'm not a baby, Gramma."

She ruffled his hair. "Of course you're not, sweet boy, but 'grand big kids' is harder to say." She put her hand on his back to steer him toward the entrance. "Come on, kids, let's go up to our room. Grandpa has a surprise for us."

Josie shot a questioning look at Hunter, who only shrugged. They helped Emmaline and the kids into the elevator, depositing them on the tenth floor before heading to their own room.

Twenty minutes later, the silence left in the triplets' wake settled over Josie and Hunter's room, half haunting, half bliss. The phone on the nightstand rang, startling Josie.

"I thought those things were obsolete. Who would be calling us on the hotel phone?"

"The front desk to inform us the children have destroyed the entire tenth floor." Hunter rolled onto his stomach and grabbed the receiver. "Hello?" He grinned at Josie. "Okay, Livvie, we'll be right down. Bye." He hung up and raked his hands through his hair. "My parents taught the kids how to use the phone, so I can see this backfiring very quickly."

Josie stood and slipped on her sandals. "It's cute though. I never got to do stuff like this with my grandparents."

Downstairs, Ben plowed into Josie's legs. "Guess what? Gramma said we get to eat dinner in a jungle."

Because every meal with triplets didn't already feel like eating in a jungle, now they got to do it for real. She took his hand and let him lead her to the door. "I heard. Isn't it exciting?"

At the kids' insistence, the family agreed to all ride in one vehicle, which meant Josie had to relocate a second booster seat to the third row and wedge herself into the narrow space between the two. Peter sat up front while Emmaline took the captain's seat vacated by Olivia's booster. While Josie prayed for a short drive to Rainforest Cafe, the triplets reported to their parents what Grandpa's surprise for them had been.

"It's like camping outside. There's a thing that makes stars on the ceiling, and we get our own sleeping bags," said

Connor.

"And they have candy and a machine that plays kid movies," added Ben.

Josie laughed. "You mean a television?"

"Oh, no," Emmaline shook her head. "Grandpa Peter hooked up our old VCR and brought some of our boys' childhood favorites."

Hunter almost veered off the road again. "Why did you save those old tapes?"

Peter and Emmaline had only moved to Oklahoma six years ago to care for her aging parents, which meant they'd packed that obsolete technology across state lines on purpose. If they'd done that, the odds were good they'd kept plenty of other ancient junk that would someday become Josie and Hunter's problem.

Olivia stroked Josie's hair, drawing her out of her emotional rabbit hole. "Mommy, can you make my hair red like yours?"

Josie melted. "Livvie, God gave you beautiful hair. I wouldn't change a thing about it."

"Harper said brown hair is boring and ugly."

Her heart may have melted, but now Josie's blood boiled. Who was this Harper person, and how could she teach her a lesson without going to jail?

Emmaline twisted to face Olivia with fire in her eyes. "The next time this Harper says something mean like that, you tell her, 'I'm gonna pray for God to bless you with some manners.'"

The van swerved. "Mom!" Hunter yelled. "You can't say that to a child. We're already on the watchlist after our meeting about Connor's disappearing act. Are you trying to get us kicked out of pre-K?"

"Sweetheart, they can't kick anyone out of school for putting a mean girl on a prayer list."

Josie gave her mother-in-law a grateful smile and patted Olivia's curls. One week in, and public school had already brought a lost child, a conference with admin, and now a pint-sized bully. What else would this year throw at them?

While waiting for their Rainforest Cafe table, the Caraways browsed the gift shop, a risky move with kids.

"Mom, I need this monkey." Ben clutched a plush toy in banana-print pajamas.

Unfazed, Josie pried it from his arms and returned it to the shelf. "Nice try, but no one needs a gorilla in banana pants."

"Uh-huh." He snatched it down again. "I do need it. I don't have any animals like this." His bottom lip jutted out. "Please, Mama. He needs me to take care of him."

At four, he'd already decoded the secret to tugging at her heartstrings—pulling out the babyish maternal moniker. Not eager to stage a public wrestling match over a stuffed primate, she went for the classic redirect. "Go ask your dad." Let Hunter be the bad guy for once. She tracked Ben as he sidled up to his dad and granddad, cradling the gorilla.

Grandpa Peter threw his head back and laughed. "I'll be. I can't say as I've ever seen a gorilla in banana pants either, Benny. Let's get him. Go tell your brother and sister they can also pick out a toy."

Ben skipped off with his grandpa trailing after him.

"That backfired," said Josie.

Hunter watched with folded arms. "Royally. But grandparents don't play by the same rules, so what're ya gonna do?"

"Babe, you need to talk to your parents about limits. They can't spoil the kids and send them back with us after three days."

He chuckled. "I think that's exactly what they plan to do. And I'm not about to tell my mom she can't. She's a little jealous your mom moved to town and gets to see them all the time. This is how she stays in the game."

"That's fair, but your parents are going completely overboard." Tea at the world's most expensive doll store for Olivia and a trip to a LEGO place for the boys. Both had the potential to cost a second mortgage if the triplets got their way. Then they would round out the day at Globe Life Field watching some baseball. That was just tomorrow. Emmaline had made reservations at an indoor water park for Sunday.

"You should at least encourage your mom and dad to pace themselves. It's fine for them to tell our kids 'no' occasionally."

Hunter jutted his chin toward his mother who was holding a pair of pajama bottoms to Ben's waist. "You want to get in the middle of that?"

"We haven't even made it inside the restaurant yet. At this rate, we will have to rent a moving truck to get back to the hotel."

"Jos, you're overreacting."

"Mom, look," Ben hollered. "I'm gonna match Mr. Banana Pants."

She pursed her lips and gave Hunter a wide-eyed I-told-you-so look. "Banana pants really are the perfect uniform for this little circus, aren't they, sweetie?"

The gift shop ended up being the highlight of dinner. The triplets alternated between covering their ears and ducking under the table every time an animatronic creature twitched to life.

The crowning disaster was the elephant stationed outside the restroom. The life-sized beast flapped its ears and trumpeted, sending the kids into a panic, using their mother as a human shield. Josie looked back toward the table where her husband and in-laws munched on fries, oblivious to her plight. She squatted and coaxed Connor onto her back and lifted Olivia to her chest. "Come on, soldier, we can do this," she said as much to herself as to Ben, who clung to her leg as she limped forward into the war zone.

By the time Josie made it back to the table, her appetite was long gone.

"What took so long in there?" Hunter asked.

She answered him with a withering glare. So much of her life as a mother was spent dealing with other people's bathroom needs. Where had that warning been in any of the parenting books she'd read?

At long last, dinner ended, and the whole group shuffled toward the minivan.

Emmaline patted her belly. "I, for one, am stuffed."

"Not too stuffed for campfire s'mores," Peter said.

Olivia tugged his hand. "Do we still get to roast smashmellows?"

"Sure do, Livvie Lu."

Josie lifted Connor into the van and wiped her sweaty palms on her shorts. She always forgot how humid it was here. "Peter, fire in a hotel room feels like a bad idea." A memory from last summer flashed through her mind—Hunter doubled over thanks to the ill-fated combo of a campfire and a rogue tennis ball. "Especially with so many little hands."

"Don't worry, Josie. We got one of those flameless electric roasters. It's kind of like an inverted heat gun. Totally safe."

Safe had never been a word Josie would've associated with heat guns. Or any sort of guns. Back at the hotel, Hunter suggested unplugging the room phone, lest the kids take turns prank-calling them all night.

"Aren't you worried they'll set fire to the bedspread with your dad's inverted flame thrower? Maybe we should leave the landline on until we're sure they're asleep."

Hunter grabbed the remote off the nightstand and flicked on the TV. "Babe, I love you, but you worry too much. The kids are fine. They're living their best lives right now." He kicked off his shoes and reclined on the bed.

"Your parents have never had them for more than a couple of hours without us. And I know they raised you and your brothers just fine, but our boys are…more challenging."

"I doubt that. We've greatly censored the stories of our childhood for your benefit." He winked at her and patted the bed beside him, beckoning her to join him. "Try and enjoy being off the clock. At least until tomorrow, you only have to worry about yourself."

Josie sank onto the mattress, unsure whether to laugh or cry. This week had been one long lesson in cutting the apron strings, but somehow, she was still tied in knots.

Chapter 11

Dana

Harvey lifted his eyes to Dana without bothering to raise his head from the bed. She snapped a photo of the dog's sulky face and sent it to Leah with the caption: **Somebody misses you.**

The only contact Dana had gotten from Leah in the last couple of days was a single text message saying, **Were you ever a maiden? I'm supposed to put your maiden name as the answer to a security question.**

Dana's explanation, that her maiden name was simply her last name before she got married and therefore the same as Pops's, earned her a thumbs up emoji. Nothing more. She'd reached out to Leah a few other times with no response. Not even yesterday when Adam came home with the news that he'd made first string running back. Hopefully Leah at least had the good sense to text her brother her congratulations.

Dana complained to Will as he reclined on the sofa reading a novel.

"Give her time, honey. She'll come around," he said.

"When?" If Dana had a timeline, it might make the waiting more bearable.

"Once she figures out how good she had it living under the umbrella of our protection and guidance, she will learn to appreciate us more."

Her heart quickened. Would Leah have to stumble into some disaster before she realized life outside their umbrella wasn't all sunshine and decaf lattes? The thought made Dana itch to drive over to campus and put eyes on her firstborn.

She picked at the hem of her tee shirt. "Do you think she's eating? I mean, you remember when she first got braces, she practically survived on milkshakes. What if she's living off nothing but cereal right now?"

Will turned the page with maddening calm. "Then she'll be like every other college freshman in America."

Dana pressed her lips together. Easy for him to say. He didn't lie awake at night wondering if their daughter would ever return home again. Or if she was walking across campus alone after dark. Or if a nefarious person might try to enter the dorm's side stairwell by having someone with a keycard hold the door.

Her phone buzzed. She yanked it up, thrilled Leah had responded so quickly. She deflated at the name on the screen. Not Leah, her writing buddy Carlos.

Anyone available to squeeze in an extra session next week? I'm up against a deadline and could use your eyes.

Dana groaned. This was the third week in a row he'd asked them to double up, and she'd barely written anything since their last meeting. While she pondered her reply, a message came through from Beverly, separate from the group.

We've got to find that man a girlfriend. He's getting awfully demanding. She tacked on a laughing emoji, but she wasn't wrong.

Nate barreled down the stairs, his little brother close behind. "Leah invited us to ride horses at Jordan's family's ranch today."

Will met Dana's eyes over his book. "She called? Is she coming over?"

So, he missed her too. Dana's mouth pulled into a half grin.

Adam bounced on the balls of his feet. "She said Jordan would pick us up. Can we go, please?" His "please" came out like it had five e's in the middle.

"I don't know." Dana may have spent most of her childhood around horses, but the boys hadn't. How could she trust a kid she'd only met once to guide them through the basics? "I'd feel better about it if Dad or I went, too." And then she could spend a little time with Leah and find out how life on campus was treating her.

Nate held his phone in both hands, thumbs poised to text. "What if she says no to that? Can *we* still go?"

Why would she say no? Sure, Leah was putting space between herself and her parents and trying to be an adult, but would she go back on her offer to the boys just to avoid them?

Will picked a junk postcard from a roofing company off the coffee table and slipped it into his place in the book. "Ask her if it's okay for us to tag along. We can take the Tahoe and follow y'all out there."

Nate tapped away at his screen, waited a beat, and proclaimed, "She said, 'fine, whatever.'"

For Dana, that was as good as an embossed formal invitation. She popped up from her seat and issued orders. "Boys, you're gonna want long pants for riding. Go change. And those crocs aren't safe for stirrups. Put on sneakers." She grabbed a canvas tote from the back of the laundry room door and filled it with water bottles, sunscreen, and hats. The kids would get hungry before they got back. She took the hats out and set them on the kitchen counter to make space in the bag for a box of granola bars. A hangry Leah was a terrifying Leah.

Will came up behind her and planted his hands on her shoulders. "Honey, we're going to a ranch for a couple of hours, not the beach. Dial it back."

"I just want everything to go right so she'll visit more often."

He turned her to face him. "It's been less than forty-eight hours. If this were a true crime show, the cops would still be interviewing witnesses."

"Okay, but wha—"

Will silenced her with a kiss. "There's no 'what if.' She *will*."

Dana whistled a low note of awe. For at least four miles, they'd driven along sprawling pastures marked by purple metal gates along the barbed wire fence. Now they turned under an overhead sign in the same bold shade. It was a brand symbol of a backward K attached by its spine to an H. "Are you sure this isn't Four Sixes Ranch?" This was nothing like the two-bit farm with a lean-to stable Dana had imagined.

Fingering the necklace at her throat, she took in the sprawling acreage and pristine white fences. *This* was Leah's boyfriend's uncle's place? She'd pictured a horse or two, maybe a rusty stock trailer out back, not something lifted straight from *Yellowstone*. Now Dana wasn't just glad she and Will got to tag along to hang out with Leah. They'd need the extra eyes to keep tabs on the boys out here.

They followed Jordan's pickup down a caliche drive lined with live oaks, past a stately white home with a wraparound porch—complete with the obligatory rocking chairs, of course—to an enormous purple building bearing the same brand over the barn doors. Jordan rolled down his window and indicated where Will should park the Tahoe, next to an old F-250 pickup.

Dana stepped out and tugged down the leg of her shorts. After insisting the boys dress in proper riding attire, she'd opted to remain in her summer Saturday clothes, lest Jordan think she was there to ride the docile old mare he'd mentioned before.

"O-M-G, Mom. What're you wearing?" Leah had such a delicate way of putting everything.

"I'm not here to ride." Dana glanced down at her bare legs and shook a rock out of her Birkenstocks. Maybe she should have at least donned sneakers.

Leah waved a judgmental hand over Dana's tee shirt. "I mean *that*. Why would you wear something so embarrassing in public?"

Will turned to get a view of Dana's top. It bore the Morton Salt trademark little girl in a yellow dress under an umbrella and the words *Stay Salty*. "I bought your mom this shirt. It's funny."

"Only to you." Leah shook her head with her eyes heavenward. "Just come on."

They fell in line behind Jordan and the boys, slipping into the massive purple barn through a gap in the sliding doors large enough to drive a combine through.

"What's with all the purple?" Will muttered to Dana.

She gave a helpless shrug.

"I'm a proud Horned Frog. Class of '97. You can never have too much TCU purple," drawled a cowboy who looked like he'd stepped off the cover of *Spur & Saddle Monthly*. He clapped Will on the back with a hearty laugh.

You really could have too much purple. Barns should be red. And where had this guy materialized from? Dana recovered her sensibilities, painted on a smile, and offered her hand. "You must be Jordan's uncle."

He leaned in to take it, his handshake firm and surprisingly bone-dry for a man working in this Texas heat. "Kendall Hirschfield." He shook hands with each of the Hardings as they introduced themselves until he got to Leah. He tipped his hat to her. "Good to see you again, girl. When you get a chance, go check out Delia's new chicks. They're in the brooder in the last stall." He nodded toward the far end of the barn.

"Oh cool! Thanks, Uncle Kenny," Leah said.

Uncle Kenny? Dana had only found out this week about the boyfriend. Meanwhile, Leah had already attained honorary niece status with his family.

"Delia's my aunt," Jordan explained.

Uncle Kenny pulled leather gloves from his back pocket. "We're glad to have you folks. Jordan will take good care of ya." He tugged on the gloves. "I've got to get back out there." He left out the door they came in, and moments later, a diesel engine roared to life outside.

Leah slipped her hands into her hip pockets. "He's working on a Saturday? That stinks."

"The cattle and horses still have to be fed and watered, even on Saturdays." Jordan laughed. "I'd be out there too except I've put in forty-two hours already this week."

Forty-two hours? Maybe some of Jordan's work ethic would rub off on Leah. After a week of volunteering at their church's Vacation Bible School this summer from 8:00 a.m. to noon, she'd declared she was not cut out for a full-time career. Good thing Dana and Will were investing so much in her higher education.

Dana scanned the cavernous space and counted eight horses in stalls. One wall held hay bales stacked to the rafters, while the tack room was better stocked than a professional riding stable. Maybe Dana should give up writing and apply for a job with good ol' Uncle Kenny's operation.

"How many horses are we saddling today?" Jordan swept his pointer finger as though taking a headcount.

Dana put both hands up. "Count me out. I'm only here to hang out and look around."

Jordan bridled a stout Quarter horse and led it outside. The family watched from the doorway as he hitched it to the pipe railing of a corral and ducked back inside to retrieve another. After tying a third horse, this one a black and white speckled Appaloosa, he declared, "And now for saddles."

"Can we give you a hand instead of letting you do all the work?" asked Will.

"Sure." Jordan passed out equipment for them to carry.

Adam draped a saddle pad over the fence and wiped his forehead with the back of his hand. "Why do the horses need blankets when it's ninety degrees out here?"

"Keeps the saddle from hurting their skin," said Dana.

Jordan patted the neck of the first horse. "This here is Copper." He stepped to the next one. "This is Rio." He put his hands on the Appaloosa's jowls and brought her face close. "And this little sweetheart is Penny Lane. I helped break her, and Uncle Kenny and Aunt Delia gave her to me for graduation."

Once introductions to the horses were made, Nate and Adam mimicked Jordan's careful movements, saddling Copper and Rio while he outfitted Penny Lane. After checking every strap and buckle, Jordan gave a satisfied nod. "Okay, who's up?"

In a rare show of generosity, Leah nodded toward her brothers. "Since I've been before, let the boys go first. Then Dad."

Jordan demonstrated the proper way to mount and showed the boys how to steer and handle the reins. "A little kick in the belly tells them you want more speed. But let's hold off on that until we've mastered trotting, okay?"

Dana couldn't help noticing he spoke to the boys as if they were toddlers. Was that the tone he used on all city slickers?

"We know what to do," Nate cut in, his voice carrying the same edge of impatience his big sister used when her tolerance ran out. "We ride at camp."

"Well, alright then." Jordan tipped his hat toward the pasture. "Let's head south and give Rio a workout."

Nate had a little trouble getting Rio to turn the way he wanted. The horse preferred to munch on a patch of clover at his feet. Nate finally tugged hard enough at the reins that Rio raised his head. Unfortunately, his timing coincided with Copper swishing away flies with his tail. Rio's bridle caught Copper's tail hair, spooking Adam's mount.

The horse reared on his hind legs, and Adam tumbled to the ground.

Dana lunged for her baby boy and squatted next to him. She checked him over. No blood. No bones sticking out.

He pushed himself into a seated position and cradled his elbow. "I'm okay."

"Can you get up?" Will asked.

Adam got to his feet and tested his arm movement. "I'm fine."

Will turned back to Dana who was still crouching. "What about you?"

"I'm gonna need a little help." She reached for Will's outstretched hand.

Leah covered her face with both her palms. "Good grief, Mom."

Dana narrowed her eyes at her daughter. She prayed to live long enough to see the day her lithe teen couldn't get her own middle-aged joints to propel her off the ground.

Jordan leaned sideways in the saddle and reached for Copper's reins.

Terror flashed on Nate's face. "I dunno what happened. Are you sure you aren't hurt?"

Adam shook his head.

Jordan pulled Copper to his side. "Ready to get back up?"

"Nope." Adam dusted his jeans off. "Y'all go ahead."

Will put a hand on his shoulder. "You've got to get back on the horse. Where do you think that saying came from?"

"I'm good." Adam crossed his arms and stood his ground.

He was always up for an adventure and had a positive attitude most of the time. But as traumatizing as it was for Dana to witness her child's fall, she knew it was so much worse to be the one thrown off a horse. If he didn't want to get back on, she fully supported that decision.

Dana shot Will a pointed look that conveyed "drop it" without having to say it. "Why don't you ride with Nate and Jordan while Leah shows Adam and I what a brooder is?"

Will would probably have words for her later about coddling the baby of the family, but she didn't care. She'd fallen off plenty of times when she was a kid. As the fences got higher, often, her confidence faltered, and she ended up on the ground. But that was different. For one, English riders always wore helmets. And for another, for all her falls, she'd never been bucked off the back like that.

If she hadn't seen what spooked the horse to begin with, she'd have been livid hearing about it later from the kids and blamed Jordan. A little part of her unfairly blamed him now.

Adam marched toward the barn.

Dana nudged Leah to go with him and gave a smile to Nate that she hoped was encouraging. "Have fun, but be careful." She jogged to catch up with the kids heading to see the chicks.

In the last stall sat a plastic tub with pine shavings, a heat lamp, and metal food and water containers. Seven fluffy baby birds pecked at the feeder and cheeped.

Leah clasped her hands under her chin. "They're so cute I can't stand it." She stooped and assumed a high-pitched tone. "You're so tiny. I could put you in my pocket."

Adam's lips pressed into a thin line. "Please don't. I would like to hold one, though. Do you think it's okay?"

"I don't see why not. Last week, before they hatched, Delia told me I could come play with them." Leah entered the stall and bent low to scoop up a chick. As soon as one touched her hand, she recoiled. "I'm scared I'll hurt it."

"Try it like this." Dana knelt beside her and cupped her hands around a yellow fluff ball. "The trick is to keep your hands loose enough not to squish it but firm enough so it can't jump out. She drew her hands to her chest and stroked the down feathers with her thumb.

Adam followed her lead and cradled a chick close to his own chest. "It's hard to believe something so small will grow into the most delicious food with a side of mashed potatoes. I shall call you Extra Crispy."

"Adam," Dana and Leah scolded in unison.

Leah swiped her sweaty palms on her sides. "Okay, I'm going in." She lifted a hatchling from the brooder.

It flapped its tiny wings, and Leah flinched. "Ack!"

The bird hopped out of Leah's grasp and onto the cement floor. She lurched forward, but the tiny thing was deceptively quick, darting out of the stall faster than the three of them could blink.

"Help me," Leah shrieked.

Dana and Adam carefully returned their chicks to the container and filed out of the pen. Who knew a three-day-old bird could sprint like that? Adam crouched low, reaching, only for the chick to zigzag and slip past his fingers.

"Don't let it get under a stall door." Leah planted herself in the middle of the aisle with her arms spread like a goalie.

If that chick disappeared into the hay beneath a horse, its fate was in the Lord's hands because Dana sure wasn't about to let her kids crawl between hooves to fish it out.

"Got him." Adam rose from the floor with one cupped palm facing up and the other clamped over it, forming a closed dome. He released his catch into the brooder, exited the stall, and latched the door behind him. "That was way more cardio than I expected for birdwatching."

Dana threw back her head and laughed. "Are you sorry you didn't go riding instead?"

He pressed his bottom lip against his braces. "Still no."

The hope that taking an interest in Leah's boyfriend's family business might buy them a few more Saturdays together evaporated with the stubborn set of Adam's jaw. Ranch excursions wouldn't be the key to bonding with her daughter after all.

Chapter 12

Josie

"**Remind me again** who in their right mind thought dragging four-year-olds to a baseball game was a good plan," Hunter said.

Josie tugged her ponytail through a Rangers cap in front of the bathroom mirror. "The same helpful people who bought a seventy-five-dollar doll for one of those four-year-olds."

"I can't believe my mom paid that much. That's a lot, right?"

She eyed him through the mirror with a look that said "duh." "You know from now on our moms will outdo themselves accessorizing this doll until Olivia outgrows it."

"What was wrong with the baby doll Livvie brought from home for the tea party?"

"Nothing until she saw the ones in the store." Josie pulled her clear crossbody bag over her head and settled it on her hip. "You should've seen that place. Toy furniture that cost more than a crib for a human baby. I made myself a human shield, blocking Olivia from laying eyes on the stroller I knew she'd beg for if she saw it. A hundred and twenty dollars. I did every breathing exercise I could think of just to keep from having a panic attack."

"Almost had one myself in the LEGO Discovery Center." Hunter tipped his head toward the large shopping bag in the floor that held two building sets, each with price tags as much or more than the doll. "I insisted on keeping these with me or else Dad would let them open the boxes and spill pieces all over the hotel."

"Are the boys even old enough for those?"

"No. Dad bought miniature construction work for me."

Josie opened the door to their room and stepped into the hall. "Maybe we can stash them somewhere for a couple of years. They'll forget about them, right?"

He smirked as they made their way to the elevator. "Sure, babe."

The kids and their grandparents were waiting in the lobby with far too much energy, considering the laundry list of activities they'd already had today. Olivia cradled her new doll and shushed it. "Gramma said I can take Basketball with me to watch the Rangers."

"Basketball?" Hunter whispered. "She knows we're going to a baseball game, right?"

Josie cleared her throat. "Livvie, sweetie. I told you; you can name your Walmart dolls whatever sport you want, but your very special doll needs a very special name."

Olivia hummed and gazed at the ceiling. Her eyes grew round, and a smile spread across her face. "Then I'll call her Josefina Camille." She pronounced it in the Spanish accent she'd heard her Abuelita use so often while proclaiming her annoyance with Josie.

Hunter met Josie's eye above Olivia's head. "That's a *very* special name indeed."

Josie rewarded his compliment with a kiss on the cheek. "Who's ready for some baseball?"

By the top of the fourth inning, the triplets had lost interest in all things baseball. Meaning hot dogs, popcorn, and the foam fingers they'd scored for free for being among the first 5,000 through the gate. The oversized red weapons had been abandoned on the sticky floor during the bottom of the second inning, to the great relief of the people in front of them who'd endured more than one thwack to the head.

Connor swung his feet, kicking the seat back.

"I told you to stop that," Josie hissed. Why had society thumbed its nose at public spankings? "Sorry. Again," she said to the lady in a Cubs shirt with a permanent scowl. Maybe it was only semi-permanent—an unfortunate side effect of sitting near triplet preschoolers. Josie glanced at her phone. The game started only an hour and a half ago. She'd have guessed double that. They'd been here for hours, and it wasn't even halftime. Did baseball have a halftime? If not, it was probably to keep the fans from leaving as they realized the game still had anywhere between two and ten more hours to go.

Emmaline leaned forward to talk to Josie across Hunter and Ben. "How about we take them to the Kids' Zone on the concourse?"

There'd been a Kids' Zone this whole time, and she was just now mentioning it? "Sure." Josie stood and began herding the children to the end of the aisle with her mother-in-law, leaving Hunter and Peter to catch a few minutes of the game in peace.

Cubs Shirt Lady applauded as they passed.

The indoor play area was crowded with families whose little ones had also given up on watching the game. Who could blame them? Baseball was interminable.

Josie tucked Baby Josefina under her arm and patted her purse slung across her shoulder. "I've got the van keys right here. I'm tempted to take the kids back to the hotel and bathe them while you and the guys finish watching the game. But it would be impossible for y'all to get a rideshare with 30,000 people making their exit at the same time."

Emmaline's weary face brightened. "There's a shuttle that drops off right in front of the hotel. You and I can take the kids back in the van, and Pete and Hunter can catch the shuttle."

"You sure you don't mind missing the other twenty-seven innings?"

"Truth be told, I'm beat. I only bought tickets in the first place because I knew how much Pete wanted to go." She praised Ben, who was showing off his climbing skills on the play structure. "And if I'm going to keep up with these guys at the water park, I need to rest up tonight." She pulled out her phone and typed a text.

Josie studied Emmaline's face, worried her mother-in-law was overdoing it with her grandkids. "Are you sure you don't want them to sleep in our room tonight and give y'all a break?"

"Nonsense. But if you and I get them to sleep before their grandpa can rile them up with s'mores, so be it." She threw Josie a conspiratorial wink and checked her phone. "All set. The guys offered to leave with us, but I told them we had it under control." Her head popped up, eyes wide. "That's okay, right? Should I have told them to come on?"

The foreignness of having a parent consider her feelings over their own stopped Josie cold. While more hands usually made lighter work when it came to the kids, that rule didn't apply in cramped hotel rooms. Getting the triplets down would probably go faster without the men.

They'd snagged a decent parking spot, thanks to their early arrival, so the walk to the minivan was mostly painless. Though nothing with all three kids was completely without punishment. Connor refused to hold his mother's hand, and in his zeal to turn back and join Emmaline and Olivia, he narrowly missed being plowed down by two senior adults on mobility scooters.

"Watch it, sonny," the gentleman scolded.

Josie barely suppressed a swear word. "Connor. Hold your grandmother's hand now or so help me, you and I will *not* go to the water park tomorrow. Do you understand?" She'd said it so loudly, everyone within twenty yards of the parking lot understood. Their eyes bore into Josie, causing heat to creep up her neck.

Josie's eyelids fluttered open at the mechanical scrape of the lock disengaging. Hunter tiptoed in, sporting a huge grin.

"How did the game turn out?"

"Rangers pulled off the win by one point. You thought

the Cubs fans in front of us were mad when the kids kicked their seats? You should've seen them when Seager hit a home run in the bottom of the ninth." He bent to kiss her forehead. "Thank you for that. I feel bad you had to deal with the kids without my help, though."

"You're welcome. I'm glad you got to spend time with your dad." She pushed herself upright and watched him tug off his sneakers. "Your mom is amazing. If she hadn't been there, I never would've gotten the kids to the car without them getting run over." Of course, if it weren't for Emmaline, they wouldn't have been at a baseball game in the first place.

He chuckled. "If anyone knows how to handle feral children, it's her."

"Our kids get it from you, don't they?" Josie resisted the urge to bean him with a pillow.

He stuck his toothbrush in his mouth and merely shrugged.

There was nothing untamed about Josie's own childhood. When her mother had so much as looked at her sideways, Josie always snapped to attention. She'd stuck with nine years of viola lessons, not because she loved it, but because her mother insisted.

"You know what's great about your parents?" Josie didn't wait for Hunter to answer. "They don't blame us for the kids' behavior. My mom criticizes my discipline tactics, and my dad avoids spending more than an hour or two at a time with the kids because any amount of disorder offends him. But your parents? They're just…happy. They don't so much as flinch when the kids are demolishing everything in sight, even though I'm unraveling inside."

Hunter peeled off his shirt and shorts and dropped them in a heap at the foot of the bed. "They've always been pretty laid back, even when they were raising three rambunctious boys, but if anyone can ruin their chill nature, it'll be the triplets." He slid under the covers beside her and was snoring softly against her neck within minutes.

Josie lay awake, staring at the ceiling. Her client Mrs. Peirce never ran out of grievances about her daughter-in-law, and after today Josie couldn't help wondering what it would take to drive Emmaline to the same brink. Even though she was sweet in person, did she secretly lambast Josie to her friends? If there was some invisible tripwire that turned mothers-in-law—Josie had googled the correct term today—against their sons' wives, she was determined to spend the rest of her life tiptoeing around it.

The family entered the water park sporting armbands announcing their status as day-pass holders. The triplets wore matching day-glow orange swimsuits, chosen for their visibility both underwater and in crowds. Judging by the swarm of neon attire, every parent here had dressed their children with the same survival strategy.

The splash pad and water playground held the triplets' attention for a stretch until Connor and Ben spotted the wave pool across the way. They bolted. Josie charged after them with as much speed as she dared on the wet cement floor.

The lifeguard blew a sharp blast on his whistle. "No running!"

The boys slowed their pace until they reached the pool

and hurled themselves into the water like expert swimmers rather than beginners who'd only graduated from Miss Mary's Guppy School last month. Hunter and his dad followed them in, keeping what Josie could only hope were close eyes on Connor and Ben.

Olivia approached with the caution of someone testing ice. She let the surf lap her toes and finally ventured waist-deep at Emmaline's coaxing. A giggle bubbled out as she waved to Josie, who was fighting to stay upright in the turbulence.

To Emmaline's left, a man held a cherub-faced toddler by his hands. The child's sagging swim diaper bobbed in and out of the water as his pudgy body rode the artificial breakers. The man's eyes bulged as a subtle brown halo fanned out around them.

Josie scrambled to the ladder a split second before the lifeguard, undoubtedly trained to detect biohazards, blew his whistle, emitting three quick blasts and bellowed, "Everyone out of the water."

The green pallor of Emmaline's grimace as she dragged Olivia to shore indicated she'd also witnessed the root of their hasty evacuation. "I'll take Livvie to the shower." She quaked with a full-body shudder.

"Relax, Mom." Hunter laughed. "They use enough chlorine here to disinfect the port-a-potties at Coachella. You're safe. Not from chlorine poisoning, but you know."

Emmaline skewered him with a glower.

"Come on," said Peter. "Let's give the lazy river a go."

The boys raced in that direction, eliciting another warning from the lifeguard. "Walk!"

Josie and Hunter fished stray inner tubes out of the

current and passed them to Peter. The men plopped each triplet onto a float, with a single safety tip, "Hold on tight."

Emmaline eased her backside into the hole of her tube and gripped the handles. At once, the gentle flow thawed her sour expression, and the easygoing woman Josie had known for half her life returned. That is until they approached the waterfall.

Emmaline dug in and paddled toward the outside edge, away from the deluge. Her floaty bumped against that of a teenage boy. With a devious smirk, he kicked it, spinning Emmaline right under the cascade. She coughed and sputtered as her silver mane plastered to her face. She flopped out of the inner tube and waded to the steps.

Josie tried to call out to her, but Emmaline only put up her hand as though she'd had enough. A few short hours ago, Josie had marveled at her mother-in-law's enduring patience and her unflappability in chaos. Now, as Emmaline marched toward the lounge chairs, the crack in her cool demeanor split wider by the second. Josie prayed the universe could withstand whatever cosmic shift the water park had unleashed as Emmaline Caraway's tolerance finally ran dry.

Chapter 13

Dana

Sunday evening found Dana with her feet propped against the coffee table, a glass of sweet tea balanced on the arm of the sofa, and fingers gliding over her keyboard. The doorbell chimed. Harvey lifted his giant head and gave a single, half-hearted yip, too lazy to qualify as a bark. Dana swung her legs down and set the laptop aside.

"You're really falling down on your one job, buddy." She stepped around him to get to the door. "If you're not even going to scare away bad guys, the least you could do is run the vacuum once in a while, considering it's your hair everywhere."

She opened the door to find Josie clutching an oversized insulated mug. She motioned her neighbor inside and reclaimed her spot on the sofa.

Josie scanned the room. "Where is everyone?"

"Boys are upstairs, and Will went over to my dad's house to help him replace a toilet supply line."

"Then who were you talking to?"

"Harv." She indicated the mountain of fur in the center

of the room. "He's a slacker, and I told him I expect to see some improvements."

The dog answered her with a sigh.

"I just had to get away for a few minutes." Josie sank into the armchair that Pops liked to claim.

"Rough weekend with the Oklahoma grandparents?"

Josie took a long drag from the tumbler's straw. "Remember how I forced my family to go camping last summer to cover up the lie I told my mom?"

Of course she remembered. Dana was there for every harrowing minute of it. She gave a slight nod.

"Well, I've been paid back in spades."

"I thought your payback was getting appendicitis in the woods."

"Me too until this road trip where Hunter acted like the GPS was winning some kind of race against him every time we stopped. I love him, but sometimes, he's absolutely infuriating." Josie pressed her hand to her temple and closed her eyes. "And then there's my in-laws who spoiled the triplets so lavishly, they put Daddy Warbucks to shame." She recounted the weekend highlights for Dana, culminating in the water park fiasco.

Dana didn't see the problem. If anything, she envied the Caraways' wealth of grandparents—four, plus a scattering of great-grands. Her own kids only had the one Pops. He did more than his fair share of spoiling, but she missed the days when her mother was alive and part of it all. And it would never be fair that Will's parents had passed before ever getting to meet their grandkids. Dana shook off the ache, forcing herself to tune back into Josie's story.

"I'll admit, Ben twinning with a stuffed gorilla is the

cutest thing ever, but I don't want my kids to amass so much stuff. Or to think it's normal to own dolls with exorbitant price tags." She shifted in her seat. "And I don't want them to expect their grandparents to take them to expensive places every time they're together. Peter and Emmaline are setting a dangerous precedent."

"Kudos to Emmaline, though, for sticking it out after the wave pool incident. I'd have bailed right then. And that teen in the lazy river was lucky. Anyone less restrained might've given in to their intrusive thoughts and yanked him straight out of his tube."

"Yeah," said Josie. "But she didn't bounce back afterward. She stayed glued to that lounge chair for the rest of the afternoon. I figured a hot shower would put everything right again, but she claimed a headache and wouldn't even go to dinner with us last night."

A day stuck in a room full of tube slides in a wet bathing suit would've given Dana a headache too.

"She insisted the kids spend last night in their room though and seemed fine at breakfast this morning."

"There you go," said Dana. "She simply needed to recharge."

"I dunno." Josie stared at Harvey with a faraway look in her eye. "When we loaded the car to leave, there was something else behind her sadness at seeing us go. Relief almost. Needless to say, I don't think she and Peter will be inviting us on anymore family fun weekends for a while."

Dana tilted her head, her mouth pressed in a soft line. "Don't read too much into it. She was probably worn out."

Josie scoffed. "Oh, I'm quite sure she was. My kids drove her to the edge, and strangers in swim trunks pushed her right over it."

"Give her time and I'm sure she'll be back to wearing you out with how well she spoils your kids." *Give her time.* Will had used the same platitude on Dana regarding Leah. But this situation was different. Dana nudged the thought out of her head and changed the subject.

She leaned forward, hands clasped in her lap. "You know how Zola's been a pain in your rear lately and how she complained about her pitiful love life Wednesday night?"

"Uh-huh." Josie arched an eyebrow, her tone flat, as if bracing for whatever wild scheme Dana was about to unveil.

"Do you remember my old writing teacher—well, not *old*. He's in his thirties—Carlos Ruiz?" Dana scratched at a hangnail, her confidence evaporating now that Josie was across from her. So much for rehearsing this conversation in her head for the last four days.

"I met him at your book signings." Josie's brows pinched, suspicion flickering in her eyes.

"He's a single dad, and lately he won't stop whining about his dumpster fire of a love life and how even his ex-wife has found her soulmate, and all he's found are women with attachments to guinea pigs."

"Guinea pigs, really?" Josie let out a chuckle.

"Something like that." Who could remember what purse animal he'd gone on and on about? "What's important is he's lonely, and it's making him cranky and overly critical, which is turning into a real problem for the romance writer in our group." Dana drew her finger through beads on condensation on her tea glass, not quite daring to make eye contact with Josie.

"And you want to set him up with Zola."

"It couldn't hurt to try, right?" Dana lifted one shoulder in a sheepish shrug. "I mean, if they don't hit it off, neither of them is worse off than they already are."

"Or they'll take it out on us for setting them up in the first place." Josie plunked her tumbler on the table. "Then, they'll be a hundred times more difficult to work with, and *we* end up being the ones who are worse off."

An even fouler Carlos, nitpicking every line of Dana's work was not a Carlos she could continue meeting with. Certainly not twice a week. She sagged against the sofa cushions, deflated. "I guess introducing them is a bad idea after all." But then a spark caught. The corners of her mouth tugged upward. "Unless…what if we don't set them up? What if they just so *happen* to meet on their own?"

Josie sucked air through her teeth. "I don't know. Still seems risky. They're bound to find our fingerprints all over it. I think it's best if we mind our own business. And with my booth lease coming up for renewal, the last thing I need is Zola looking for an excuse to toss me."

She glanced at her phone. "I better get home. Lots to do before tomorrow." She scooped up her tumbler, stood, and flashed a wry smile over her shoulder. "Thanks for being my escape."

Dana walked Josie out and pulled a few random weeds in the front yard as Josie crossed to her own side of the cul-de-sac. The more she thought about it, the more defensive she got. Setting up Carlos and Zola was not as disastrous as Josie tried to convince her it was. They were both basically good people who'd helped Dana achieve her dreams—one of becoming a published author, the other of having shiny hair with no pesky grays. Besides being single parents, they also had Dana in common. How were they not made for each other?

Okay, she had no idea if their foundational beliefs, such as faith and thermostat settings, aligned. She couldn't recall if these were ever topics of discussion back when Zola had been Dana's hairdresser. And they sure didn't come up in critique group. So what if they didn't make a love connection and live happily ever after? Carlos hated that term anyway, but there was still a chance he would enjoy hanging out with Zola and lighten up on Dana and Bev for a while.

"Come on, ref. Open your eyes!" shouted the owner of the backside currently blocking Dana's view of the football field.

She might've minded more if the sun weren't roasting her. It was probably a state law that mandated stadiums be built with the setting sun blinding the visiting opponents. As it was, the reprieve of the man's broad shadow was almost worth the racket.

The only thing worse than having a son playing middle school football was one competing at the junior varsity level. The bigger the kids, the harder they tackled, and the louder their parents got. The worst part though, was out-of-town games.

Dana and her dad left Lubbock midafternoon to make it to Odessa in time for the 6:00 p.m. kickoff. Will was already in the Permian Basin for his usual Thursday business meeting and was supposed to be here by now, but he'd missed half of the first quarter. And whatever play prompted

Sunblock Guy's scorn of the ref.

At least tonight they had their own section. Some stadiums crammed both JV home and visiting crowds onto the same side, which only stirred up more bleacher drama. A few parents always took the game way too seriously and acted as if their kids were being scouted by the NFL.

"Marco, you better hit somebody," shrieked a zealot to Dana's left in a tone sharp enough to rattle the aluminum bench.

Dana slid her eyes to the woman, memorizing her face so she wouldn't repeat the mistake of sitting so close at next week's game. She'd be easy enough to spot in the custom jersey with Marco's name and number and his face on a button pinned to her team hat.

The ref blew his whistle, and within seconds, Marco's mom shot to her feet squawking, "That's my baby, number seventy-two. Way to pound him, Markie!"

Dana leaned close to her dad and whispered, "I feel sorry for Marco."

He pointed at the wilting figure next to her. "I feel sorry for his dad."

At last, Will waved from the bottom of the bleachers, shrugging out of his suit coat as he climbed. By the time he reached their row, his tie hung loose, and his hair stuck damply to his forehead. "It's hotter than blazes out here." He dropped the coat on the bench beside him. "How's the game going?"

"Who can tell?" She motioned toward the rear end in front of her. The scoreboard read zero to zero, and third down, and that was the best she could offer. If Will wanted more insight, he'd have to ask Marco's mom.

Will rolled his sleeves to the elbow and leaned forward. "Hey buddy, you mind taking a seat?"

Dana froze. Confrontation turned her stomach. If this guy decided to go a few rounds with her husband, she had no plan, short of hiding behind her elderly father.

"Oh, my bad." The man sat, and Dana flinched as the sun once again seared holes in her corneas.

She covered her eyes as they adjusted to the abrupt change in light intake. On either side of her, Will and her dad sprang to their feet amid the angry shouts of many parents voicing their dismay at the lack of a yellow flag being thrown. Had she been watching the game, Dana would've seen Nate take a late hit from a linebacker three times his size. By the time she registered the commotion, a hushed silence fell over the crowd.

"What'd I miss?" Dana looked between her father and Will, their faces filled with fear. "Is that Nate on the ground? Why isn't he getting up?" Dana shoved past Will, but he caught her arm.

"You can't charge onto the field because your kid got hit."

The players dropped to one knee.

He was lucky she didn't hit *him*. "That's my son." First, Will had tried to toss Adam back on a horse that had already bucked him, and now he wanted her to sit still while Nate— She couldn't even finish the thought. All she managed was a single desperate word, *Jesus*.

Trainers swarmed Nate, and after the longest minute of Dana's life, he wobbled to his feet. A thunder of applause broke out on both sides of the stadium. The game lurched back to life while Nate was led to a bench behind the sideline and a man shined a penlight into his eyes.

"I'm going down to see what I can find out." Will took the steps two at a time.

Dana held in the urge to ask why it was different if he went down to the field than if she did.

Her dad patted her knee. "I'm sure Nate's fine. Try not to worry."

Easy for him to say. "Dad, you only raised a girl, and they're far less injury prone than boys are."

His mouth quirked a thin, half-smile. "Really? You seem to have forgotten your trip to the emergency room for stitches when you fell out of that tree. Or your own daughter's broken wrist playing soccer last year."

"Yeah, yeah." Sometimes his dementia symptoms scared her. Other times, like this, his memory was sharp enough to drive her crazy.

Eventually, Will returned. "Got the wind knocked out of him, but otherwise fine. The head trainer checked him for a concussion. He's going back in."

"Back in the game?" Dana's pitch nearly rivaled Marco's mom.

"Honey, he wants to play. It's what we're here for."

Nate didn't take the field again until the second half, and every time he did, Dana laced her fingers through Will's and squeezed until he pried her hand away. "You're crushing my bones."

In the fourth quarter, Nate caught a punt return and ran it into the end zone, but the team still lost by ten points.

On the way home, her dad nodded off, which suited Dana fine because it gave her time to think. She'd never been one of those bubble-wrap moms, not even after Leah's accidents. Plural. There was the fire hydrant she hit her first day with a license, a fender bender in the school parking lot junior year, then the broken wrist. Kids got hurt. That was life, but then again…

The Creed family from church flashed through her mind. Their son had been three years ahead of Leah and just seventeen when a football tackle crushed his spine and left him paralyzed. What if that happened to Nate or Adam? Today's close call was enough for Dana to know her heart couldn't take a worse injury. Texas might worship Friday night lights, but surely there had to be a way to convince Will to pull the boys out of football for their own protection.

Dana perched on the edge of their bed, arms crossed, while Will reclined on one elbow, still unbothered by Nate's brush with death.

"What happened to that Creed kid was a one-in-a-million hit. It's awful, sure, but hundreds of boys and a handful of girls take the field every week across the South Plains, and ninety-nine times out of a hundred, they walk away unharmed."

"And what about the one time?"

"Minor bumps and bruises. Stories they'll brag about someday. Teaches them grit."

Dana didn't care if her boys had cool stories. And they could learn grit in safer ways. "I'm putting my foot down on this."

He swung his legs over the side of the bed and wrapped his arms around her. "Dana, I know you don't want to hear this, but you're being irrational."

Her mouth dropped open. She clenched her jaw and shrugged away from Will's embrace. "Are you kidding? I'm the only rational one here. My kid got flattened by Goliath's descendant. We aren't waiting until he's in a wheelchair before we put a stop to this nonsense."

He shifted to face her. "Let me get this straight. Nate gets tackled—while wearing protective gear designed to prevent injury—in a game where tackling is the literal point, and you want us to pull him and Adam out immediately. But two days ago, when a thousand-pound beast threw the little one on the ground—on his back, no less—with *no* protective gear, you let our other son ride away like it was no big deal."

"That was different." Dana rubbed her forehead. "We didn't force Adam to keep riding."

"And no one is forcing either of them to keep playing football. But mark my words—if you pull them out of a sport they love because of your fear, you'll do more damage than football ever could. Leah will come around in time. But the boys? They'll look back on this as the moment everything shifted. They'll wonder how far they could've gone—in football, maybe in life—if their mom had believed in them and been less controlling. And they might not forgive you for it."

She hated when he used logic against her.

Chapter 14

Josie

Josie slid her scissors and comb into their drawer as Elisa stormed into her booth. "Can you believe her?"

In a salon full of women, that could mean anything. "Believe who?"

Elisa gave her a look. "Check your phone."

Josie's jaw flexed as she opened the group text Zola had blasted to every operator.

I shouldn't even have to say this, but Sanctuary isn't your personal dumping ground, and newsflash—your mothers don't work here. Stop leaving messes for other people to deal with. I won't tolerate sloppy shampoo stations or pigsty booths. This isn't summer camp, and you're not twelve. Start acting like professionals or find somewhere else to play hairdresser.

Elisa shook her head. "Could she be any more condescending?"

Not without hurting herself. "She's something else." Josie seethed. "I love this location because it's close to my house, but I'm sure my clients would understand if I moved to another salon where the owner was less of a…" The right word eluded her.

"Jerk? Dictator?" Elisa checked over her shoulder and lowered her voice. "You know, when she wears that long jacket, she does kind of resemble Napoleon."

Josie chuckled. "Be nice."

"I was. I didn't use any of the descriptors I wanted to." Elisa flipped her hair over her shoulder and smirked. "I've got a client under the dryer. I better go before Her Eminence has me beheaded for abandoning my post."

None of the booths at Sanctuary were sloppy. Each stylist followed state licensing standards, and they worked together to keep the shampoo room spotless. Zola hadn't just overstepped with her harsh message. She clearly needed glasses if she thought the place was in disarray. And who wanted a cut and color by someone squinting at their head because she was too vain to wear corrective lenses?

That night at MOMS, Dana cornered Josie by the refreshments. "What's going on with you? You keep glaring at the door like you're about to deck somebody."

"Read this." Josie thrust her phone at her, Zola's message glowing on the screen.

Dana's eyes went wide. She mouthed an exaggerated, "Wow."

"I know, right? I left to pick up the kids soon after she sent it, so I didn't see her. I figured she'd either text an apology for being rude or I'd calm down. But nope. No apology, no calm. I've been stewing all day." Josie shot another look at the door. "If she shows up tonight, I don't know if I'll be able to hold back."

"Tell you what, if she does, I'll run interference so you don't have to face her alone."

Josie nodded. Dana's level head would make a solid buffer. Between her and Mrs. Steen, Josie might actually keep her cool and not throttle Zola. At least not in the church building.

A small bell tinkled.

"Good evening, ladies. Let's find our seats and get started." Serena, the pastor's wife and group leader, set the bell on the lectern in the corner.

"Well, that's new," Josie muttered.

"Yeah, I'm sure a bell won't get old at all." Dana rolled her eyes playfully, not in the scathing way Leah often did.

Josie slipped into the empty seat between Mrs. Steen and Kathy. Just in time, too. Zola settled into the chair beside Dana as Serena launched into her announcements.

"As many of you know, this semester we're partnering with Agape House," Serena said. "It's a haven for women leaving domestic violence and substance abuse. Women ready to begin a new life. I know everyone here has struggles, but most of us have been spared the deprivation and hardship the women at Agape House have had to overcome." She paused while a couple of latecomers found their seats.

"Tonight, we'll hear from the director and learn how we can make a real difference for the residents. You'll find cards at the center of your tables to fill out afterward with your strengths and how you can best be used in this ministry."

Zola reached for a card and scanned it. Josie quickly snapped her gaze back to Serena before Zola caught her staring.

Serena introduced the director, Yolanda, who spoke with a mix of fire and tenderness. She painted a picture of women stepping into Agape House after unimaginable turmoil—women for whom a plain room and a bed of their own was a luxury.

Josie would trade her left arm for one night alone in a quiet room. She hadn't gotten to sleep past the break of dawn since the triplets came along. But for these brave survivors, a night of peace wasn't indulgence; it meant security.

"Safe housing is only the beginning." Yolanda clicked a slide on her PowerPoint presentation. "Our goal is to see every Agape House resident rebuild her life and step into independence. That can mean help with job applications, practice through mock interviews, even a makeover in our on-site boutique where she can borrow a professional outfit for her interview."

Bile rose in Josie's throat. Here she was fuming over a nasty text, while women in the same city were clawing their way out of nightmares Josie could barely imagine.

During the Q-and-A portion, hands shot up all over the room, moms eager to learn more about this worthy cause and how they could contribute. Some took notes, but all leaned in, captivated. When the director finished, Josie's earlier worries about whether she had the time to commit to Serena's pet project faded. She wasn't only interested. She was all in.

Josie grabbed a card and checked the box next to "hair and makeup." Across the table, Mrs. Steen stared at the ceiling, tapping the paper absentmindedly. Dana fixed the end of her pen between her teeth as if thinking what to write, and Zola scribbled intently. How much was there to say on the little notecard? Josie flipped it to the back, wondering if she'd missed the essay portion that stymied her friends and captivated her landlady.

After the meeting, Josie tried to duck out quietly and avoid Zola altogether, but luck wasn't on her side.

Zola snagged her by the arm as she slipped toward the door. "Josie, do you have a sec?"

"I really need to get my kids home and bathed."

"I've got to pick up Beck, too. We can walk down to the children's area together."

Perfect. Dana wouldn't be there to run interference after all. Josie muttered a silent prayer for self-control and for her face not to betray her real feelings. "What's up?"

"As I sat there tonight, listening to story after story of how Agape is saving women's lives, I just felt this gnawing in my gut about the group text this morning. I owe you and every stylist at the shop an apology."

Owed one but had yet to offer it. Josie let the unsaid apology hang in the air and pressed her lips together to keep from shouting, "That's the Holy Spirit convicting you." Instead, she simply said, "It was pretty brutal."

"It's not an excuse, but I had a crummy morning." Zola hugged her arms around herself, shrinking inside her already-petite frame. "A few people were late on their rent, which meant I had to cover overhead out of my own pocket this month. Meanwhile, Beck has a dental appointment I can't afford to cancel but just spent our deductible ordering shampoo and paying the receptionist."

At the bottom of the stairs, she pulled a tissue from her purse and dabbed the corner of her eye. "Then while I was cleaning out a dye tray someone left in a sink, I overheard a couple of stylists who still owe rent chatting about how much they spent on new shoes and going out Saturday night, and I lost it."

Josie's irritation softened into real sympathy. She wouldn't trade places with the salon owner for anything—raising a child alone, dealing with client complaints, late shipments, and bills on top of it all. "It might help if you raised late fees. Or offered a small discount for stylists who pay at the first of the month instead of breaking their rent into installments."

"If I can barely afford to keep the lights on now, why would I offer a discount?" The edge in Zola's tone chipped away at Josie's compassion.

"Weekly payments are more likely to be late than a lump sum on the first of the month. A discount offers an incentive for stylists to pay up front, which would be cash flow security for you."

"Hmm." Zola's scowl morphed into a cheerful smile as Beckett waved from the doorway of his classroom. "You've given me something to think about. Again, I'm sorry for the text this morning." She greeted her son with open arms.

It was as if two women lived in that tiny body—an arrogant hardnose who called herself a girl boss and a mom who was doing her best and still scared she was falling short. Lately, every encounter with Zola set Josie's teeth on edge, but then she ended up feeling sorry for her. Could there be a simple solution to dialing back Zola's sharpness?

Josie paused outside the preschool hall and pulled out her phone.

I changed my mind. How soon can we set up Carlos and Zola?

Josie's phone vibrated in the cupholder as she backed out of the church parking lot. No doubt Dana was full of questions at the sudden change of heart, but Josie ignored the Bluetooth notification on the Odyssey's screen until she pulled into the garage at home.

Dana: Why the sudden about-face?

Josie: Zola's unraveling, and I'm desperate. She added a shrugging emoji.

Dana: When can you meet to make a plan?

Josie: Your patio as soon as the trips are in bed.

Dana responded with a thumbs up emoji.

"Mom!" Connor kicked his feet against his booster seat. "Can we get out now?"

Josie unbuckled her seatbelt and opened her door. "Sorry, guys. Let's go see Daddy."

Some days, she wished the kids could free themselves from their seats. It would speed up getting into the house. Then again, Connor and Ben rarely sat still unless confined with no other options. If they could unbuckle while she was driving, her minivan would become a rolling bounce house, and she'd probably find herself on the shoulder of the road with a state trooper at her window. No, their buckle ineptness was a blessing.

The kids barreled into the house with Josie on their heels. Hunter stood over the sink with a plate of spaghetti in one hand. He quickly set it on the counter a split second before three short humans tackled his legs.

"Daddy, you're here." Olivia reached up, bouncing on

her toes.

He knelt to hug each of them and lifted Olivia into his arms. "Hey, baby girl. How was your day?"

"Connor cut in line at music, and Miss Piper made him go to the back."

Connor folded his arms and tucked his chin with all the indignation his four-year-old self could muster. "Miss Piper's mean."

"Sweetie, there are consequences to making bad choices, and cutting in line is a bad choice." Josie raked her fingers through Connor's hair as she kissed Hunter. "Hey, babe. How was your day?"

"The usual. The kitchen cabinets at the Elm house were the wrong size, and the garage doors showed up in white instead of black."

Hunter's construction business routinely hit snags like that, but he thrived on the work as one of the most sought-after builders in West Texas.

"At least no one got hurt. It could've been worse." It was her standard pep talk whenever minor problems or picky buyers put him in a mood.

"Joseph got hurt today," Ben said.

"Oh no. Who's Joseph, and what happened?" Josie braced for the rundown on a classmate's playground scrape.

"His brothers dropped him in a hole and smeared blood on his coat."

"Yeah," Olivia chimed in. "Then they told their dad Joseph was dead."

Josie caught Hunter's eye and grinned. At least the kids were paying attention in Wednesday night Bible class.

Connor yawned, Josie's signal to get the bedtime

routines started.

Awhile later, with the triplets tucked in and Hunter settled into his recliner, remote in hand, Josie slipped across the street to hash out a plan with Dana to tame Zola. Or at least one to trick her into becoming Carlos's problem for a while. Dana met her at the door and steered her toward the back patio, where candles ringed the brick firepit and flickered between two Adirondack chairs.

Josie raised an eyebrow. "Please tell me we aren't casting a love spell. I'm not comfortable with magic or voodoo."

"Don't be ridiculous. They're citronella." Dana sank into a chair. "Unless you'd rather donate your blood to the neighborhood mosquito population."

"If there were a spell to wipe out mosquitoes, I might could get on board with the dark arts."

Dana shook her head. "So, was it Zola's text that sent you over here after you swore the whole thing was a terrible idea? Or did she pull something else after the meeting?"

"I never said 'terrible.'" Josie tilted her face toward the sky, where the day's last streaks of orange and purple rimmed the clouds. "After the Agape House presentation, Zola admitted she felt bad about her appalling message. She's dealing with some things and took her frustration out on the rest of us. She could use some sensitivity training. Makes me wonder, though, if she'd be a happier person if somebody took an interest in her." Josie held up a finger. "And no, I'm not saying every woman needs a boyfriend to be happy. But in Zola's case, something's gotta give before she drives all the stylists out of Sanctuary."

"Still think we should nudge them together without

tipping them off?"

"More than ever. If we set them up outright and it backfires, or Zola falls for Carlos, but he doesn't like her, she'll make my work life completely miserable."

"So…" Dana tapped her nails on the arm of her chair. "Any suggestions on how we introduce them without implicating ourselves?"

Josie exhaled. "I wish I knew." Cicadas droned in the trees, loud enough to rattle her thoughts. So much for a peaceful evening. Josie's mind snapped back to the Agape House presentation. "Hey, what'd you think of Yolanda's talk tonight?"

Dana shifted in her seat. "That place is doing remarkable work. MOMS will be blessed to serve there as much as they are a blessing."

"What did you put on your card?"

"Card?"

"The one on the table. I checked the box for helping with hair and makeup. What about you?"

Dana squirmed. "I…didn't fill one out."

"A second ago, you called it a remarkable cause. Why wouldn't you want to help change more lives?"

"I don't have a gifting to offer those women."

Right. The twice-published author who'd gotten some shiny plaque from the PTA for masterminding the school's most profitable fundraiser had nothing to offer. Dana could probably singlehandedly find employment for all the Agape House residents while tripling their annual donations.

"You're selling yourself short. You've practically transformed half this city through Moms on Mission."

"That was all Serena." Dana waved a hand. "My only

contribution was griping about how building adult Sunday school classes around the ages of their children limited learning from parents who'd already survived the trenches. She ran with the idea of a mentoring group."

Josie folded her arms. "Are you forgetting the small matter of you being a school fundraising machine?"

"That was luck. One dad was an anesthesiologist going through a bitter divorce. He made an absurd donation so he wouldn't have to split it with his ex. Had nothing to do with me."

"Well, I give up." Josie planted her hands on the armrests and levered herself to stand. She wasn't getting anywhere with Dana, and those blasted cicadas were blocking all her creative matchmaking ideas. "I'll let you know if I think of something for Zola and Carlos. You need to fill out that card."

"I'll think about it." Dana stood and blew out the candles.

Harvey nudged Josie's thigh as the women made her way through the house. "Hey, big guy. Did you finally decide to get up and say hi to me?" She scratched his giant head.

Dana smiled as they said their goodbyes, but it stopped just below her eyes. Josie should've asked more questions, should've probed why her friend, who made everything look effortless, was suddenly so unsure of herself that even a simple volunteer form left her flustered.

As she turned the knob of her own front door, it hit her. Josie had made the conversation about herself, and she hadn't thought about how Leah's departure was affecting Dana. Shame crept in. What business did she have investing in a colleague's love life when she was neglecting her closest friendship?

Chapter 15
Dana

Dana turned the deadbolt and sagged against the door. Josie was right, of course. Filling out that volunteer card should've been straightforward, the least complicated part of Dana's week. Writing her name and checking a box was easier than cranking out another scene in her latest crime novel. A cinch compared to watching her sons get pummeled in the name of football, and far less complicated than pretending it didn't sting that she hadn't seen her daughter in a week and a half. But somehow tonight, she'd run out of pieces of herself to give, even to the worthiest of causes.

Will's booming laughter, mingled with Nate's howls and Adam's protests, filtered down the stairs. No doubt the three of them were huddled around a glowing screen, locked in a video game battle—the easy camaraderie she used to be part of before Leah moved out.

Harvey cocked his head and whimpered as if calling Dana out for lying to herself. He circled his favorite patch of rug three times, laid down with a huff, and gazed up at her.

"Oh, what do you know? You don't have a daughter."

In truth, nothing about Leah had been easy lately. She had grown increasingly outspoken, stubborn, and impatient with her mom as college loomed closer. And now that it had arrived, she couldn't even make time for her family. She didn't even attend church with them anymore, opting instead to go to the popular student ministry across town with her dorm friends.

"Just be glad she's going to church," Will had said. "Most kids quit once their parents stop dragging them."

Maybe so, but his words were no comfort. Leah didn't miss her mom the way Dana missed her. She hadn't even been home since she picked up the boys for the Hirschfield Ranch trip.

Guilt clawed at Dana. She'd failed to check on her own parent today, and he was far less self-sufficient than Leah. With a sigh, she headed for the kitchen to dig up her phone.

Her father answered with little more than a grunt.

"Hey, Dad. What are you up to?"

"I thought I might watch the climax of this *NCIS* episode, but between the dog needing out and you calling, I guess I'll have to wait for the rerun."

She rubbed her temple. "You know your streaming platform lets you rewind and pause your show." On good days, the man could book rideshares through apps on his phone and download digital books from the library. But today, the TV remote was too advanced for him?

Patch Johnson barked in the background.

"Did you call for something?" he asked, clearly not in the mood for small talk.

"Just checking on you."

"No change since you saw me at Adam's game last night. And I reckon there won't be one before I see you at Nate's tomorrow."

So much football. In time, she'd probably miss yelling for her kids, but right now she was counting the days until their seasons ended. "Did you eat today?"

"Maggie made flapjacks this morning, and she put a plate of roast with all the trimmings in my fridge for dinner. Heated it up before I sat down to watch my show. Now if you'll let me go, I might get to enjoy it before it gets cold."

Well, alrighty then. "Dad, I love you."

"Love you too. I almost forgot. Don't pick me up tomorrow. Leah said she'd swing by and take me to Nate's game."

"That's nice. See you then." Her heart did a little flip as she ended the call. Leah was coming to the game. Maybe she'd stop by the house for a late dinner afterward.

"What are you grinning about?"

Dana startled. She hadn't heard Will walk down the stairs. She clapped and twirled in a happy dance. "We get to see Leah tomorrow. Feels like it's been two months rather than two weeks since she left us."

He rested his hands on her waist. "Hon, I think you would've taken her leaving better if she'd gone farther than across town."

"What do you mean?"

"If she'd gone to…say, Texas A&M or that burnt-orange school in Austin we don't speak of, we wouldn't see her until Thanksgiving. You wouldn't wait on edge, wondering when she'll grace us with her presence."

She shoved his hands away. "So, you wish our daughter had picked a college across the state? I don't even know what to say to that."

"Not at all, honey." He softened. "But I hate watching

you get your hopes up. You probably figured Leah would come over for dinner once a week, maybe bring over her laundry and crash in her old room on the weekends."

Dana opened her mouth to protest, ready to tell Will how ridiculous he sounded. But the words stuck because he was right. As much as she wanted Leah to thrive on campus, she secretly hoped her little girl would still need her, still miss her. And like Dorothy leaving Oz, sooner rather than later, Leah would discover there's no place like home.

Right or not, Dana wasn't about to give him the satisfaction. "Doesn't matter. She's bringing Dad to the game tomorrow." She spun on her heel and breezed out of the kitchen.

Dana, Will, and Adam arrived at the high school stadium early, which had given Adam more than enough time to raid the concession stand before kickoff. He plopped onto the bleacher, arms loaded with a soda, nachos, and a pickle.

"Want a nacho?" he asked through a mouthful.

"No thanks. I'm too nervous to eat." Dana thumbed out a quick text to her dad and Leah. **North forty-yard line, four rows up.**

Will laid a hand on her bouncing knee. "What are you nervous about?" He leaned across her and swiped a chip oozing with liquid cheese.

"Careful. I don't want you dripping that on me." She put her hand between her lap and Will's chip as he drew it to his mouth.

They'd promised last week not to share her football-injury worries with the boys. Which left her with no way to explain the knot in her stomach over Nate playing without Adam catching on.

Adam slurped his soda. "Is it because Leah's bringing Jordan?"

"She is?" Will practically choked on the boy's name and clamped his fingers tighter on Dana's knee. "Did you know Jordan was coming, honey?"

"Why would Jordan make me nervous?" More like disappointed. Dana yanked her leg free. "This is the first I've heard about it, anyway." Now Leah would split her attention between the field and her beau, and Dana would be lucky to get two sentences out of her.

"You and Dad act weird around him. Like you can't relax," said Adam.

Since when did the youngest child get so perceptive? "That's silly. Jordan's perfectly lovely," she trilled.

Will snorted. "Perfectly lovely? I've never heard you use that phrase before. I'm surprised you didn't say it with a British accent."

Adam jumped in with the worst Cockney brogue imaginable. "How lovely. Here they come now, just in time for high tea with the royals."

"Hilarious." Dana stole a sip of his drink and gagged. Root beer, gross.

"Hey, you got your germs on my straw." He wiped it with the hem of his tee shirt, already a petri dish of middle school locker room funk.

Leah waved as she guided her grandfather up the steps, her hand looped through his elbow.

"I'm not an invalid, granddaughter. You can let go."

She lifted both hands. "Sorry, Pops. You struggled getting out of the pickup, so I wasn't sure."

Pops lowered himself beside Adam and ruffled his hair. "Lifted trucks are murder on my arthritic knees. But I can climb stairs just fine."

Dana rose to hug Leah, but Will beat her to it. "Hey, baby girl. Glad you could make it." He offered his hand to Jordan. "Mr. Hirschfield. Welcome."

The two exchanged stiff nods, casting their eyes downward.

Leah and Jordan squeezed between Dana and Adam. Jordan declined Adam's offer to share his nachos, but they bantered over the size of the opposing team's defensive line, which was warming up on the field.

Nonchalance wasn't Dana's strong suit, but she refrained from throwing her arms around the prodigal daughter, instead offering a casual conversation opener. "How are your classes?"

"Seriously, Mom?" Leah hissed.

"What?" Dana made sure to wear a plain tee just to avoid causing a stir, and somehow, she did anyway. So much for casual.

"You know Jordan's not in college, and you're just asking me that to rub it in his face. Like, 'hey, my daughter's smarter than you'." Her hushed tone was sharper than a paring knife.

As if that were Dana's fault. "So, even though we forked over your tuition, which, by the way, cost more than your car, we're not allowed to ask how it's going?"

The voice over the loudspeaker cut her off, instructing

the spectators to rise for the national anthem. An instrumental version of *The Star-Spangled Banner* blared from the P.A., and with her hand over her heart, Dana fumed. Were there no safe topics that wouldn't send Leah into a rage?

Their outing to the ranch had been amicable. Could she bring up the baby chicks without Leah trading places with her little brother to get away from her?

Nate strode to midfield as one of the team captains for the coin toss. The whole family sprang up and cheered.

They won, opting to receive, and Nate took his place on special teams. Dana's legs turned to jelly, and she sank onto the bench. She held her breath through the kickoff. Her fingers dug into the hem of her shorts until Will pulled her hand onto his lap and covered it with his own. "It's all going to be okay," he whispered.

Will turned out to be only half right. Nate's team won by two touchdowns, and there were no injuries on the field. But Leah ignored her parents for the rest of the game, her two sentences wasted on that biting accusation.

As they made their way to the parking lot, Will invited everyone over for pizza.

"No thanks, Mr. Harding. I've got an early morning," said Jordan.

Dana's mouth twitched before bowing into a less-than-heartfelt smile. "Well then, it was great to see you. Remember, you're welcome to come over anytime." Whatever it took to get Leah there.

"Thanks, Mrs. H. Will do."

She wrapped Leah in a side hug, the most affection she dared for now. "If you and Pops want to stay for dinner, you can ride with us, and I'll take you home later."

Her firstborn recoiled. "That would be rude to Jordan."

"We couldn't have that, could we?"

Dana kissed her dad's thin, weathered cheek. "Blink twice if you're their hostage and need help."

He patted her forearms. "Patch probably needs out by now. I'll call you tomorrow."

And just like that, time with Leah went up in smoke faster than a West Texas grassfire in July.

Dana returned from dropping the boys at school on Friday and started a load of laundry before opening her laptop at her desk. It dinged to life with a barrage of notifications.

Serena had emailed twice in the wee hours with ideas she wanted to bounce off Dana. Toy and clothing drives for Agape House, a cookie decorating party to kick off the Christmas season, and a Bunco night in the church rec center where residents of Agape House could get to know women from MOMS. Nothing outlandish until Dana read the last suggestion on the list.

"Wouldn't it be great if you taught a creative writing class?"

No, quite the opposite of great. Dana wasn't a teacher, and she failed to see how a writing class would help employ someone or secure permanent housing. She reached for her phone to advise Serena to dial back her exuberance and maybe take things one step at a time.

The pastor's wife picked up on the first ring. "You're

never going to believe it." She didn't wait for Dana to respond. "I just got off the phone with Yolanda. She wants to schedule an employment-readiness fair in three weeks," she squealed.

"Would this be a day of resume-building, makeovers, and mock interviews?" Dana asked.

"You guessed it. I can't believe how quickly it's coming together."

Neither could Dana. "How are you going to pull off such a big event on short notice?"

"*We,* not me. Almost everyone at Moms on Mission filled out cards with their specific volunteer interests and skills. The sooner we get started, the sooner residents at Agape House can get a jump on their new beginnings."

If the Wednesday MOMS were excited to volunteer, it made sense to capitalize on their eagerness.

Serena cleared her throat. "I noticed *you* didn't turn in a card. Don't you want to help make a difference for women in transition?"

Well sure. The problem was, Dana couldn't think of one thing she did well that might help another mom get hired or move into a home of her own. Her skills were limited to developing surprising plot twists and characters with quippy one-liners. And rooting for her kids. Mostly.

Half the stands gave her the evil-eye at Adam's last game because she'd cheered at the opposing team's interception. It wasn't her fault everyone on the field had on blue pants and white jerseys. All gawky middle schoolers looked the same when you slapped a helmet on them. So, she was good at one thing only, and unless any aspiring crime writers attended the job-prep fair looking for advice getting started, her skill wouldn't be all that helpful.

"I'd be happy to arrive early and set up," she offered.

"Did you get a chance to look at the email I sent you?" Serena had the hopeful timbre of a kid asking Santa if he'd read her Christmas list.

"Yes, and inquiring minds would like to know when you sleep since you were up at all hours of the night composing electronic dissertations."

"Then you'll do it?"

Dana sucked in her bottom lip. "Coordinate a toy drive? Why not? I'm already sitting on a tub of building bricks ready to go." And it was the most elegantly sorted bin there ever was, but now that it was organized, Adam had mixed feelings about letting it go.

"I already have a volunteer coordinator for the toy and clothing collections. I was talking about teaching creative writing."

"About that." Dana rubbed her forehead and said a silent prayer for the right words not to offend her friend. "A writing class won't get anyone hired."

The silence on Serena's end stretched for an uncomfortable few seconds. "Sometimes the best way to process heartache and tragedy is through journaling and creative writing. For many, it's even a form of worship."

By the end of the conversation, Dana had promised to think about it. After all, she'd joined Carlos's writing class while grieving the passing of her mom. Escaping into worlds she created had soothed her broken heart. Now, her writing served as an income stream that almost covered the cost of Leah's textbooks.

Dana set the phone down and tapped a restless rhythm

against the desk. The cursor blinked on the empty page, mocking her. Serena and Yolanda already had momentum, real plans, real ways to help. Agape House had built something that mattered, lifting women, reshaping their futures. The Wednesday MOMS could carry that reach even further, helping change entire family trees. Kids who watched their mothers break free from abuse and addiction wouldn't have to repeat the same patterns.

Everyone else seemed to know exactly how to pitch in, while Dana only stewed in her own uselessness. If she couldn't reach her own daughter, what business did she have pretending she could help a stranger?

Chapter 16
Josie

"Mo-om-uh. I need you."

Josie dried her hands on a dishtowel and hurried to the boys' room. "What's wrong, Benny?"

"The tablet died." Ben sat cross-legged on his bed, holding out the device in its indestructible blue case.

He was on day three of a mild case of strep throat with a stubborn fever that refused to break. Josie and Hunter had been trading off staying home with him and scrubbing down every surface of the house. By some miracle, Connor and Olivia hadn't caught it yet, but keeping Ben quarantined to his bed was getting harder by the hour.

"I'll bring you a charger. But don't get up except to go to the bathroom. Got it?"

He glared up at her with pouty eyes, ringed in feverish halos. "I want to go play outside. This is not fun."

"You're too sick to have fun. Your body needs rest." Josie sympathized with him, though. She was going stir-crazy herself, but the only thing worse than a sick kid was a houseful of sick kids, and his entertainment wasn't worth spreading germs.

She brought a charger and plugged in the tablet, loaded

with educational games and preschool shows, then snuck into the garage. It may have been almost October, but the heat still pressed in.

Praying the hum of the motor wouldn't draw Ben's attention, Josie hit the button to raise the overhead door. A fall breeze rushed in, stirring dirt and leaves on the concrete floor. She cleaned out the back seat of the Odyssey and grabbed a broom to sweep up.

Dana crossed the cul-de-sac balancing a foil-covered plate on her palm like a server in a restaurant. "Thought y'all could use some chocolate chip cookies."

Josie peeled back the foil and grabbed a cookie still warm from the oven. "When do you even have time to bake?" she asked through a mouthful.

"When I'm procrastinating writing, I can find time to do all kinds of things. Need your gutters cleaned or your trees trimmed? I'm your girl."

Josie took the plate and set it on the hood of the minivan. "Thank you. I'd invite you in, but I don't know if Ben's still contagious." She took another bite and wiped melty chocolate bits from her lip. "The doctor said he would be fine after twenty-four hours of antibiotics, but that doesn't make sense. Why would he need to take them for ten days if one day kills enough bacteria for him to safely return to school? Besides, he's still running a fever."

"After eighteen years, I'm probably immune to strep by now. Want me to pick Connor and Livvie up from school or stay with Ben while you get them? You sound like you could use a break."

"My mom's getting them. Thank you, though." Josie propped the broom against the wall and gave Dana her full attention. "So why are you procrastinating writing?"

Dana shrugged. "Serena's gung-ho about implementing her ideas to change lives at Agape House, and I still don't know how I can be useful there." She put up her hand as if reading Josie's mind. "Before you disagree, hear me out. The residents need help polishing their resumes and learning how to budget. Things that will sustain them in their new lives. All I have to offer is a working knowledge of how to kill victims with unconventional murder weapons."

Josie folded her arms and snorted. "Theoretical."

"What?"

"If you had *working* knowledge, it would mean you'd tested them out, right? What you've got is *theoretical* knowledge." She took a wary step backward. "At least I hope so."

"See? I don't even have a good handle on the English language. How am I supposed to help a former addict rebuild her life?"

Josie bit back the urge to tell her neighbor how absurd she sounded. They'd been over this before, and whatever Dana was wrestling with, she needed to work it out for herself.

"I volunteered to coordinate the toy and clothing drives, the one thing I would've been good at, but Serena's already got them covered."

"What do you mean by 'the one thing'?" In the four and a half years they'd been neighbors, Josie had yet to see Dana try something she *wasn't* good at.

"I can oversee organizing like you wouldn't believe. Last month, when Leah and Nate were on my last nerve, I made them sort a ten-gallon tub of LEGOs by size, shape, and color. If I'd been thinking, I'd have made them arrange the pieces by which set of instructions they matched, but that might've gotten me reported to Amnesty International for cruel and unusual treatment of prisoners."

Josie snickered. "At least you're getting them out of your house. My in-laws bought the boys some LEGO sets that are well above their age level. Before I know it, they'll be strewn everywhere, stabbing my bare feet."

"Adam has a renewed interest in ours now that they're neat and orderly, so we'll see if they actually get donated. Which brings me back to my limited helpfulness."

"Any woman conniving enough to dream up a punishment like sorting LEGOs has plenty to offer." Josie reached for the broom and regathered the debris the wind had scattered. "And that's not even including your ingenious killing expertise."

"Serena wants me to teach a creative writing class. How ridiculous is that?"

"Hmm." Josie snagged a second cookie and leaned on the broom handle.

"What's that supposed to mean?"

"Seems like your creative writing skills could be useful for plumping up a resume." She left off how Dana could've come to that logical conclusion on her own.

Dana folded her arms, one elbow propped thoughtfully. "You mean like turning 'fry cook at a fast-food joint' into 'ensured health-code compliance and thrived under high-pressure in fast-paced conditions'?"

"Exactly. And maybe Professor Carlos would lend his expertise for a couple of hours. After all, he's the one who convinced you to write a novel." Josie's eyes went wide as the thought clicked. A sly smile tugged her lips. "And if a certain hairdresser-slash-salon owner happened to be volunteering too, well, that wouldn't be the worst thing, would it?"

A grin spread across Dana's face. "Why, Josie Caraway. You're a more devious schemer than I ever imagined. Have *you* considered writing murder mysteries?"

The door to the house swung open, and Josie and Dana swiveled toward it. Ben stood in the doorway, his gaze darting from his mother to the half-eaten cookie in her hand.

"I want one."

"What are you doing out of bed?" Josie slid a cookie out from beneath the foil and passed it to him.

"I heared you talking. Hi, Dana."

"Hi, Benny." Dana waggled her fingers. "I hope you're feeling better."

"Cookies make my tummy feel better." He took a bite the size of his entire mouth.

"Then you can thank Dana for making them."

"Oh, thank you." Ben's affection for chocolate chip cookies ran as deep as his love of playing outside and climbing on…well, everything.

Josie turned toward Dana. "I'd better get him inside. And you, my friend, have some calls to make to Serena and Carlos."

As she settled Ben back in his bed, with an extra cookie for good measure, Josie mentally patted herself on the back for helping Dana out of her woe-is-me funk. How had the writer not been able to pick up on her ability to help other people?

"Mom, can I build the LEGOs Grandpa Peter bought

me?"

She cringed. Hunter and Josie had been so sneaky to stash the building sets after their trip to the Metroplex in hopes the boys would forget about them. A safe bet since their attention spans resembled a fruit fly's. Ben must've been eavesdropping on her and Dana's conversation.

"Not today, sweet boy. That's a toy for when you're well." And hopefully when she wasn't home. "Tell you what, why don't you draw out a design to build when you're feeling better?"

He pressed his lips together and gave her a look that said she was not using her brain. A look she suspected would become a fixture as her trio of headstrong children grew into adolescence. "There's are-dee a picture on the box of what you're 'posed to build."

Well played. "You and Daddy can get them out another time." She pressed the back of her hand to his forehead. "Take a nap, and if your fever goes away when you wake up, I'll let you play in the backyard for a little while."

He bounced on his knees. "Yay!" Unlikely he heard the part about a little while.

Josie washed her hands at the kitchen sink for the nine hundredth time in three days and went looking for her phone. Even if Carlos agreed to help at the job-readiness fair, if Zola was busy that day, it was back to the drawing board for her and Dana's matchmaking scheme.

She retraced her steps to the garage, where the plate of homemade cookies still rested on the Odyssey's hood. She picked it up, slid open the van's side door, and leaned across the middle row. Maybe she dropped her phone when she took out the floormats to shake off a layer of crumbs.

Ben tapped her on the rear. "This is buzzing." He held out her phone and swiped his other arm across his runny nose.

"Thank you. Where was it?"

"In my room."

With the contaminated phone in one hand and the cookie plate in the other, Josie debated how to close the car door without spreading strep to any other surfaces. She bumped the button with the back of her knuckle. "Back to your room, mister." Besides isolating patient zero to protect the rest of the family, Josie figured the more boring sick days were, the less liable the kids would be to fake it and play hooky down the road.

"Ah, man. Can I be well tomorrow?"

Please, Lord, let it be so. "That fever's gotta go away. How about we say another prayer for God to heal you?"

He clasped his hands and bowed his head. "You know why we bow when we talk to God?" His tone suggested he was testing to see if she knew as much as he did rather than asking out of curiosity.

Reverence. A term he didn't know yet. "Why, Benny?"

"Jesus lives in our hearts, so He can hear us better when we put our mouth down like this." He dropped his chin and pressed his mouth as close to his chest as he could.

His answer was better than hers. "Do you want to ask Jesus to take away your fever, or do you want me to?"

"Your hands are full. I'll do it."

She suppressed a smile.

Once the patient was back in bed, Josie took the cookies to the kitchen, scrubbed her phone with a disinfecting wipe, and washed her hands yet again. Then, she sent a text to Zola.

What are you doing three weeks from Saturday? That'll be the first day for the volunteer salon at Agape House.

Zola: I've got two clients in the morning, but Beckett will be with his dad, so I should be free to help after lunch.

Josie blew out a slow breath. That had gone easier than expected. Zola hadn't even thrown in a single biting remark. She tapped out a message to Dana.

Zola can only work the afternoon. Any news on the professor?

Three dots stayed on the screen for several seconds, disappeared, then returned. Dana was a decade older than Josie, but her texting wasn't usually that slow.

He can only volunteer until noon. We'll have to think of something else.

Bummer. It had been a long shot, anyway. Even if Carlos and Zola both made it to Agape House, Carlos would be styling resumes, far from the boutique where Zola would be styling hair.

Hunter called later in the day to check on Ben.

"He's the same. Too sick for school, but not sick enough to keep him from climbing the walls."

"Surely he'll be well by the weekend, right?" Hunter asked.

Just in time for the other two kids to come down with strep. "I hope so. I've got several clients on Friday. We can't ask my mom to stay with sick kids."

She clicked on the speaker, opened her calendar app, and scanned her appointments.

"Jos, we need a night out."

"Where's this coming from?" Not that she was objecting. Their last real date had been before school started.

"We've both had a long week already, and I miss hanging out with my wife."

It was only Tuesday, but yeah. All their time hanging out together lately was with little people hanging *on* them. "We haven't even had a real conversation without the kids interrupting since the Dallas trip."

Ben tugged on Josie's shirttail. "I napped. I can go outside now."

Josie picked up the phone and took it off speaker mode. "Perfect timing. You were saying?"

"Why don't we try to get Leah for Saturday night? We'll cancel if anyone's sick."

"Better make it Friday. She'll probably choose College Game Day over babysitting if we ask for Saturday."

"Good point. I want to watch that game, too. Do you have a restaurant preference? I'll make a rez if Leah says yes."

"Nope." Josie could've teased him for picking football over romance, but she liked watching the Red Raiders as much as the rest of the alumni, or, for that matter, the rest of the city, regardless of their college background.

They said their goodbyes, and Josie released Ben into the yard for some much-needed fresh air. From a patio chair, she texted Leah about Friday night, not expecting an answer anytime soon. The phone buzzed almost instantly, making her jump.

I'd love to babysit! Low on funds, and my parents are being annoying about me using the emergency credit card.

Josie chuckled. Many a freshman had been lured by free food and fast cash. Sometimes even by a free T-shirt. Much to her mother's dismay, she herself had applied for three different credit cards during her university years, sucked in every time by the promise of swag at a folding table. She and Hunter were protecting Leah from a similar fate by giving her a flexible side hustle and access to their fridge.

So what if her and Dana's scheme to unite their relationship-challenged friends had died in the water? The Caraways had a date night on the books. Strep might've come to steal Josie's joy, but a scheduled babysitter and a husband with dinner reservations offered her a beacon of hope. A chance at least for a moment's peace before the next round of chaos.

Chapter 17
Dana

Dana left a voicemail Leah would never hear because teenagers didn't check voicemail. "Hi, sweetie. I'm about to run to the store and wanted to see if you need anything. Snacks? Toiletries?" She cupped her hand over her mouth. "Feminine hygiene products?" Why was she whispering? No one else was home, and even if they were, the boys knew what a period was. "Text me a list, and I can drop your stuff off whenever is convenient. For you, I mean. Convenient for you." She swallowed. "Anyway, let me know. Love you."

The *Friends* episode where no one is ready for Ross's award ceremony played in her head, specifically the part where Monica tries to leave Richard a breezy message on his machine and instead says, "I'm breezy." Dana played it cool about as well as Monica did. Parenting a mostly-grown daughter had a lot in common with dating. Act casual but not *too* casual. Be supportive without smothering. Inevitably, she just came off awkward and weird.

Dana piled her cart high with teenage-boy survival food—Pop-Tarts, string cheese, single-serve pretzels and chips, and a variety of fresh fruit, half of which would probably rot untouched. She shifted things around to wedge in two gallons of milk when Leah finally replied.

I'm good.

Code for "I don't need or want your help."

Raising children not to need their mom was the end goal of the motherhood profession. By that standard, Dana was successful. So, why did it feel more like an occupational hazard?

The Tahoe drifted over the white stripe, eliciting a honk from the wild-eyed driver of a red corvette in the right lane. Dana mouthed an apology as Nate jerked the wheel, recentering them in the lane.

"Hey, Mom." He glanced over, while Dana yanked her seatbelt tighter with both fists.

"Eyes on the road."

"What do you call those flower things girls wear to Homecoming?"

"A mum. Well, technically that's the flower, but the whole contraption is more like a corsage with a hundred yards of ribbon and mini cow bells. Every now and then, you'll see one so elaborate it's more like a sandwich board." Texans liked to do their Homecoming mums up big.

"A what?"

"Slow down a little. You know, those signs people wear on their front and back when they hand out flyers."

"Can you make one before next week?"

"A sandwich board?"

Nate checked all three mirrors with practiced intensity. "No, a homecoming thingy."

Dana blinked. Crafting was not in her wheelhouse. "Wait. Did you ask someone to Homecoming?" Under normal conditions, she'd be screaming inside that her fifteen-year-old had a date, but this driving lesson had wrung every ounce of adrenaline out of her. That Nate even liked a girl was so unexpected. Last she'd checked, he was still geeking out over the same video games as his little brother and more invested in sports than in girls.

"Kinda. It's just my Pixel Pastures buddy. She's also in my biology class." Nate slammed on the brakes for the stop sign a quarter mile up ahead. "So can you make a…mam?"

"A Mum? Maybe. I'll have to look it up. Blinker, son!"

Dana staggered into the house, her muscles still twitching from bracing against Nate's erratic driving. Another hour of practice down. After surviving rush hour on the south Loop, they'd picked up two of Nate's buddies for a Friday night movie at the mall.

Will met her in the kitchen with a kiss. "Hey, where've you been?"

"Auditioning for the role of a crash test dummy in Nate's rendition of *The Fast and the Furious.*"

"Yikes. That sounds like a horror flick."

She leveled a glare at him. He joked as if he understood, but he always used work as his get-out-of-driver's-ed-free card. "Did you know your son has a date to Homecoming?"

Will's face lit up. "That's fantastic!"

Now she regretted telling him. "Isn't he a little young to be dating? When Leah was his age, you wouldn't have let her go out." She flopped onto the sofa and massaged the tension from her temples.

He tipped his head to the side. "That's different."

"Because she's your daughter?"

"Yeah."

Dana shook her head and rolled her eyes. "Your son wants me to whip up a mum, so I hope you're happy."

He gestured to his shoulder with fingers splayed. "You mean one of those fluffy monstrosities? Honey, I love you, but you're not exactly a Pinterest mom."

"Then you and Nate can have a nice father-son night figuring out how to make one together." Every florist in town sold homecoming mums this time of year, and they would probably save money ordering one over buying the supplies and courting disaster with a hot glue gun. And by "they," she meant Nate. No way was she financing his dating life. However, he'd asked her to make it, and it was the least she could do for one of her kids, especially since she apparently couldn't even buy groceries for the oldest.

"What do you say we grab stuff to make our own pizzas with Adam?" asked Will.

Why hadn't he suggested it before she spent half the afternoon in the supermarket? They made a list, and Will—bless him—offered to run to the store. It was only fair after she'd put her life on the line to help Nate get one step closer to his driver's license.

Will lifted his keys off the hook and opened the garage door. "Hon, did you know Leah was babysitting for the Caraways tonight?"

"No." She rose and peeked through the blinds. Sure enough, Leah's SUV, with her graduation tassel still dangling from the rearview mirror, sat against the curb across the street. "I wonder why Josie didn't tell me. Or why Leah wouldn't."

"Should we run over and say hi? That'd be fine, right?" Hope mounted in Will's questions.

She shrugged. The triplets would still be up, so no disruption there. But if Leah wanted to see them, she'd have mentioned the babysitting gig.

He rattled his keys in the open doorway. Was he arguing with himself about dropping by? "Come on. It'll be weirder if we pretend we don't know she's there."

Dana followed him through the garage and stood a few feet behind as he knocked on the Caraways' door so Leah would see him first. Will elicited a milder response from their daughter than she did these days.

"Who is it?" a little voice called from inside.

The handle rattled. "Connor, no. We never open the door without checking who's there."

"That's why I asked 'who is it.'"

Will leaned close. "It's Will and Dana."

Three kids tumbled out as Leah turned the knob. "Come play with us." They tugged at Will and Dana's hands.

Leah crossed her arms, a scowl pulling her mouth down. "What are you doing here?"

"Just saying hello," Dana said evenly.

"You're checking up on me."

"Why would we check up on you? You've been babysitting these guys for years." Dana should've let Will speak first.

"Might as well come in for a minute." Leah held the door, motioning them inside.

Will wrapped her in a bear hug. Leah offered a half-hearted pat on his back in return. Dana went with a one-armed side squeeze. Leah bristled but didn't pull away.

"Look what we got." Ben brandished a yellow LEGO box with a treehouse splashed across the front.

"Oh." Dana arched a brow. Leah had never been big on construction toys. Probably even less so after the tub-sorting punishment. "That looks…fun."

"The mosquitoes are too bad for the boys to play outside, so Josie thought this might keep them out of trouble until bedtime."

Will examined the box. "This looks a little advanced for preschoolers. I think they'll get frustrated and lose interest once they start."

"Great." Leah huffed. "Josie said it's all Ben's talked about for days."

And yet, Josie and Hunter held off breaking out the set until they were out for the night. Convenient. "Want to ask Adam to help?" Dana braced for a sharp retort.

Instead, Leah perked up. "Do you think he would?"

"Let's go ask him." Will herded the boys to the door while Olivia scooped up her baby doll and followed suit.

"We'll never get them back over here." Leah sighed. "Poor Harvey."

The triplets were the dog's best friends and worst nightmares.

"I'll get him." Connor ran ahead and barged through the garage door. "Adam!" His screech could've summoned the neighbors two doors down.

The gangly preteen stopped in his tracks as the parade met him in the kitchen. "What?" He held a corndog in one hand and a bag of chips in the other.

"I told you I was going to the store to get stuff to make dinner," said Will.

Adam pursed his lips. "Did you go already?"

"Not yet."

Adam bit off a chunk of corndog. "Then I don't see a problem. I'll eat again later."

Ben pushed past Will's legs. "Adam, you wanna help us build a treehouse?"

"Uh…" He looked between his parents, his eyes full of questions.

"He means a LEGO treehouse." Leah twirled her finger in Olivia's curls.

"Sure. I'll help," said Adam. He locked eyes with his sister. "But I'm coming home before their bedtime. Not doing your dirty work for you."

"Whatever, dude," said Leah.

Olivia hefted her baby doll onto her shoulder and patted its back. "Shh. Don't cry, Josefina. It's okay."

Leah's expression softened in a way Dana rarely saw from her fierce firstborn. "Hey, Livvie. I think I have something your baby might like in my room." She turned to Dana. "Is it okay if I give her my old doll accessories?"

A soft ache spread through Dana's chest. Of course, her college-age daughter would eventually want to part with childhood keepsakes, but hearing it still caught her off guard. What surprised her more was Leah's willingness to hand them over so freely to Olivia. Some of those pieces could bring in real money online.

"They're yours to do with as you please." Dana followed the girls into Leah's room and stood by silently as

Leah pulled a tote from the top of her closet.

She set it on the floor, popped off the lid, and nodded toward the contents. "See anything Josefina might like?"

Olivia peered inside, her doll still pressed to her shoulder. A delighted smile stretched between her rosy cheeks, and she laid the baby beside her. "Pajamas and a bottle. How 'bout these?" She held up a pink duck-print set of footie pajamas. "Gramma got me jammies on our trip, but not Josefina. She needs some."

"Anything else?"

"I can just take them?" The child's eyes grew wide.

"Sure. My dolls don't use them anymore," said Leah.

Olivia's mouth dropped. "You have baby dolls? Show me."

"I think you just got out of building a treehouse with the boys." Dana laughed. "But you might have to take Samantha and Kimmy back to the Caraways'."

Samantha and Kimmy were the dolls Leah had once begged her grandparents and Santa for. Samantha, the "Doll of the Year" when Leah was seven, came with a gymnast backstory. Her balance beam and bars, sold separately, had cost nearly as much as a semester of Leah's tumbling lessons.

Kimmy made her debut the next Christmas, her box barely open before Leah squealed, "She looks like me!" The doll's long blond hair, blue eyes, and dusting of freckles across her plastic nose sealed the resemblance.

Dana's lashes fluttered as she chased away the tears threatening to spill onto her cheeks.

"Oh, this is pretty." Olivia held up a turquoise dress with a ruffled hem.

"It's building time," announced Connor as he led the charge toward the garage.

"Livvie, let's take the box to your house." Leah reached for the lid.

"Okay. Get your babies." Olivia scooped up Josefina and filed out with her brothers.

Leah ducked back into the closet, metal hangers jangling as she rummaged.

"Can I help carry anything?" Dana kept her tone neutral. What she longed to ask but couldn't was why Leah hadn't told her parents she'd be babysitting across the street. Or why she'd been keeping her distance lately. But she swallowed the bitter words. If writing crime fiction—and watching *Die Hard* a thousand times with Will—had taught her anything, it was never to spook the captor with the hair-trigger fuse.

"Here." Leah produced a small wooden crib with purple flowers painted on it. "I want Olivia to have this. You don't think Josie will get mad that I'm cluttering up her house, do you?"

The Caraway home was a monument to childhood. Riding toys littered the back patio, and cars, puzzles, and blocks of every imaginable size and shape spilled from containers in the living room. The bedrooms brimmed with endless items to entertain busy kids. What was one more thing? "She might not even notice."

Leah emerged from the closet with two dolls in hand. She studied them both, then tucked the one that looked most like her back onto the shelf. "Samantha's Olympic training makes her better suited for a field trip across the cul-de-sac. She's used to extreme physical activity." A grin flickered at the corner of her mouth.

"Good thinking." Dana picked up the box of accessories, set the crib on top, and walked out behind Leah. "Remember when Kimmy had to go to the doll hospital because Harvey chewed her foot?"

"Yes. I still can't believe Dad made me pay for her repairs."

"We warned you not to leave your stuff out with a new puppy. Shipping a doll off for leg replacement must be among the weirdest things I've done for my children."

Dana shifted the tote onto her hip and pulled the door closed behind her.

"Hey, Mom." Leah didn't turn around, just kept walking across the yard. "I'm glad you came over."

No apology. No explanation. Just that. And it was enough. Dana's chest constricted. "Me too." For the first time in weeks, she let herself believe they would be okay.

Chapter 18
Josie

Josie and Hunter both reached for the last breadstick in the basket and chuckled. He broke it and handed half across the table as Zola walked into the restaurant on the arm of an older man in a leather sport coat. His thinning hair was slicked into a low ponytail, and even from across the room he emanated a vibe that made Josie's skin crawl.

She caught Zola's eye and waved. Her landlady veered over and introduced her date. He had one of those first names that should be a last name. Or a fancy car. Bentley, was it? Josie hadn't heard over the commotion of the restaurant and the man's loud Hawaiian shirt peering from beneath the camel-colored coat. The heat that thing must trap. Josie shuddered.

Bentley's glassy gaze never lifted above Zola's neckline, proof he'd pre-gamed and had only one thing on his mind, and it wasn't her sparkling conversation. Smarmy. That was the word Josie's mother would've used.

As the plates were being cleared, Josie brushed Zola's arm on her way to the restroom and gave a pointed tilt of her head. Zola arched her brows in mock innocence, but Josie held her stare until she finally sighed, muttered an excuse, and rose.

Josie waited with the door open, catching the echo of Zola's stilettos across the tile. The moment they were alone, Zola folded her arms and spun to face her. "What?"

"I don't think you should get in a car with Bentley. He looks like he's been overserved already. We can give you a ride home."

Zola shifted her weight to one hip. "I drove. And his name is Royce." She shook her head. "Where'd you get 'Bentley?'"

"I knew it was a car name. In my defense, it was noisy when you introduced him."

"Uh-huh." Zola shot daggers at Josie. "I know you're judging me for going out with an older man, but don't. He's fine. Probably. This is our first date, and Royce thought a highball would calm his nerves. But I'm taking him home after this, and he doesn't know where I live."

"Why would you have agreed to pick him up if this is your first meeting?"

"Josie, you've been married for like forever, so don't condemn those of us who are still putting ourselves out there. The fish in the sea everyone talks about are not as abundant as you think." She scrutinized the tile floor and cleared her throat. "Royce has a suspended license."

For driving under the influence, no doubt. "Promise you'll call me if you need an out from this guy."

"Fine." Zola's fight drained from her demeanor. "And Jos, it means a lot that you care."

"Thanks again for babysitting tonight." Josie pulled a wad of bills from her purse and pushed them toward Leah, who wrinkled her nose.

"Don't you have Venmo or the Cash app? No one uses actual paper money anymore."

Hadn't they always paid Leah in cash before? Josie shoved the money, for which she'd made a special trip to the ATM, back into her handbag. "Sure, I use Venmo for my business. Lemme just—" She fished her phone out, swiped her thumb across the screen, and typed Leah's Venmo username into the app.

The device in Leah's hand vibrated, confirming the transaction. She scanned it and gave a tight-lipped nod.

The beauty of handing off folded bills was that the grateful teen—make that *formerly* grateful teen—would pocket her pay, not bothering to count it in front of her employers. That she agreed to babysit the next time meant the amount had been sufficient. But this transaction was different. Had Josie done the math right in her head? She always paid well because…triplets, but Leah's unreadable expression made her second guess herself.

Leah picked up a plastic tub from the coffee table, next to a three-dimensional LEGO treehouse.

"I can't believe y'all built this whole thing before bedtime." Hunter traced the edges with his finger. "Incredible."

"That was mostly Adam's doing, but Ben and Connor helped, of course." Leah shook the bin. "Olivia and I played babies while they put it together. Oh, and I hope it's okay I gave Livvie some of my old doll clothes and a crib for Josefina."

Josie blushed, still not used to hearing her name regarding a toy. "How generous and sweet. Thanks." She pointed to the box. "Are you taking that back to your parents' house?"

Leah nodded.

"While you're over there, will you deliver this to Adam for his hard work?" Josie held out the bills again. Good thing they didn't go on dates often since she was paying double the usual rate.

"Sure. Let me know when you need me to babysit again." Leah gave a small, grateful smile and ducked under Hunter's arm as he held the door for her.

He lingered in the doorway, probably making sure she got inside the Hardings' safely. "I hadn't even considered hiring Adam to build the construction kit with the kids. That was even smarter than waiting until we left to let them open one."

"Smart indeed." Josie tried to stay in date mode and be present with Hunter, but her mind kept drifting to Zola. If she couldn't make better choices in men on her own, Josie and Dana would have to intervene sooner rather than later. What began as a mission to get an overbearing colleague off Josie's back was turning into one to save Zola from herself.

Josie unlocked her phone and sent a quick text asking for confirmation Zola had gotten home safely and then typed one to Dana. **Saw Zola on a date with a creep. We've got to steer her toward Carlos before chasing losers puts her in a dangerous situation.**

Hunter sank onto the sofa instead of the recliner, an unspoken invitation. Josie curled into his side, and they drifted into a rerun of the comedy-drama procedural they used to watch together in college.

Half an hour later, Josie's phone buzzed with a reply from Dana.

What if we could convince them to help with the toy drive? They both have kids, so it's a safe bet they have donations.

Donations, sure. But getting the two would-be lovebirds to show up at the same time? Nearly impossible. Josie tapped her phone against her palm, hoping for inspiration that never came. **Keep thinking. Your writer mind can do better than that.**

Dana replied with a laughing emoji.

Another hour passed before Zola's proof of life text came. Hunter snored softly against Josie's shoulder, snorting with a start at the vibration of her phone.

Zola: Home. Alone

Josie: That good?

Zola: I'm so tired of kissing frogs. When does one of them finally turn into a prince?

Josie gagged at the thought of Royce's mouth on Zola's. **The only thing you get from kissing frogs is a lip infection.**

Zola fired back a barfing emoji, followed by: **It was metaphorical. And don't worry, I blocked Royce after depositing him on his mother's doorstep. Last thing I need is a fifty-year-old child to raise.**

Josie mulled over an idea. She'd been so adamant that Carlos and Zola never know they were being set up, but what if they were open to it? Getting them together would sure be easier if they were on board with the process. She typed, deleted, retyped. Finally, after a quick prayer that Zola would take it the right way, she sent: **If I knew an age-appropriate, gainfully employed guy with his own transportation, would you want to meet him?**

The row of laughing emojis Zola sent back told Josie everything before the words appeared on her screen. **Only if he has a pet unicorn. Otherwise, spare me the mythology lesson.**

One date with Rolls Royce—proof that luxury names didn't guarantee class—had done little to soften Zola's salty attitude. Josie and Dana would have to take the covert matchmaking route after all. **Don't forget the clothing and toy drive for Agape House is coming up. Let me know if you have donations or want to help set up.**

When Zola didn't respond, Josie gave up waiting and got ready for bed. Life would be easier if she found another salon and left Zola and all her drama behind her.

Monday morning came too soon, but at least Ben's strep was gone, and the triplets made it to school without incident. With only one client on her schedule, Josie headed home early to gather donations for the toy drive. No way was she risking three pairs of watchful eyes suddenly rediscovering their long-forgotten treasures. She reached under the kitchen cabinet for a garbage bag and thought better of it. The kids would be leery of a trash bag that didn't find its way to the dumpster. They might even make out shapes and colors through the plastic. Instead, she grabbed an old Amazon box from the garage and set to work excavating the kids' graveyard of misfit toys.

The boys' room yielded a trove of outgrown playthings they'd never miss. By the time Josie migrated to Olivia's, sweat trickled down her temple. She dug to the bottom of the toy chest, where a beaded abacus and a shape sorter had somehow escaped previous purges.

The doorbell rang.

Josie stood, swiping her sleeve across her face as she headed for the front. Impatient knocks followed, layered with another ding.

"Hold on, I'm coming." She glanced through the peephole, then yanked open the door to find her mother, poised for another round of knocking.

"Why didn't you punch in the code and let yourself in?"

"I didn't want to interrupt you and Hunter if you two were having a mid-morning rendezvous."

"Mom." Heat flooded Josie's cheeks. "You think we send the kids to school and—." She put up her hand. "You know what, forget it. I'm not having this conversation. What's so urgent you had to beat down my door instead of calling?"

Marie Saldana clutched her purse to her chest as she stepped over the threshold. "I did call. And when you didn't answer, I called the salon. They told me you were gone for the day. Which is why I thought better of barging in."

"My phone never rang." Josie reached into her back pocket and found it empty. "Maybe it did ring. It seems I don't actually know where it is."

"What if the school tries to reach you? Really, Josefina, you should be more responsible."

"If the school can't reach me, they'll call Hunter. And if they can't get him, they'll call you. Then Dana." The tension on her mother's face shut Josie up. This wasn't about her negligence. "Mom, what's wrong?"

Marie perched on the edge of the sofa, hands trembling as she laced them tight against her knees. "I've got to get to Albuquerque as soon as possible."

Josie's heart pounded. Her three aunts still lived there. Had something happened to one of them? "Oh no, what's wrong?"

"A pipe burst in Clara's attic, and the entire house flooded. They're staying at Flor's for now." Marie bowed her head and inhaled a ragged breath. "All my parents' beloved memories are stored there. Now Clara needs our help to sort through everything to see what's salvageable."

Our? Josie swallowed the lump in her throat. No one was sick. No one had died. The only tragedies were a few waterlogged keepsakes, forgotten longer than the toys she'd just boxed up. Relief should've been her first reaction, but her mother had said "our help" as though she expected Josie to drop everything and drive three hundred miles to sift through soggy photo albums. Marie's eldest sister never threw away a single "sentimental" scrap. Clearing out Tía Clara's house would take a backhoe. Maybe "our" meant Marie and her sisters. *Dear Lord, let it be so.*

She patted her mother's back. "I'm sorry, Mom."

Marie pressed her hands to her knees and straightened. "I'm going to leave this afternoon, and I don't know how long I'll be there. Do you think you can get someone else to pick up the kids on Friday?"

Friday's problem could wait. "Mom, are you sure about this? Where will you stay?"

"Flor has plenty of room for Clara's family plus me. Or

maybe I'll go to Mirabel and Tino's. Tino smokes, but at least it's quiet over there." She shrugged. "That's the beauty of a big family. There's always an extra bed somewhere." Marie stood and pulled Josie into a hug. "Te amo, mija. Kiss my nietos for me."

"I love you, too, Mom."

Her mother left in a rush, and Josie whispered a prayer of thanks she hadn't been roped into going with her. The last place she wanted to be was in her obsessive neat-freak mother's path when there was a deep-cleaning project on the line.

Now, if only Josie could find her phone. She turned the house upside down, grumbling. Hunter had lobbied to buy her a smartwatch for her birthday, but she'd insisted it was impractical. Her hands were always in hair dye, shampoo, or some sticky concoction courtesy of the triplets. Still, a smartwatch might've helped track down the phone she constantly misplaced.

By the time she located the missing device in the minivan's cupholder, her toy cleanout window had vanished. She tucked the overstuffed donation box between the lawn mower and the Christmas lights, hopefully hidden well enough for her to smuggle it to the toy drive before the kids rediscovered their treasures.

Maybe as MOMS got more involved with Agape House, the need for donations would increase, and Josie would finally be motivated to clean out closets more often. She backed the van out of the garage and steered toward the school. Surely it would get easier to tidy up as the kids got older, she mused. The lone child-size sneaker on her passenger seat testified otherwise. Who was she kidding?

The only way their house would ever get a proper cleanout was if it flooded.

Chapter 19
Dana

Dana squatted in her dad's entryway and scratched Patch Johnson behind the ears. "How are you, boy?"

His tail thumped.

Edward Johnson grabbed a trucker cap from the table and shoved it onto his head. "Maggie baked him homemade dog biscuits. He's living the dream."

"Wow, she really spoils both of you." Dana straightened and glanced around the living room. Not a thing out of place. A wicker basket she'd never seen before sat near Dad's recliner, filled with Patch's toys. "The house looks great."

"Yeah well, don't check the kitchen. My latest lesson was blueberry muffins, and it didn't go as well as Bundt Cake 101."

"That bad?"

"Even the dog won't touch 'em. I'll clean up when we get back and give it another go for Maggie's sake."

"Why are you punishing that poor woman after everything she does for you and Patch?" Dana stepped outside and drew in the crisp air. Crisp-ish anyway. The high today would still reach almost eighty, but fall had finally arrived, carrying the faintest hint of pumpkin spice.

"Funny," he muttered, shuffling past her. "Mags will worry about my mind failing if I can't produce an edible batch."

When had his walk slowed like that? Dana followed him to the car, making a mental note to bring it up at his next neurology appointment. She started the Tahoe and let the engine's rumble drown out the worry creeping in. "Mind if we swing by Hobby Lobby before the supermarket?" Even without looking, she felt the weight of his displeasure.

"Why on earth would I want to do that?"

"Because your grandson has a Homecoming date on Friday, and I need supplies to make a mum." She finally turned, wanting to catch his reaction to the news that Nate had asked out a girl.

Dad's jaw hung slack. "And they want *you* to make the thing all her friends are going to see?"

Right reaction. Wrong reason. "Yeah, yeah. I didn't inherit Mom's crafting abilities. Did you miss the part about Nate going on his first date? *Nate.*"

"Don't act so surprised. The boy's got my blood in his veins. The ladies were bound to notice him. How about we stop by a florist instead and order the mum? It'll be my gift to you." He rested his hand on her forearm. "And to Nate because I've seen how you wrap presents, and it'll be in everyone's best interest if we leave this to the professionals."

"Hey." Indignation sparked a stubborn urge to prove herself to her dad and to Will, fanned by the maternal longing to create the kind of handmade magic her kids believed she could. Pride collided with practicality. In the end, the lure of working on her novel without drowning in glitter and ribbon tipped the scales. "Any preference on florists?"

Dana stood at the stove, stirring macaroni when movement caught her eye. Adam carried the infamous LEGO bin through the kitchen and set it on a dining chair.

"You decided to let them go, huh?" she asked.

"Yes, helping Connor and Ben build their treehouse made me think other kids could enjoy these."

"And you won't regret getting rid of them?"

He shrugged. "Nah. It'll be a while before the triplets are old enough to put their sets together on their own, so I can have fun coaching them. Besides, Josie paid me, so if I get desperate, I can use the money to buy new ones."

The boy who completed their family tugged at Dana's heart. His mix of wide-eyed wonder and the awkward angles of adolescence reminded her how quickly the years slipped by. When her kids were small, she couldn't imagine loving older ones as much as toddlers, but every stage proved fascinating in its own way.

"I'm proud of you."

He pressed his lips together. "You won't be when I tell you this." He stepped closer and flashed his teeth. "I broke a bracket on my braces."

She set the spoon aside and planted a hand on her hip. "Why did you wait until now to tell me? I can't call the orthodontist until tomorrow."

Adam's grin turned sly. "Because I wanted to come home and relax without somebody's hands in my mouth."

"I didn't pay all that money for the metal in there to

dangle uselessly. If you're not interested in straightening your teeth the right way, you can use your LEGO money for the next braces payment."

His eyebrows shot up. "That's not fair."

"Then take care of them." She leveled the spoon at him. "And speak up when something breaks."

His shoulders slumped. "Yes, ma'am."

She wrapped her arm around him. "You're a good egg. Now, move the LEGOs to the garage and set the table, please."

Her phone rang from inside the purse perched on a stack of mail. She swiped across a photo of Josie with the triplets. "Hello?"

"What are you doing Friday around 11:30 a.m.?"

Dana glanced at the ceiling as if her calendar were posted there. "Let's see…I'll be in a cardiologist's waiting room, wondering if they forgot about us because Dad's appointment was supposed to be an hour earlier. He'll be grumbling at me about my lack of patience while I march up to the desk for the second time."

"The short version is, you're taking your dad to the doctor."

"Yes, and then I have my shift at the Agape House toy drive, finishing just in time to drive my little boy on his first date." She was rambling. "Why?" Dana clicked to speaker mode, set it on the counter, and splashed milk into the pan. Close enough to a quarter cup. Probably. Mac 'n cheese didn't have to be an exact science.

Josie sighed. "My mom's in Albuquerque, so I either find someone to watch my kids, or I reschedule my clients. Some of whom I cancelled on last week because of Ben's strep."

"Hunter can't take off?" Dana shook a packet of powdered cheese over the noodles.

"He's meeting an inspector on a building site after lunch."

Any other time, Dana would've been happy to watch the triplets for an afternoon. They filled that maternal longing for the old days when her own kids were sweet and cuddly, while simultaneously making her thankful for independent teenagers. "What about Leah? She gets out of class at noon on Fridays."

"That could work if Hunter picks them up from school. I'll text her. Any more thoughts on the Zola-Carlos front?"

Oh, she'd had plenty of thoughts. In their last critique group, Carlos huffed so many times while reading Beverly's kissing scene, they thought he was having an asthma attack.

"Why does the man always 'cup' the woman's face? Never in my life have I done that," he'd groused.

"Maybe that's why you have so much trouble keeping a woman's attention," Bev shot back.

Their meeting ended early and on a sour note. If Carlos didn't find a love interest soon, the critique group might break up.

She snapped from her reverie. "I haven't come up with a great way to force them together yet."

Getting them to bump into each other at the toy drive was unlikely to begin with and even more improbable now. Serena had emailed the MOMS detailing the schedule for the event. Dropoff would begin Thursday evening, and those who volunteered to sort would take two-hour shifts from Friday morning through Saturday afternoon. Zola and Carlos would bring their donations at their own convenience, never seeing one another.

"Although…" An idea took shape. "What if we threw an end of summer get-together in the cul-de-sac and invited the two of them?"

Josie groaned. "We could. But then we'd have to host a party. Let's file that in the last resort column for now."

The gears in Dana's brain finally ground into place as she processed the reason for Josie's call. "Wait, why is your mom in Albuquerque?"

"There was a flood in my aunt's house. The home that belonged to my grandparents."

Dana paused her stirring to consider Josie's words. "That's awful. I didn't realize it rained enough there to cause flooding."

"A pipe burst." Josie laughed. "But yes, there is occasional flooding in monsoon season. I'll let you go so I can check with Leah, but I want to hear all about Nate's date later."

Dana ended the call and set her phone aside. She said a quick prayer for Josie's aunt's house and mulled over the notion of a summer block party. Technically, it was already fall, though the thermometer still climbed close to ninety most days. Even so, celebrating the death of triple-digit heat had a certain appeal. How hard could it be? A few folding chairs on the lawn, snacks on a table. Bug spray was nonnegotiable. Without it, the party would end in ten minutes with everyone scratching themselves raw.

The more she thought about it, the more she warmed to the idea of a casual gathering for introducing Carlos and Zola. Josie was right, though. They would have to tame their houses first so guests seeking a restroom didn't stumble into squalor. Or worse, catch sight of unmentionables drip-drying on the shower rod.

She carried the macaroni pot to the table as her phone buzzed.

Josie had already reconsidered her stance. **Is Saturday evening too soon for a block party? Zola just asked me to be her wingman at ladies' night. If I can sell her on our cul-de-sac as the happening place to meet guys, I won't have to turn down going to a seedy bar and put my already shaky job at risk.**

Dana: I'm willing to clean house if you are.

Josie: Anything to get Z off my back.

Dana: Wait, should we clear it with our husbands before we execute a plan?

Josie: I already checked, and it's a bye week for Tech.

Bye week. Dana's two favorite fall words.

Dana stretched to release the tension in her lower back. She'd spent the last two hours at Agape House steaming dress clothes and hanging them by size. There had been no shortage of donations, and she prayed the women and children who would receive them would be blessed with bright futures.

"You don't have kiddos to pick up today?" Her friend Kathy sat on the floor, polishing scuffs from a pair of black pumps.

"Will's getting them, but I do have to get going soon.

Nathan has a date to Homecoming, and I want to be there to take a million pictures." And to drive them. At the rate he was mastering turn speeds and stopping distances, she'd be chauffeuring him to his own wedding.

"Awe. That's so sweet."

"Sweet wasn't my first reaction to my boy's first date. Why can't they stay little, Kathy?"

"Older kids aren't so bad. And the hope is that once you finally adjust to them being grownups, they have little ones of their own, and you get to experience it all over again through the lens of grandparenthood."

The steamer nearly slipped from Dana's grasp. "Are you going to be a grandmother, Kath?" Her daughter, Naomi, was a twenty-four-year-old newlywed in law school.

She chuckled. "Not yet. Not that I know of anyway. But the deeper we get into the teenage years with Titus, the more I long for Naomi to have a little nugget I can spoil and send home."

Dana picked a piece of fuzz from a blazer and hung it on the rack. "Did your daughter pull away and treat you like her enemy when she graduated high school?"

A snort escaped as Kathy pulled another pair of shoes from the heap beside her. "Are you kidding me? She barely talked to me her freshman year unless she needed money."

A rock sank to the pit of Dana's belly. Last weekend had been a breakthrough in her relationship with Leah, but this week had been much of the same old radio silence. "Were things better that summer?"

"Yes. It's as if being on her own and then coming home made her a little more grateful. But it was a gradual change, and I'm still the recipient of the occasional eye roll."

Oh good. Dana would hate for the eyes to quit rolling. She checked her watch. "Our shift's over. Need a hand getting up?"

"Thanks." Kathy took Dana's hand and stood, unfolding slowly like a middle-aged pretzel. "Good luck tonight. I'm going to be heartbroken when Titus asks out a girl for the first time."

Dana was waiting in the kitchen when Will got home with the boys. Nate dropped his backpack and stopped in front of the Homecoming mum Dana had hung on the laundry room door. "Whoa, that looks awesome! Thanks, Mom." He gave her a quick hug.

"Your Pops bought it, so be sure you thank him." She braced for another snide remark about her inability to craft, but it didn't come.

He grabbed a snack from the pantry and charged up the stairs. "I'm gonna take a shower and get ready."

Adam trudged in and tossed his own backpack onto the heap. "If a girl is all it took to get him to shower, you should've let him date years ago."

Dana took in his sweaty hair. "You're one to be talking. Judging by the smell, I'd say you had an intense practice today."

He raised an arm and sniffed his pit. "It's not that bad. But yes, practice was rough." He opened the fridge and grabbed a yogurt cup and cheese stick.

"Not that bad?" Will pecked her cheek. "The upholstery in my car is peeling from their stench."

The Tahoe permanently reeked of a locker room. Dana routinely drove with the windows down and spent half the grocery budget on air fresheners, so Will complaining after picking them up once only grated on her nerves. "Bless your heart."

A little later, Nate strode downstairs in a polo shirt and khaki shorts. His hair was combed, and he'd spritzed himself at least twice too many times with cologne. Dana's eyes watered. Hopefully, the cloud would thin before they got to the young lady's house.

"Do you have enough money for dinner, Nate?" asked Will.

"I guess. Can I borrow your credit card just in case? I don't know how much the food trucks at the tailgate party will cost." Nate lifted the Homecoming mum from its hanger on the door frame and draped it over his arm.

Will fished his wallet from his back pocket. "Don't lose it."

Dana waited for him to impart more fatherly instruction to their son, like "make good choices. Don't drink. Call us for any reason." But he didn't.

"Have a good time," was all Will said as Nate left carrying the jangling explosion of ribbons and glitter.

He laid it across the back seat. "How is she supposed to even wear this thing?"

"In my day, we pinned them to our shirts, but that satin bow probably ties around her neck," Dana guessed. Leah hadn't been into Homecoming, so this was the first mum Dana had seen up close since her own high school days. As far as she was concerned, the floofy eyesores were an odd Texas tradition that grew bigger and gaudier every year.

She backed out of the garage and cleared her throat. "Dating comes with responsibility, and I want to make sure you—"

"Let me stop you, Mom." Nate held up his hand. "Faith and I are just friends. She made that very clear when I asked her to go with me."

Dana let out a breath and then tensed her grip on the wheel. How could anyone not like Nate? "I'm sorry, kiddo. I'm sure you'll meet a girl who likes you soon enough." Not *too* soon, hopefully.

He shot her a look. "I don't like her that way either. We just don't want to be the only ones in our group not in pictures because everyone else is paired up. Don't make it into something it's not."

"Then we're good on the talk about respectful behavior and kissing?" She squirmed as she said it.

"Dad already covered all that last night," Nate said. "And he told me to hold the door for her and be a gentleman, even if it's not a real date."

So, Will hadn't slacked off on parenting after all. Dana eased back against her seat, watching her freshly scrubbed son beside her. The smell of his cologne was still strong enough to burn her nose. Not so long ago, it was a nightly chore to get him to use soap in the shower.

All three kids had grown up practically overnight. Last year, Dana had to remind Leah to pack extra socks for their camping trip. Now she was on her own and dating a cowboy. Adam had shot past his mom in height, and his quick wit took her by surprise, a charming twist on the fun-loving kid whose inside voice hadn't developed until he was almost ten.

As their childhoods whizzed by, Dana was struck with

the realization that letting them go wasn't one big moment, but a hundred small ones that slipped quietly past while she wasn't looking.

Chapter 20

Dana flitted about the kitchen on Saturday afternoon, a college football game droning from the living room TV. The smell of chocolate fused with melted cheese as she slid a pan of brownies onto the stove to cool and gave the crock pot of queso another stir. She shook tortilla chips into a mixing bowl and checked the front window for Nate and Adam.

No boys in sight. Just Will yanking the cord on the leaf blower. When she asked him to get the front yard ready for guests, she meant putting out chairs and dragging the large gray garbage can out of the garage. Not yard work.

"Boys," she hollered.

"Yes?" Nate's voice floated from upstairs.

"Why aren't you outside setting up?"

The blower roared to life, drowning out his answer. Perfect. If only she could curse in Spanish like Josie, this would be the moment.

"Nate, go remind your dad he's supposed to pick up Pops. And maybe tell him the trees are still green." In a couple of months when the yard really was blanketed in leaves, he and his leaf blower would pull a ninja-worthy disappearing act.

By six o'clock, the cul-de-sac hummed with chatter. Friends and neighbors milled about, sampling offerings on the snack tables. The Wednesday MOMS had brought everything from homemade ice cream—thank you, Anita Steen—to pigs in a blanket. Josie set a piping tray of empanadas down as Hunter wheeled an ice chest to the edge of the sidewalk.

"Is Carlos here yet?" Josie murmured.

Dana tipped her head toward a knot of guys hunched around a tablet, probably watching football. So much for Texas Tech's bye week. "Over there. When's Zola getting here?"

"Any minute. She likes to make a grand entrance though, so there's no telling."

She'd need one big enough to pull Carlos away from the screen.

Dana checked her phone. Leah's response to the party invitation was a noncommittal, "We might swing by," but the faint glimmer of hope it offered tempted Dana to track her daughter's location to see if she and Jordan were on their way. She stopped herself. Better not to know than to be disappointed. Instead, she channeled her energy into the matchmaking task at hand.

"What do we do when Zola gets here?" Dana asked.

"I thought *you* would figure that part out." Josie popped the top on a soda can and sipped the fizz. "After all, you were the one who suggested throwing this party."

"That's why the next step was supposed to be *your* idea."

Josie waved to Ben, who raced by on a scooter. "We'll just introduce them. Single parents of boys should be able to come up with enough common ground to cover a couple of minutes of polite conversation."

Simple enough. Dana sank into a chair and dug into a plastic bowl of vanilla ice cream. "Anita, this is divine. I can't remember the last time I had homemade ice cream." The only person in her family who ever made it was her mother, and she'd been gone for five years.

Her dad caught her eye over his own bowl and winked. He must be thinking about Mom, too.

As the sun set behind the rooftops, Leah and another girl walked from around the corner. Dana placed her bowl aside and met them halfway. "You made it." She gave Leah the briefest of hugs.

"I didn't expect so many cars. We had to park a block away."

Dana shoved her hands in her pockets. "Word got out about our cul-de-sac shindig."

Leah's wide-eyed glare warned Dana she was treading into embarrassing territory. "Anyhoo. This is my roommate, Skylar." She nodded to her companion with shoulder-length jet-black hair.

Skylar's presence instead of the boyfriend's was a curious but welcome surprise, and Dana dared not ask about Jordan's whereabouts.

Adam came barreling up. "We have a problem. You know how Mrs. Pruitt has that bare spot where the grass won't grow?"

The Harding family knew all about the next-door neighbor's grass, or lack thereof. Mrs. Pruitt had long blamed their oak tree for casting too much shade and causing the eternal mud puddle.

Dana straightened, already bristling. "Did she say something to you again?" Confronting her cranky neighbor in front of a yard full of guests wasn't her idea of a good time, but the woman couldn't keep scolding kids over a patch of dirt she could easily fix with a few squares of St. Augustine sod. Will had even offered to buy and install it. Mrs. Pruitt, however, preferred to complain.

"No, but she might when she hears what happened. That kid Marco swerved into the grass to avoid hitting Olivia with my bike and wiped out in the mud."

Dana looked past him to see Carlos's younger son, dripping brown sludge from head to toe. "Oh, no." She hurried toward them as Marco's predicament pulled his father's attention from the game.

The boy tugged his shirt away from his skin as his ears flamed red.

"Adam, show Marco to the bathroom, and loan him a fresh shirt and shorts," Dana said.

"Thanks, but we'd better head home." Carlos put his hand on Marco's one unsoiled shoulder. "Have you got a trash bag he could sit on to protect my car seats?"

"On it." Adam jogged into the house.

"Are you sure you don't want him to clean up in our bathroom first? I feel responsible." Dana grabbed napkins from the table and handed them to Marco.

Carlos gave her a weary smile. "It's technically their mom's weekend, but she let me pick them up while she went to dinner with her fiancé." He practically spat out the last word. "So, I better get these clothes in the wash before she gets back, or she'll think twice about letting them hang out with me the next time."

"Thanks for coming. We're glad you could make it," Dana said.

Carlos nodded. "It was fun, wasn't it, boys?" Both sons mumbled agreement as Adam appeared, shoving paper towels and trash bags into his hands.

Dana looked on as Carlos layered plastic across the car seat before letting Marco climb in. She shook her head. Dads had the strangest methods—equal parts practical and panic. A mom would've hosed the kid off, borrowed a clean outfit, and called it good. She waved as Carlos got in and pulled away from the curb.

"Alright, party people, I'm ready to meet someone handsome, stable, and emotionally available." Zola's lilt pulled her back.

"Hey." Dana turned to find the petite stylist, who ordinarily came up to her chin, standing at eye level. Her gaze drifted to Zola's feet. "Are those six-inch stilettos?"

Zola lifted one shoulder. "I like to make a good first impression. Now, point me to my future ex."

If only there were someone on whom to make one. Dana swept the crowd looking for Josie. She spotted her biting her thumbnail and staring at her phone. "Josie, look who I found."

"Zola, hey." Josie tucked her phone into her pocket and painted on a bright smile that looked forced. "Let me introduce you to Car—"

Dana shook her head fiercely. "Didn't you see him leave?"

Josie frowned. "No. Why would he take off when the party's just getting started?"

"You really didn't see his son fall in the mud? It was a

whole thing," Dana said.

"I must've missed it. My mom called, so I've been distracted. Is he alright?"

"You dragged me to suburbia instead of going with me to ladies' night for what appears to be the *only* single guy you know, and he *left*?" Zola planted her fists on her hips until she zeroed in on the food table. "Is that homemade ice cream?" Without waiting for an answer, she click-clomped up the driveway in her skyscraper heels.

"So much for Operation Cul-de-sac Cupid." Josie's shoulders sagged. "We threw a party for nothing."

Dana waved her hand toward the surrounding scene. Neighbors laughed, their plates piled with snacks balanced on their knees, while kids chased each other through the grass. "Not for nothing. We might not have made a love connection, but look at this fellowship."

"You're right." Josie stood taller and smiled. "We did a good thing. It's almost like we know what we're doing."

A shriek erupted from the food table. Zola's heel sank into the grass, and her bowl of vanilla ice cream launched skyward.

"Almost," Dana said.

Chapter 21
Josie

Josie leaned against Olivia's door and dragged her hands down her face.

"What's wrong?" Hunter asked. "That was the easiest bedtime all week."

She pushed off the wall and trudged toward their room. "It's not the kids. Mom called during the party."

"That can't be good. What did Marie want?" He dropped onto the edge of the bed.

"Mom threw her back out and can't move, let alone help with Tía Clara's house. My aunt and uncle think insurance is trying to lowball them, and supposedly the restoration specialists are tearing through the place without respecting the 'heirlooms'." She threw up air quotes.

Hunter raked a hand through his hair. "Can't they roll Marie onto a stretcher and park her in the middle of the room? I have no doubt she could command an army even flat on her back."

"Funny." Josie flopped down beside him. "I hope she's better soon because the sisters can't agree on what should stay, what should go, or what qualifies as treasure versus trash."

"Wasn't she down for several days the last time she threw out her back?" he asked.

"When she rearranged her living room after the movers left because she didn't like the way they angled her sofa? Yes."

He rested a hand on her hip. "She's tough. I'm sure your mom will bounce back and run the show again in no time."

"I hope so." Josie couldn't help but think if the roles were reversed, her mother would have packed a bag and been on the way to help as soon as she got word Josie was hurt.

Before she retired and moved to town, Marie still visited once or twice a month, stocking their freezer with homemade meals so they wouldn't starve while figuring out how to keep three newborns alive. And when Josie's appendix burst in the Colorado wilderness, Marie had dropped everything in the middle of a work week to care for the triplets, in a camper no less. And now that she was flat on her back, literally, Josie was too busy to do the same for her.

The next morning, Hunter and Josie dropped the kids off in Sunday School, made a detour by the coffee station, and slipped into their own class as the teacher was taking prayer requests. Josie kept her head down, focused on the paper cup in her hand. Hunter elbowed her. She should've asked them to pray for her mom and Tía Clara's home, but her problems seemed small compared with what their classmates were going through. Abigail Benton asked for prayers for her sister's family, who had lost everything in a house fire, and the Masons' five-year-old daughter had leukemia. There was no need to burden their friends with their own minor issues when other families were in crisis.

Serena Pendleton caught Josie's arm on the way into the sanctuary. "There's my favorite hairdresser. Last night was so great. I can't remember when I've sat outside and laughed with friends like that."

"It was all Dana's idea." Josie smiled. She'd hardly spoken to Serena at the party, thanks to her mother's phone call. Then she had to deal with a pouty Zola after she took a tumble on her ridiculous heels.

"Are you ready for the employment-readiness fair?" Serena gave a little clap. "Can you believe it's only a week away?"

A week? Josie swallowed. Time really did fly when you were juggling a sick kid and playing matchmaker. "Can't wait." She *had* been looking forward to the event. Using her talent to bless others was a small way she could be the hands of Jesus when she was too busy raising preschoolers to do much more for Him. But now all she could think about was her mom lying in bed in Albuquerque. Josie felt torn between the mother who raised her and the one she was trying to be.

She paused by a trashcan in the foyer and threw away her coffee cup. "Serena, out of curiosity, how many hairdressers signed up to participate?"

"I've got two in the morning and you and Zola after we break for lunch. There's not much space for more than that in Agape House's tiny salon."

Great. If Josie did leave to take care of her mother, Zola would be on her own. Working with her had been miserable before, but there was no telling what fury she'd bestow on Josie for ditching her.

Josie was twisting her hair into a topknot when Hunter poked his head in the bathroom. "Babe, have you seen my work boots?"

"You always take them off by the garage door. Where else would they be?"

He narrowed his eyes at her reflection in the mirror. "That was the first place I checked."

"Well don't look at me. I have no need of steel-toed work boots."

She brushed past him and walked down the hall, calling, "Boys, have you seen Daddy's—"

Her words cut off at the sight of Connor wobbling across the room in his dad's boots. She turned back to Hunter and jutted her bottom lip in mock sympathy. "I guess you'll have to wear Connor's sneakers to work today." She scooped little red shoes off the floor and handed them to Hunter. "Here, babe."

He made a show of cramming his toes into Connor's shoes. "You're right. This could work."

Connor threw his head back and let out the kind of belly laugh only a small child could manage—pure and contagious. Soon, Hunter and Josie were laughing right along with him, and Ben and Olivia wandered in to see what was so funny.

When Connor finally caught his breath, he said between giggles, "Dad, your feet are too big for my shoes."

"I guess we'd better trade then, so we don't both fall over." Hunter punctuated the point by prancing across the floor on tiptoe as Connor's sneakers flopped from his toes like clown shoes.

The kids erupted into another fit of cackles.

Josie's abs hurt from laughing so hard. "Hurry up and swap or you'll be late for school." She said a silent prayer that Connor's frivolity was out of his system and wouldn't be an indicator of how the rest of the morning would go. Some of the light had gone out of Miss Piper's eyes since Meet the Teacher night, and Josie couldn't help but think Connor was to blame, at least in part.

Once the kids were safely deposited at school, Josie took a detour to her favorite coffee shop on her way to work. She fiddled with the radio while idling in the drive-through line. Why did morning DJs have to talk so much instead of just playing music? Her phone rang over the van's Bluetooth, and her sister's name lit up the screen. "Hey, Laurel. You're up early."

"I teach an eight o'clock class this semester, and the commute to Boulder is killing me."

Josie inched up to the intercom and rolled down her window. "Hold on, Laur." She ordered a caramel macchiato and a blueberry scone. "Okay, I'm back."

"Do you know how much money you could save—not to mention all the chemicals you could keep out of your body—if you made coffee and muffins at home?"

Laurel was a crunchy, modern hippie, though she preferred the term *eco-chic*. Criticizing others for their indoorsy, consumeristic choices was practically a hobby of hers, but Josie had grown used to it over the years.

"It's once a week. I'm not breaking the bank, and I doubt whatever chemicals are in my corporate scone and flavored syrup are going to kill me." At least not faster than raising triplets would.

"I'm worried about Mom," Laurel said. "Did she tell you she has to use Abuela Susana's old walker just to get to the bathroom?"

"I guess it's lucky Tía Clara kept it, then. What a miracle they were able to locate it."

"I'm serious, Josie. Do you even care that our mom is suffering?"

Of course she cared. She and Hunter had discussed him taking a few days off work so she could go to Albuquerque if

Marie didn't bounce back. But Laurel's accusation made Josie prickle.

"Did Mom tell you Tía Clara expects the sisters to pay for whatever insurance won't?" Laurel asked.

"Why would they do that? She's the one who got the house in the estate. It's her and Silvio's responsibility now."

"I don't know. They're all stubborn as mules. And with Mom literally unable to stand up for herself, she's at the mercy of whatever the other three decide. I feel so bad for her."

"Hold on again." Josie held out her phone for the barista to scan her app and took her purchases. "Thank you."

Josie bit into the warm pastry as she drove away, but its usual comfort failed to satisfy. The promise of a pleasant morning was sullied by guilt and something heavier—a quiet dread that she would actually have to go to New Mexico. "Can't you get someone to cover your classes for a few days and drive down?"

"I'm farther away than you are," Laurel said, her tone tight and defensive. "Besides, it's not a big deal, but Jefferson is having some skin cancer removed tomorrow, and I need to be there for him."

Seemed the granola, outdoor lifestyle had challenges of its own, but now wasn't the time to point that out to Laurel. She was clearly masking her worry under a layer of practiced composure and a touch of big-sister condescension.

Josie softened. "Look, Hunter and I are already trying to sort out our week so I can go. Everything will be fine." She hoped Laurel knew she meant Jefferson as well as their mom.

The morning flew by, despite Josie being preoccupied with her mother's situation. She pushed it to the back of her mind and pasted on a bright smile to pick up the kids.

"Connor was an absolute gem today," said Miss Piper. Her hands were clasped in front of her, and her relaxed smile held no hint of sarcasm.

Olivia nodded as if sensing her mother's incredulity. "He

listened good and did his work."

"Yep. I minded, even in P.E." Connor beamed.

P.E. should've been the class a wiggly little boy excelled in, but he preferred to make up his own rules for the games and exercises Coach gave them.

Josie bent to hug him. "I'm very proud of you."

Mrs. Tyson had a positive report on Ben as well, and Josie pinched herself to be sure she wasn't dreaming. Maybe the key to a good day was a round of side-splitting guffaws after breakfast. She and Hunter would have to brainstorm a daily stand-up routine. Anything to ensure neither pre-K teacher quit at Christmas break. Or at least if they did, no one would be able to blame the Caraways.

Hunter stood in the kitchen, slathering peanut butter onto bread when they walked in.

"This is a nice surprise. The kids all had great mornings, and now we get to eat lunch with you." Josie kissed his cheek. "To what do we owe the pleasure?"

He didn't look up from his sandwich making. "Thought we could talk."

So much for a good morning.

Once Connor, Ben, and Olivia were settled at the dining table with a show playing on the tablet, Josie and Hunter slipped into the backyard, where they could keep an eye on the kids through the French doors but still have a modicum of privacy.

She lowered herself into a patio chair and folded her arms. Hunter never came home at lunch to talk, so his news had to be serious. She braced for the worst—death, financial ruin. They'd never thrown around the D word, but the gravity in his face sparked a flicker of worry. Whatever it was, they'd face it together. Except divorce. Even then, he wasn't leaving her without a fight.

Hunter took the chair opposite her. "I booked you a plane ticket to Albuquerque for tomorrow morning. My mom will be here Wednesday, and she and I will hold down the fort so you can take care of Marie."

Josie stared at him, her mouth hanging open. Of all the disasters she'd imagined, this one hadn't even made the list. Still, it was an answer to her prayers. As much as she didn't want to go to New Mexico, her sense of family obligation was stronger than self-preservation.

"I know I should've included you in the decision," Hunter said, "but you would've found a way to talk me out of it. Marie does so much for us, and I feel bad for her being laid up at her sister's while your aunties railroad her about the house. Because we both know they are."

He waited a beat, but Josie's brain was still buffering.

"Say something, Jos."

She buried her face in her hands. "I can't believe you did that."

"I'm really sorry. I thought it was for the best. And my mom agreed."

"Thank you."

"You're… not mad at me?" Hunter rested a tentative hand on her knee.

"No. I'm relieved. Laurel can't go because Jefferson's having a procedure tomorrow, and while she didn't come right out and ask me to take care of Mom, she probably pulled a muscle from hinting at it so hard." Josie slipped a hand behind his neck, pulled him in, and kissed him. When she let go, she sat back and asked, "How'd you get your mom to drive down?"

Hunter shrugged. "Easy. She was suffering from grandkid withdrawals and asked when a good time to visit would be. When I told her about Marie, she said she could be here in two days."

After how Labor Day weekend ended with Emmaline, Josie had expected her to keep her distance, not jump in on short notice.

"You know school is out on Friday for parent-teacher conferences, right?"

"I didn't, but we'll handle it. You take care of Marie. I'll go to the conferences, and Mom will keep our kids from burning the house down. Hopefully."

She clapped her hands on her knees and stood. "I guess it's settled then. I'll reschedule my clients and pack." She started for the door. "Are you sure you and your mom can handle everything here?"

"Jos, it's not like I've never taken care of my own kids before. We'll be fine. You have nothing to worry about."

"That's the same thing Miss Piper said at Meet the Teacher night." After losing Connor on the second day of school, she'd all but developed an eye twitch. What could possibly go wrong?

Chapter 22

Josie dropped the kids off at school Tuesday like it was the last time she'd ever see them. "Remember, Daddy's picking you up today, and Gramma will be here tomorrow. I'll be home as soon as I can."

Ben bounced on his toes. "I can't wait to see Gramma!"

Olivia and Connor echoed his excitement without the slightest hint of concern over their mother's departure. Little traitors.

She crouched with open arms. "Give me hugs and take care of Daddy for me."

"Okay, Mom. We will."

The kids laughed, and Josie drove home with a heavy heart. She'd hoped to run across the cul-de-sac to check in with Dana before leaving for the airport, but her neighbor was just backing out to take Nate and Adam to school and wouldn't return before Josie had to go. Instead, she paced and added to the already growing list of instructions she'd left on the kitchen counter.

By the time Hunter emerged from the bedroom, coffee mug in hand, the list was three pages long. He'd been fielding work calls all morning, but now he leaned in the doorway and asked, "Ready?"

As ready as she'd ever be.

The rideshare driver stopped in front of an adobe home with a cactus garden where a lawn might've been. Josie approached the front door, typed in the code Tía Mirabel had texted, and let herself in.

The ticking of the enormous grandfather clock in the living room echoed through the house. It looked out of place among the Saltillo tile and southwestern décor, and it took up far too much space in the modest home. But it had stood in that very spot for as long as Josie could remember, booming out the hour with a haunting chime that seemed to ricochet off the tile.

She smiled at the memory of the time it struck just as she was about to win a heated Checkers match against her cousin. She jumped, sending the board flying, and Junior had declared Josie the loser by forfeit.

"Josefina, is that you?" her mother called.

"I'm here, Mom." Josie carried her bag down the hall to the bedroom, where her mother reclined in a nest of pillows.

"Wouldn't you be more comfortable lying flat?"

"I've been supine for three days, and no position is comfortable at this point," Marie said. "We were starting to make headway until I pulled a drawer out of your Abuela Susana's hutch, and I swear my spine snapped in two. Now there's no telling what's going on over there. If they could, those sisters of mine would box up every last thing in that house, store it, and then put it all right back exactly the way it was." Her face twisted in disgust.

Josie sat gingerly on the edge of the bed. "Isn't everything water-damaged?"

"If it was touching the floor, yes. The ceiling collapsed over the main bedroom, so the worst of it hit Clara and Silvio's personal things. But the restoration crew came through and did what they could—extracted the water and got most of the furniture out of harm's way. Now they'll have to replace all the floors, a ceiling, and some drywall and baseboards." Marie put her head in her hand. "It's such a mess, Josefina. You just can't imagine it."

She could, and it wasn't a pretty sight. Even when her grandparents were alive, the house had been bursting at the seams. Books and magazines stacked on every surface. Shelves and cabinet tops crowded with pottery and crystal. Knickknacks and travel souvenirs displayed as if they were priceless mementoes. When Josie and Laurel were little and asked why their grandparents collected so much, their mother only shrugged and said, "They left everything behind when they came to America and had to start over with very little. So, what they've accumulated over the years is precious to them."

Josie scratched her eyebrow and handed her mother the glass of water from the nightstand. "Why is it so hard for your family to understand that people matter more than things?"

Marie sighed. "When someone we love is gone, it's hard to part with what they've left behind. It feels like losing them all over again. Clara remembers how hard our parents worked to give us the life they never had in Mexico." She stared into the distance, lost in a past only she could see. "What started as a tribute to their memory—guarding what they built—has turned into a monster of sorts."

"And what is it you hope to gain by being here? I mean, if they want to save everything, and you don't, why do you care what happens to all the junk in that house?"

Marie's eyes flew wide, and she jerked her head toward Josie, immediately wincing in pain.

"I-I don't mean *junk*, per se," Josie added quickly. "But I can't imagine you were planning to hire a moving truck to take that hutch back to Lubbock, were you?"

Her mother eased back into the pillows. "Heavens no." She inhaled a shaky breath. "When I was a girl, I used to visit my grandparents in Cuauhtémoc during the summers. My Abuelita taught me to crochet lace. She'd squint and strain to see the tiny stitches, but together—over several summers—we made the most beautiful tablecloth. It looked like a giant doily." A far away smile touched her lips. "When we finally completed it, Abuelita wrapped it in butcher paper, and I couldn't wait to give it to Mamá for Christmas. It ended up being the last time I saw Abuelita, and that tablecloth holds special memories for me."

Marie's countenance hardened. "But after Mamá passed away, I never got it back. At first, I didn't press because it was a sensitive subject for Clara. Then, in time, she said she lost track of it. Now I don't know if my sister lied to keep it or if it's just buried somewhere in the chaos of that house. I came to lend a hand and moral support, but I also want to find my tablecloth. For the same reasons my sisters have clung so tightly to our parents' belongings."

After an uncomfortable beat, Josie stood. "So, what can I do to help?"

"I can't lift my leg more than an inch off the ground

without excruciating pain." She swept a hand over the pink, billowy swath of satin and ruffles cocooning her frame. "Hence Mirabel's nightgown. But between the two of us, I think we can manage to get pants on me."

Josie cringed but tried to keep her expression in check. "And then what, Mom?" She braced herself, knowing some hairbrained scheme was incoming.

"And then," Marie said, index finger shaking at the ceiling fan, "we march right down to Clara's and get to work hunting for that tablecloth. Cleaning as we go of course, because we aren't animals."

How her mother planned to clean anything when she couldn't even push herself upright was beyond Josie. "What if we—" She tried to pull her up by the arms but dropped them when Marie yelped. "How are you getting to the bathroom?"

"Move, and I'll show you." As Josie stepped aside, Marie rolled onto her stomach and inched her legs over the edge of the bed, letting them slide to the floor, much in the same way the triplets used to climb down from the sofa. She shuffled her hands along the mattress until the metal walker was within reach and gripped its handles.

"That was… hard to watch." The nightgown had ridden higher with every scootch that got her feet closer to standing, and Josie barely managed to look away before getting mooned.

"Don't tease me, mija. You must know this is killing me. I hate being incapacitated."

"I know, Mom. That's why I'm here." Josie cleared her throat. "Now, about those pants."

Marie tipped her chin toward the dresser. "Top drawer."

Josie pulled it open and sucked in a sharp breath at the sight of neatly folded unmentionables. She pinched a pair of underwear and lifted it gingerly by the waistband.

After devising a system that allowed both women to retain as much dignity as possible, Marie was finally dressed and reasonably presentable. Normally, she wouldn't step outside without perfect hair and a full face of makeup, but today she conceded to let Josie pull her long bob into a low ponytail.

"You're going to a chiropractor when we get you home. This back problem is getting worse every time you throw it out."

"Pish. I don't believe in those witch doctors."

"*You* might not, but I believe in anyone who keeps me from having to pull up your underwear."

Her mother mumbled something in Spanish as they made their slow procession to the beige Camry parked out front.

"Any bright ideas about how we're going to put you in the car?" Josie doubted her mother could hunch over to get in.

"What if you folded down the back seats, and I laid across them like a gurney? Reach through the trunk and pull my legs around."

It was Josie's turn to mutter in her grandparents' native tongue. Marie fixed her with a withering glare. The only thing saving Josie from getting smacked was the vice-like grip Marie had on the walker.

"Mom, if I have to slam on the brakes, you'll become a human torpedo."

"I think there's a bike helmet in the garage. Just put that

on me.”

“You can't be serious.” Josie rubbed her palms together. “I have a better idea. Lock your hands around my neck, and I'll wrap mine around your middle. Then let your legs go slack, and I'll lower you into the seat.”

Josie towered over her mom, so the plan was simple enough, but the execution lacked finesse. By the time she got Marie's legs in and buckled the seatbelt, Josie was panting.

She stood at the back of the car, gathering herself before the drive to her aunt's. The worst should've been over, but they were just getting started.

A storage container sat in front of Tía Clara's house, and a roll-off dumpster parked at the curb announced renovation—new life on the way, at least to anyone driving by. In truth, three generations of clutter were actively rotting inside, tethering the house's inhabitants to the past and to a future weighed down by it.

Josie tugged the walker from the trunk and unfolded it, then jogged to the dumpster. She grasped the top edge and planted a foot on the metal support for a quick look at what had been tossed since the flood. Damp, crumbling sheetrock littered the floor, along with a few warped books and papers too soggy to save. Otherwise, the dumpster was far too empty for her liking. She jumped down, carried the walker to the passenger door, and braced herself both for lifting her mom out of the car and for whatever they were about to walk into.

Chapter 23
Dana

Some days, Dana wrote thrilling pages, even full chapters, in her laundry room/office. Today, the space only added to the clutter in her already muddled mind. Tools from Will's weekend fix-it project lay strewn about the counter, and for the love of everything holy, what was that smell?

She rolled her chair back and tugged on the drawer where the hammer and screwdrivers belonged, but it jammed halfway. No wonder Will had left the tools out. With a sigh, she slid her fingers into the narrow gap and worked to dislodge the wedged pliers holding the whole thing hostage. Once it slid free, she found the drawer's contents were a jumbled hodgepodge, so she set it on the floor and organized it. Then she tidied the rest of the area, even vacuuming lint from behind the dryer.

The odor remained. She opened the washer, instantly regretting it. Friday's load of towels had soured. Even after adding bleach and restarting the cycle, the stench clung to the walls. Could she be imagining it? That was a sign of a stroke, wasn't it—phantom smells?

Dana ducked into the powder room and studied her reflection. Her smile looked symmetrical enough, and the scent of lilac air freshener lingered. She rubbed her temples. Clearly, she was inventing problems to avoid the blinking cursor mocking her from the laptop. Writing required focus, something impossible to muster with everything else on her mind.

Since last week, when Leah babysat the Caraways, her daughter had been more responsive. Granted, not by much, but at least she answered texts. Leah wasn't actively keeping Dana at bay anymore. Her improved communication and Jordan's noticeable absence from the block party suggested a disturbance in the force. Had the happy couple broken up? Or maybe Jordan simply had to work late Saturday night, and Leah had been out of the house long enough to finally realize she missed her mom. Dana longed to ask what had changed, but pressing the issue would send Leah back into her emotional foxhole.

And then there was football. A high school kid from a neighboring district had collapsed on the field and had to be shocked back to life with an AED. What if Nate or Adam had an undetected heart condition waiting to surface? The odds were low, which should have given Dana peace of mind, but it didn't.

The one thing that did settle her was that for once, the person who usually gave Dana the most to worry about was behaving himself. Her dad had been taking his meds, getting exercise, and sharpening his mind. The cardiologist even told Edward to keep up the good work and to climb a few stairs now and then.

She plodded back to the desk, intent on pushing through the mental distractions only to realize the awful smell hadn't been wet laundry after all. Something had died in there.

After several minutes of rooting around like a bloodhound, she gambled with her life by standing on her swiveling office chair and unmasked the smelly culprit—a plastic bowl of nightcrawlers Will and the boys had bought to go fishing after church yesterday. One of those yahoos had left the container atop the drink fridge, behind the yellow emergency flashlight they kept for power outages.

Dana gagged. She pulled the neck of her shirt over her nose as she reached for the container. Just carrying it to the dumpster made her dry heave, and she had half a mind to hide it in Will's car later as payback. Instead, she filed away dead worms in her repertoire of villainy for a future novel.

She washed her hands before rampaging through the house with a Febreze bottle. Every surface may have been soaked, but at least the malodorous particles were drenched in aromatic "morning spring showers." Her phone buzzed with a call from Serena.

"Hey, lady. I want to touch base with you about the job fair thing before Saturday."

"I've got it on my calendar." Dana patted her leg and lured Harvey outside with a treat. They both needed fresh air after all the chemicals she'd sprayed. "Should I bring anything?"

"If you and your friends each come with your own laptop, it'll speed up the resume writing. Yolanda also mentioned helping a few ladies set up email accounts."

How did anyone get by this long without an inbox full of spam and discount codes? Must be nice. "Will do."

"And Dana." Serena was hesitant. "Do you mind checking in with your writing group to remind them about Saturday? I've already heard from one hysterical Zola this morning about how Josie roped her into this gig and then bailed."

Dana bent to pull a stray weed and threw it in the firepit. "That's a little harsh. Josie had a family emergency. She might even be back by the weekend." After all, no one would willingly spend more than forty-eight hours with Marie Saldana without receiving combat pay.

The summer before last, Marie had blamed Dana and Will for coercing her daughter into that ill-fated camping trip where Josie had an emergency appendectomy. Marie had swooped in to help, never having camped a day in her life, and the great outdoors hadn't brought out her nurturing side.

She and Dana had been cordial since her move to Lubbock, but Dana still gave her a wide berth.

"I wouldn't be a bit surprised if Zola strong-arms one of her stylists into coming on Saturday to take Josie's place," Serena said.

"I don't know about that. She's a spitfire, but I can't picture her being that controlling." Then again, Josie might have a different opinion.

"Just know, Dana Harding, I'm grateful for you. None of this would be happening if you hadn't had the genius idea to start a mentor group. You should be proud of the difference you're making in Lubbock."

Dana opened her mouth to protest, to remind Serena that MOMS had been *her* idea, not Dana's, but the words caught. It was nice to hear that her suggestion had mattered, and not just in the fleeting way that being the only Harding who could find lost items mattered—appreciated in the crisis, forgotten five minutes later.

She ducked her chin, reluctant to accept the compliment. "I'm glad my very small part in starting MOMS helped people."

They ended the call, and Dana sent a group text to her critique partners. **Y'all are both coming Saturday, right?**

Bev: 9a.m. sharp! I wouldn't miss an opportunity to pitch in at Agape House.

Carlos: I'll be there, but you both owe me an extra chapter edit next week to make up for waking up early when I don't have my boys.

A moment later, a message from Beverly popped up outside the group chat. **Lord Jesus, we kindly ask you to please find that cantankerous man a girlfriend.**

Dana chuckled. Zola and Carlos were both volunteering Saturday, and the only thing standing between them and a Hallmark ending was the fact that they were equally impossible lately. Did a grumpy always need a sunshine, or could two grumpies melt each other's frozen hearts?

A thought needled at her until it finally clicked. Beverly and Carlos were working the morning shift. Dana scrolled through her old texts with Josie. Zola was working the afternoon shift. Her heart pounded.

"Not again," she said aloud. Harvey put his head on her lap. She scratched him behind the ear. "Oh, Harv, how are we going to fix this?"

She started typing a message to Josie but reconsidered and texted Carlos instead. **I can take your 9 a.m. shift so you can get your beauty sleep. Come at 1 p.m. instead.**

There. Problem solved.

Carlos: No can do. Got an indoor soccer game at 2.

Dana: Soccer at your age? Did Medicare sign off on that?

Carlos: Funny. You should try adding in some of that wit to your writing.

Dana closed her phone and pinched the bridge of her nose. This matchmaking scheme was officially sunk.

Chapter 24
Josie

Josie had lost track of how many times she'd trudged back and forth to the storage container in the last two days. Every time she thought they were making progress, the house mocked her—still cluttered, still damp, the faint odor of wet cardboard still hanging in the air. Ten days since the flood with very little change. Her mother's crocheted tablecloth was still missing, and at the rate they were cleaning out the house, the triplets would start high school before they unearthed it.

She navigated a tower of furniture to get out of the container with her phone pressed to her ear.

"How's your mom?" Hunter asked.

"She overdid it yesterday, so she's back in bed." Josie scanned the yard to make sure no one was within earshot. "Babe, if I don't get out of here soon, I'm going to need the rest of her muscle relaxers just to survive my aunts."

"Hang in there. I know it's rough, but your mom's counting on you."

"Yeah, yeah." She exhaled. "Promise me that if I die first, you will get rid of my belongings. I don't want my stuff turning into a burden for you and the kids."

"Sure, we'll dump everything in the hole with you so there's plenty of space for my new wife to move in."

"You'll still have several children, so I hope your standards for the next Mrs. Caraway aren't too high."

"Josie, you're the only wife for me, and I miss you. Find that blasted tablecloth and bring your mom home."

She smiled. "If you were a second-generation hoarder, where would you store a lace tablecloth your sister and grandmother made?"

He sighed. "I couldn't begin to guess, but I'm praying you find it."

"You might want to have a word with your mother about her VHS tapes. That's a gateway collection to hoarding. That and her cabinet of Tupperware. Nip it now before the Oklahoma house ends up just like this one."

"Sure, Jos, but your relatives have a fifty-year head start on my parents."

Heated Spanish drifted out from the house, punctuated by clattering furniture.

Josie slumped. "I better get back in there. I'd say tell the kids I said hi, but with your mom there, they've probably forgotten I exist."

"Well, *I* haven't forgotten about you."

The front door flew open. Flor and Mirabel waddled backward, gripping two corners of the dining table, while Mirabel's husband, Tino, staggered on the other end with an unlit cigarette dangling from his lips.

Josie scrambled toward them. "Hunter, I've got to go. I love you." She clicked off the call and shoved her phone in her back pocket. "Tías, let me help." She squeezed between her aunts and lifted their side of the table with ease.

Flor and Mirabel dropped out of the way, rubbing their hands with dramatic moans.

"Watch your step," Tino warned as Josie approached the end of the storage container. Once inside, he pointed to the desk behind her. "We better flip it over and set it on top of that or this thing is going to run out of space pretty quickly."

They muscled the table into place, and Josie dusted her hands on her jeans. They stepped back into the sunlight, sucking in fresh air untainted by mildew and years of built-up dust. Tino didn't look any more eager to go back inside than she was.

He plucked the cigarette from his mouth and jabbed it toward the house. "This is getting ridiculous. They should've let the restoration crew haul everything out. Then the contractors could've started already. But no, Clara and Silvio are attached to everything. They're out of control." He pitched his voice high and fluttered his hands, mocking his sister-in-law. "'Careful with that, it's a priceless heirloom.' If you ask me, it's all worthless junk, and the way they're drawing this out, the repairs will never get done." He popped the cigarette back between his lips, puckering as he struck a lighter.

Josie leaned her back against the side of the container. "Have you come across a crocheted lace tablecloth in all that mess?"

"No, sorry." Tino took a long drag and let the smoke rise. "Heard your mom going on about it, but as far as I know, it hasn't turned up. Wouldn't surprise me if Clara hid it just to be spiteful. Nobody loves as fiercely as those sisters, but they can be vindictive, too."

"Tell me about it." Josie folded her arms and laughed. "Remember the Christmas Flor and Mirabel went to war over candlesticks?"

Tino waved his hand toward the ground to shush her. "It's still a sore subject around here. Don't let anyone hear you mention anything about candles. Or sticks." He took another puff and ducked his head conspiratorially. "There's a cedar trunk at the foot of Sil and Clara's bed. It's impossible to get to right now, but my money's on the tablecloth being in there. I'll see what I can do about keeping the troops distracted so you can slip in and dig around. It won't be easy, and you'll need to be discreet."

Josie suppressed a giggle. "Okay, Tino. What's the signal so I'll know when it's go time?"

Tino had always been the fun uncle, equal parts ornery and charming. He refused to be called *Tío Tino*. "Sounds like a Saturday morning puppet show," he'd say when Josie and her cousins would tease him. "Pick one—Tío or Tino. Not both."

He tapped the side of his nose. "When you see me do this, you slink off and dig like your life depends on it."

"Josefina. Tino. *Andale*." The gruff bark came from Tía Mirabel.

"Coming, tía." Josie's shoulders sagged as she pushed off the container.

Her uncle stubbed out the cigarette under the toe of his boot, picked up the butt, and flicked it into the dumpster. Together they trudged to the door.

Inside, Tía Flor was sealing a cardboard box labeled "Fragile" in thick black marker. "We took a vote and decided you should have Mamá's leaded crystal. Papi bought it for their twenty-fifth anniversary."

"Me?" Josie held up her hands. "Oh, I can't—"

"Of course you can." Flor motioned with the packing tape dispenser for Josie to take the box now. "It's a family heirloom."

That word again. Josie had heard it at least a thousand times in the last two days.

"You're the only granddaughter with a daughter of your own to pass it down to," said Clara.

Josie stared at the box, willing it to disintegrate, along with most of the other artifacts in this house. She scanned the room. There were no empty spaces where glassware and dishes had been removed, boxed up for Josie to cherish. The cache that had always cluttered the hutch and tabletops remained untouched. From where had the contents of this box even been resurrected, and how could she put it all back without anyone noticing?

Crystal in a house full of four-year-olds was a terrible idea. Like storing open paint containers where little hands could reach, except with sharp edges. And even if by some miracle the set survived her kids, Josie doubted grownup Olivia would have any interest in inheriting dishes made with lead.

Vibration from her hip pocket interrupted Josie's hemming and hawing as she grasped for a reason to refuse her aunts' gift. Tino caught her eye and pointed at his own phone. She pulled hers out and read his message. **Just say thank you. Drop it at the Goodwill off Del Norte Rd on your way back to my house. No one will be the wiser.**

"Thank you for the crystal, tías. I'm sure it will be treasured." By whoever buys it at the thrift store.

Tino clapped once and flashed a toothy grin. "Allow me to put that in Marie's trunk for you, and let's get this house cleaned out." He hefted the box and carried it outside.

His rallying cry did little to stir the rest of the family, but Josie stepped over a pile of photos Clara was sifting through and patted the large hutch with its one missing drawer. The top section was bare, evidence of Marie's handiwork before she threw her back out removing the drawer.

"How about we make space to move this to storage?"

"We need to go through all the drawers first," Clara said without looking up.

Josie put her hands on her hips and lifted her eyes to the ceiling. *Dear God, why couldn't you have sent a fire instead of a flood?*

"Sure," she said brightly. "How shall I sort what I find in the drawers?"

Clara pointed to an overflowing box on the sofa. "If it looks important or valuable, it goes there." She gestured to a second box labeled *TRASH* with three question marks. "If you think something can be thrown out, put it there, and I'll go through it."

They were getting nowhere.

The door banged open, and Tino lumbered in. "Now we're onto something. Let's all take a drawer and make it our goal to get that armoire out the door before dinner."

"It's not an armoire, you neanderthal. It's a hutch." Silvio puffed up, pushing his glasses higher. "You can tell by the open shelving up top. Much more valuable at antiques shows."

"Right." Tino tapped his temple like he was filing away

that important furniture-identification tidbit. "We'll make it a game. There are five drawers, so let's each take one, and the last one to get theirs emptied buys dinner."

Silvio glanced between the sisters who nodded. "You're on."

"And...go." Tino tapped his nose furiously at Josie as everyone else scrambled to the hutch.

"Ladies, allow me to pull your drawers," said Silvio.

Josie snickered.

He frowned. "I meant because they're so full they're heavy. We don't need anyone else getting hurt."

"Because their drawers are so heavy," Josie repeated, and this time she couldn't hold it in. She burst out laughing.

"I was *trying* to be a gentleman, Josefina." Her uncle—the so-not-fun one—skewered her with a glare. "Don't make it dirty."

More than a half century of mindless collecting made it dirty, not her. Tino tapped his nose again, his silent reminder she had a mission to fulfil. She tipped her chin and ducked out of the room. Operation Tablecloth was officially a go.

Chapter 25
Dana

A screaming child and Harvey's worried yips sent Dana to her front window. Across the cul-de-sac, Josie's red minivan sat in the driveway, side door open, while Ben flopped in the grass, absorbed in a full-on tantrum.

Dana dashed outside and jogged across the street as Emmaline Caraway flung two cartoon backpacks over her shoulder and blew a strand of silver hair out of her eyes.

"Welcome back to Texas, Mrs. Caraway."

"Hey Dana. Glad to be here. Were you drawn by the siren song of the tired preschooler who desperately needs a nap?"

Ben screamed louder as if to confirm.

"Something like that." Dana walked to the driver's side, opened the sliding door, and unbuckled Olivia. "Hey, Livvie. What's wrong with Ben?"

"Gramma said we have food at home. He wanted Chick-uh-lave."

"We had Chick-fil-a last night," Emmaline huffed. "I don't suppose you have a minute to help me wrestle him inside, do you?"

"Sure thing. Or…" Dana stepped neatly over Ben, who

was still kicking at the grass. "We could just leave him here and go inside for lunch and cookies. What kind do y'all have?"

Without missing a beat, Dana and the non-screaming Caraways marched through the garage.

"I want cookies too," Ben shouted, springing to his feet and racing after them. He caught up to them as his grandmother held the door for them to parade into the kitchen.

"How's it going so far?" Dana jerked a thumb over her shoulder. "Other than that back there."

Emmaline flashed a weary smile. "Oh, about like you'd expect when this is the first time their M-O-T-H-E-R has been away. The routine just isn't routining well. Grandmas are supposed to be fun, not enforce the rules."

Dana nodded with understanding, not because she knew what it was like to be a grandmother, but because she'd babysat the triplets enough times to appreciate the importance of their schedule. "Hang in there. I know Jos—" Emmaline's wild-eyed alarm stopped her from saying Josie's name. "I know everyone's thankful you're here."

"Me, too. It's tough living 350 miles away from the kids. In between visits, they grow so much, I hardly recognize them." Emmaline pulled colorful plastic plates out of the fridge and set them on the dining table. "I premade their lunches to save time so hopefully they'll R-E-S-T for a bit before we go to the park."

"I know what you spelled, Gramma," Olivia piped up.

"You do, sweetheart?"

The little girl nodded. "It was nap."

The women exchanged grins. Busted.

"That's because you're very intelligent. Now please go wash your hands." Emmaline aimed the same order at the boys. "You too, fellas. And not just water. Use soap."

As the triplets stampeded down the hall, Dana opened a cabinet for cups and pulled milk from the fridge. The quiet that followed made space for the ache she'd been tamping down.

"Did your sons pull away from you when they first left home?" she asked, trying to sound casual.

"What do you mean?"

"Leah rarely calls these days." Dana poured the milk and handed the filled cups across the counter to Emmaline. "She'll answer a text with fewer than three words now and then, but it's different. I thought maybe it was her boyfriend, but then they invited us to his uncle's ranch a few weeks ago and we had a lovely afternoon." She stopped herself before mentioning Adam's fall from the horse. No need to overshare with someone she hardly knew, more than she already was, anyway. "From talking with another mom, this seems to be the norm with girls, but I was hoping to learn whether this is my one go-round, or if I get to look forward to it twice more when the boys graduate."

"I wish I could tell you it's just a phase with daughters, but Stephen and Hunter also went through it." Emmaline leaned a hip against the counter. "Of course, we didn't have unlimited data or texting back then, so parents weren't used to this constant connection."

"And your youngest?" Dana asked.

"Kyle enlisted, so we didn't hear from him much at all. Still don't. I'd hoped by now he'd be out, but he loves what he does. Hard to fault him for that." Emmaline cleared her throat.

Connor clomped into the room with his hands in front of him like Frankenstein's monster. "Smell 'em, Gramma. Soap."

She leaned down and took an exaggerated whiff. "Excellent. You're ready to eat."

He scrambled into his chair. "Nuh-uh. We hafta say the blessing first."

Dana touched Emmaline's arm. "I'll get out of your hair. And I didn't mean to wax so sentimental. Being around the triplets just reminds me how fast it all goes. I'm still trying to adjust to one of mine being out of the house."

"Don't you apologize for that." Emmaline slipped an arm around her as they walked to the door. "Moms are supposed to share their burdens and borrow a little strength from each other, which is why I'm so thankful you're right across the street. Josie and Hunter wouldn't have made it this far without you."

The brief conversation with Emmaline had somehow given Dana the peace of mind she craved, freeing her, at least for now, to focus on her main character tracking down a serial killer on the loose at a music festival.

After football practice, Adam hopped into the SUV and chatted about his day, much to Dana's delight and surprise. "Coach let me fill in at defensive tackle. It was fun, but we agreed I'm better at running back." Halfway to Nate's school, he asked, "Do you think Leah would take us to Jordan's family ranch again sometime?"

"That's funny. I was thinking about that place today." She glanced at her little bedraggled running back. "You want to try riding again?"

"No." He didn't even pause to consider it. "But I liked being out there. The animals were cool."

"Why don't you ask your sister?" Dana's pulse quickened. She'd wondered about Leah's relationship status since the block party but resisted the urge to pry. Whatever Leah said to Adam would tell Dana everything without blowing her cover as a non-meddlesome mom.

Adam pulled out his phone and started typing.

As he did, Dana's thoughts wandered. One perk of raising teenagers was watching how their sibling dynamics evolved. Leah used to find Adam unbearably loud and annoying, but her opinion shifted on their first family camping trip, where his preparedness had saved the day more than once.

Then a couple of weeks ago, she welcomed his help with Connor and Ben's LEGO project, and she cheered louder than anyone at his football games. Watching her kids care about each another was akin to winning Mother of the Year, which was probably better than making the New York Times Bestseller list.

She pulled into the field house parking lot and found a spot among the other freshman and sophomore moms secretly pining for the day their kids could drive themselves.

Adam grumbled and dropped his phone into his lap. "Well, I guess we won't be going back."

"Why not?" Dana held her breath.

"Leah and Jordan broke up."

She exhaled. Being right wasn't at all satisfying when

her kid's heart was on the line. "Oh no. Is she okay?"

He shrugged.

"Ask her."

"Mom." His eyebrows dipped low. "You can check on her if you're so interested. I just wanted to pet a cow."

Sibling evolution at its finest. No point in explaining to him that Leah hadn't opened up to *her,* and therefore, she couldn't press for more information.

Nate opened the door behind Dana, tossed in his backpack, and dropped into the seat. "What's with him?"

Adam's elbow was propped on the armrest, the heel of his hand pushing up his cheek. "Leah can't keep a man, so we all have to suffer."

"Hey, that's not fair. Your sister's dating life isn't for your entertainment. Besides, you don't know what happened." Dana backed the Tahoe out of the space, catching a glimpse through the rearview mirror of Nate's confusion. "He wanted to go back to the Hirschfield ranch," she explained.

"Just buy your own baby chicks. They sell them at the feed store." Older brothers were so helpful.

If Dana could've reached Nate, she might have smacked him. "We are *not* getting chickens. Would it kill you two to show a little compassion for Leah? This is her first breakup."

In the most dramatic fashion, Adam rolled his head toward Dana. "Mom, you didn't even like Jordan."

"Sure, I did."

He narrowed his eyes. "I thought we weren't supposed to lie."

"I *never* said I didn't like him." Thought it a few times but kept it to herself. "We all need to be supportive of Leah, and no matter how disappointed you are about losing Jordan as a buddy, or the perks he brought, like the ranch, neither of you are going to mention that to her. Is that clear?"

The boys mumbled half-hearted "yes ma'ams."

"Can we at least go by the feed store and *look* at the chicks?" asked Adam.

No good could come from that field trip. It was bound to turn out as well as just looking at the litter of Bernese Mountain puppies had the day they brought Harvey home.

A simple, yet brilliant alternative came to Dana. Her mouth twitched. "Sure, I'll take you to the feed store to gaze upon barnyard animals right after you clean out your closet."

"Who gets to decide what constitutes clean?"

She darted a look in his direction. "Me, obviously."

"That means we never get to go." Adam slumped in the seat.

Back home, Dana traded the ground beef she'd thawed to make tacos for a bag of chicken breasts from the freezer and set to work on a new dinner plan. Then she sent a message to Leah. **Making chicken fettucine for dinner. You're welcome to join us.**

She wasn't above baiting Leah with her favorite meal. After all, comfort food was the best emotional support she could offer the prickly teen in her time of need.

Can you save me some for tomorrow? Going to play sand volleyball with friends.

If Leah had the emotional resilience to socialize, she must not be too brokenhearted over ending things with Jordan. She hadn't even given a sullen retort about Adam blabbing, and she mentioned coming over tomorrow. All good signs that eased the heaviness in Dana's heart. She typed: **Will do. I love you, sweetie.**

A heart popped up over her message. Almost as good as an "I love you, too."

The hum of the garage door signaled Will's arrival, and Dana grabbed him by the arm as soon as he stepped inside. "I need you right now." She pulled him into the laundry room and shut the door.

He set his hands on her hips, eyes sweeping over her with longing. "Whoa. This is the best welcome home I've had since…well, since the kids came along."

"Sorry to disappoint, but I just want to talk."

His face fell, hands dropping. "What's wrong now?"

"Why do you assume something's wrong?"

Will tipped his head. "Because if you didn't drag me in here to ravish me, it must be bad enough you don't want the boys to hear. It's your dad, isn't it? It's been a while since the police brought him home, so I guess we were due."

"Nothing like that." Dana sighed. She really needed to work on how she dropped social cues. Teasing and scaring people in the same breath was hardly a skill worth bragging about.

"Leah and Jordan broke up," she said.

"Is she okay?"

Dana shrugged. "She's going to play volleyball with friends. I would think if she were upset, she'd hole up in her room. Unless she's past that stage and has already moved on."

"Then what are we in here for? If she's fine, I don't see what's so pressing we had to hide in the laundry room to discuss it."

He had a point. The boys already knew about Leah's

relationship status change. There was no crisis. What was she hoping for in telling him—that he'd have the same internal freakout she'd had so they could comfort one another?

"Honey, I know you want to jump in and fix things for the kids, but it's good when they learn to handle life's curveballs on their own. It means we've raised them well."

She gazed up at him with an adoring smile. "How did you know what I needed to hear?"

He wrapped his arms around her. "Because I know your heart, and it's my job to reassure you when you're overthinking."

Maybe she should've just ravished him after all.

Chapter 26
Josie

Josie snapped a photo of the cedar chest at the end of Tía Clara's bed to ensure she could restack everything exactly as she'd found it. Not that anyone would notice. The restoration crew had rearranged half the room, and the gaping hole where the ceiling had collapsed tended to draw the eye first anyway.

She worked quickly, keeping her movements quiet until the lid was clear. As she lifted the front edge, the hinges creaked, but the lively accordion music pouring from the living room mercifully drowned it out.

Bless Tino for cranking up the Norteño under the pretense of "boosting morale" during their drawer-cleaning race.

White lace, yellowed with age, peeked out between folded patchwork quilts. This was it, finally! Josie's heart skipped as she took hold of the edge, only to discover it wasn't crocheted after all. She dug deeper. The lace belonged to a wedding dress, yet another sacred relic left to disintegrate in this cedar coffin.

Her fingers brushed something cold and solid. The bumpy texture was what her mother would have called "fluted," just as she'd described the infamous silver candlesticks that had nearly sparked a family war. Josie pushed aside a brown paper package and wrestled the fluted object out of the chest. It had to be one of them. How many silver fluted candlesticks could one family possibly hoard? At least two, as they were a pair.

She glanced behind her. The problem with music covering any sound she made was that it would also cover footsteps leading her way. She and Tino really should've planned a warning signal.

The candlestick had tarnished almost to black, but its silver form was unmistakable. Josie turned it over in her hand and briefly considered marching into the living room, brandishing her find like a trophy. It might be worth getting scolded for snooping if it meant ending her sentence in the Great Reshuffling-But-Not-Eradicating of Tía Clara's collections.

She set the discovery aside and delved back into the trunk. Beneath the paper bundle lay its twin. When she yanked it free, the brittle wrapping tore. Josie froze, eyes darting to the door again.

Torn paper or not, short of getting caught in the act, no one would even know she'd nosed through the cedar chest, but she should still cover her tracks. She reached in to push the damaged end under a quilt when the texture beneath her fingers stopped her cold. The contents were flimsy. Fabric maybe.

Her mother had carried her precious tablecloth home from Cuauhtémoc wrapped in brown paper all those years ago. Could it be—? Josie poked a finger into the tear and touched fine threads looped into elaborate configurations.

Not woven, crocheted. Her breath caught in her throat. She sat back on her heels and drew the bundle into her lap, peeling away each fragile fold until they revealed a giant doily.

Tino's voice rose above the music. "It's going to be close. Remember, the loser buys dinner for everyone."

Josie took that as her cue to move it along, though she'd have guessed drawer emptying would've taken longer. She scrambled to her feet and reset the stacks on the chest, but the fresh prints in the dust were a dead giveaway. Wincing in disgust, she used the inside of her shirt hem to wipe them away, only to realize the newly polished spots were even more suspicious. She scattered the piles again, muttering under her breath.

"Have you got a good grip on your end, Silvio?" Tino asked at an abnormal volume.

The hutch was on the move. Josie scanned for a place to stash her loot until she could smuggle it to her mother, but where? Desperate, she settled on stuffing the parcel under her shirt and folded her hands over it. Was she really considering theft? Sure, the tablecloth rightfully belonged to her mom, but she'd still acquired it in a deeply underhanded way.

She retreated into the bathroom across the hall, keeping her back to the living room, and examined her odd shape in the mirror. The corners protruding from her top made her look like a giant pregnant Lego figurine. She'd never make it out of the house.

Above the toilet was a cabinet. Josie opened it, releasing an avalanche of towels and washcloths. She shoved them back in, holding the heap steady with one hand as she closed the door with the other. Between the cabinet molding and the ceiling was about a foot of space where no one would think to look.

Josie raised her shirt enough to pull out the bundle and laid it on top of the cabinet. A bit of the brown paper stuck up above the molding. She stepped onto the side of the tub, pressed the bundle flatter, and hopped down again to check her work.

A sliver still showed, but when she bent her knees to look from a shorter vantage point, it disappeared. Since Josie was taller than anyone on her mother's side of the family, it should be safe up there until she figured out what to do.

A sharp rap on the door made her jump. "Josefina, are you alright? You've been in there a long time."

"Uh, I'm fine, Mirabel." Josie flushed the toilet and ran water in the sink so her aunt would think she was washing her hands. The layer of dirt from all the rummaging changed her mind, and she actually washed them. She opened the door and gave Mirabel a sheepish smile as she stepped out.

"Let's go eat. Clara has to buy dinner. No surprise there." Mirabel hooked her arm through Josie's and led her out the front door. "We'll have to take two cars, so you ride with Tino and me."

The candlesticks. In her haste to hide the tablecloth, Josie had left them sitting right in the middle of the bedroom floor. She spun and jogged back just as Silvio was pulling the door closed. "I forgot my…" Her brain scrambled for something. Anything. If she said phone, he'd spot it in her pocket the second she slipped past him. "Stuff." Smooth one, Josie.

Much to her relief, Silvio didn't follow her in.

Josie grabbed a candlestick in each hand and did the only thing that came to mind—stashed them behind an assortment of uranium glass plates perched atop a console TV that hadn't worked in her lifetime.

"I'm going to gut the picture tube and install a custom fish tank," Silvio always said when asked why he kept the antique eyesore.

In their tarnished state, the candlesticks wouldn't shimmer, betraying their hiding place through the translucent green glass.

She eased the door shut behind her and jammed one hand into her pocket, as if tucking away the "retrieved" item. "Got it. Thanks." *Dear Lord, please don't let him ask what* it *is.*

Mirabel waited beside the dumpster and led her to the black pickup parked behind Marie's Camry two houses down. With the storage container taking up the driveway and the dumpster blocking the curb, the family's vehicles were scattered down the block. One hoarder's den wasn't enough. They were cluttering the entire neighborhood.

Josie held the door for her aunt, then climbed into the back seat. Tino caught her gaze in the rearview mirror, one brow raised in question. She tapped the side of her nose, and he grinned.

Mirabel might not share her sister's obsessive pack rat tendencies, but she was still fiercely protective of anything deemed *family treasure*. Josie wasn't about to trust her with the tablecloth secret.

The aunts voted to call it a night, promising to start fresh in the morning, which meant they'd eaten too much Chinese food to rifle through any more precious garbage.

Josie loaded a bag of takeout containers into the Camry's passenger seat and fell in behind Tino's truck. He'd insisted she not drive home alone after dark, even though she was nearly forty. The gesture was sweet in a fatherly way, and she didn't have it in her to argue.

Her mother met them at the door. "Notice anything different about me?"

"You're upright." Josie gave her a once over. "And dressed. I'm assuming you did that all on your own?"

Marie pulled Josie's face down and kissed her cheek. "I'm a new woman, Josefina." She turned and walked to the kitchen with normal strides.

This morning, her mother needed help getting up to go to the bathroom. When Josie brought her lunch, she was still barely moving, so her newfound mobility was a confusing sight.

Josie set the bag on the counter and assessed her mother more closely. "How many of those muscle relaxers did you take after I left?"

"It's the darnedest thing," Marie said. "I was lying there going out of my mind when I found this lady on a Facebook video talking about sciatica. Turns out she's what you call a *wellness influencer*." Marie pronounced the words slowly, as though unveiling a new species. "She's got a whole social media channel—nutrition, fitness, at-home physical therapy—the works. And millions of people watch her." She made a grand sweep with her hand. "Which is how she's become so influential."

What was the appropriate facial expression when one's retired parental unit just mom-splained influencers?

"I found several helpful videos on how to bounce back from a strained back." Marie threw her hands up. "What are the odds? It's like God sent her to me in my time of need."

The odds were high her phone was spying on her and had caught wind of her predicament. Josie glanced at Tino, hoping for a shared smirk, but his rapt expression said he was actively converting to the gospel of Facebook wellness.

"Right there in bed, I started doing the stretches," Marie continued. "The more I moved my hips, the better I felt. I can even lift my leg to step into my own pants now."

Where was this miracle-working influencer when Josie had to help her mother put on underwear?

"Marie, I'm glad you're feeling better." Mirabel squeezed her sister's shoulders. "I'm going to soak in a hot bath and wash the grime off me." She turned and made her way down the hall.

"And I'm going to leave you to catch your mama up on your acquisition." Tino put a hand to the side of his mouth and spoke low. "The less I know, the better." He kissed Josie's forehead and retired to the living room.

Marie opened the container of General Tso's Chicken. "What's he talking about? Did you find the you-know-what?"

Josie nodded.

"Mija, that's wonderful!" Her mother wiped her hands on a napkin and held them out expectantly. "Gimme. I've been waiting thirty-five years to see it again."

"Here's the thing," Josie started. "Maybe you better eat and let me explain everything. Then we can figure out what to do next."

"Clara wouldn't let you have it, would she? I knew it. She's been a control freak her whole life."

Oh, hello, pot. Josie put a hand on her arm. "Just listen." She launched into a retelling of the afternoon's events, leaving out Tino's involvement. "When everyone was busy going through the hutch drawers, I snuck into Clara's cedar chest and found the tablecloth."

Her mother choked on an egg roll when Josie got to the part about smuggling the package under her shirt and hiding it on the bathroom cabinet. Josie had to wait for the coughing fit to pass before continuing. "You okay, Mom?"

Marie patted her chest. "I wish I could've been there to see it."

"I don't know how to get it out of the house without stirring up a ruckus, and I also don't feel right about just taking it."

"But it's—"

"I know, Mom. You made it as a gift for Abuela Susana, and it's rightfully yours. That's why I'm glad you're up and walking again so you can sneak it out of the house or confront your sisters, whichever you think is more appropriate."

"Believe me, Josefina. I will do exactly that." Marie narrowed her eyes and stabbed a bite of chicken with her fork.

Josie almost felt bad for Tía Clara. She stood from the table. "I'm going to go call the kids and tell them goodnight. One more thing, take a peek behind the dishes on Silvio's future aquarium tomorrow." She winked and strode away to the guest room.

Tía Mirabel made a big breakfast before the four of them headed back into the fray. The chorizo and eggs did little to boost morale, though, based on the glum faces around the table. Josie had only spent three days mining the flood damage, which was more than enough to make her feel like a prisoner with a life sentence on Alcatraz.

"I don't see how you guys can stand to do this day after day," she said. "There's no progress. None. I try to haul out garbage, and someone stops me. The musty smell is so bad that my head is pounding within the first hour. When does the madness end?"

Marie's mouth dropped open. "Josefina, I did not raise you to speak of your family that way."

Tino set his fork aside. "No, she's right. Every day we go over there and do the same thing over and over expecting different results. It's an exercise in futility."

"Aye, what are we supposed to do then?" A blaze burned in Mirabel's eyes. "Turn our backs on Silvio and Clara? Let our parents' belongings be cast aside?" Her tirade drifted into Spanish, the gist of which was, "Families are supposed to support one another, and where is your sense of loyalty?" She finally got quiet and sighed. "What are we to do?"

Tino covered her hand with his. "We've done all we can. That house is no closer to being ready for renovations than when the pipe burst. Until those two get therapy, there's nothing more we can do."

"Where does one even find a therapist for this sort of thing?" asked Marie.

Josie opened her phone with the idea a reality television show might be interested in her family's story and intervene. She typed "help for hoarders" into the search bar, and a familiar face popped up. One of her high school classmates was a licensed professional counselor specializing in obsessive-compulsive disorder. She turned her phone around. "We call her."

Chapter 27

Dana

Dana and Beverly stepped into the coffee shop together but didn't get any farther. The line to the counter snaked all the way to the door, and every table was full.

"I don't think we're getting much critiquing done today," Bev said.

"We could try The Latte Lounge again." Even as she suggested it, Dana knew how Carlos would feel about that. Sharing a wall with a dog groomer meant an endless chorus of barking. Not ideal for reading and writing.

Bev's grimace confirmed it. "Hard pass."

"We could work at my place." Dana mentally flipped through the state of her house. She'd given it a good scrub before the block party last weekend, but with three boys—counting Will—the results had been… fleeting.

"I'm game."

Just then, Carlos walked in and muttered a mild expletive. "Well, this is no good."

"Change of plans," Bev announced. "We're meeting at Dana's."

He raised an eyebrow. "You got coffee there?"

Dana tilted her head, lips pursed in the universal sign for *obviously*. "Did Hemmingway like rum?"

"I'm not comfortable drinking this early, and I *never* touch the hard stuff." Beverly's stern expression could've landed her the starring role in a *Just Say No* commercial from the eighties.

Carlos tugged her arm to move her out of the path of another customer. "That's Dana's literary way of asking if the sky's blue. What are we waiting for? Let's get out of here."

The critique group spread out around the Hardings' dining table, swapping paper copies and making changes on their laptops. Dana scribbled a notation in the margin of Carlos's chapter and rotated the page toward him. "I wonder if this sentence would work better if you moved it over here." She pointed with her pen. "Then it packs a bigger punch. See?"

"You're right." He transcribed Dana's edit on his laptop as the doorbell rang.

Harvey barked once.

"Thanks for the heads up, boy." Dana opened the door to a frantic Emmaline, wearing a knit winter beanie pulled low over her silver shoulder-length hair, and the triplets. "Good morning."

"You have to help me," Emmaline pleaded.

The kids pushed past her and fell all over Harvey, who hadn't had the good sense to hide before they crossed the threshold.

"Shouldn't they be in school?" Dana asked.

"Student holiday for the elementary. Lucky me." Emmaline pulled off the hat, revealing a fist-sized section of half-inch sprigs bursting from the left side of her scalp.

"Oh my." Dana covered her mouth, both from shock and to suppress the laugh threatening to burst from it. "Come inside." She waved Emmaline inside as Beverly and Carlos looked on. "These are my writing buddies. Bev, Carlos, this is my neighbor's mother, Emmaline."

"It's lovely to meet you." Emmaline pointed to her chop job. "And this is my granddaughter's handiwork."

Connor picked up a chew toy and dangled it in Harvey's face. "Livvie cut Gramma's hair, and it looks bad."

The little girl threw her hands onto her hips. "Nuh-uh. She's beautiful."

"You let a four-year-old cut your hair?" Dana asked.

"Not on purpose." Emmaline pulled the beanie on again. "When Olivia wanted to play beauty shop like her mommy, I thought, well sure. If letting her brush my hair and put a bunch of clips in it makes her happy while her mom is away, let's do it."

Emmaline paced the entry way. "I didn't know she got her hands on real scissors until I heard and felt that tell-tale snip of doom right next to my scalp. Of course, right before I took my place in her beauty chair, I was a bit distracted by Ben trying to play Candy Crush on my phone while I cleaned up the kitchen from breakfast. It didn't end so well."

She held up the screen which read "disabled for five minutes."

"I don't know what to do, Dana. My hair looks like, well, it looks like a preschooler got a hold of it. I'm gonna have to wear this hat for the rest of my life."

Dana looked to her critique partners for ideas, advice maybe, but all they offered were enthralled stares. Right up until she made eye contact with Carlos, that is, who suddenly busied himself with a stack of paper on the table.

"Use mine." Dana grabbed her purse off the kitchen counter and dug out her phone. "I have Hunter and Josie's numbers saved. She can probably get you an appointment with one of her coworkers." She gave herself a little pat on the back for such quick thinking.

Emmaline stopped pacing and took Dana's phone. After a beat, she said, "Hey, Jos. It's Em. You're not going to believe what happened." She smiled. "You're right. You probably will." She poured out the whole chaotic tale in one breath. "Please tell me someone can make me look like a person again instead of the creepy doll head in *Toy Story.*"

Even as she stifled a chuckle, Dana sent warning looks to Bev and Carlos, who were on the verge of crumbling.

"Okay, thank you. Yes, I will discipline the mini hairdresser and phone saboteur both soundly," Emmaline promised Josie while emphatically shaking her head at Dana. She ended the call and handed the phone back. "She's going to do some checking and let me know. Is it okay if I wait over here? Feels safer where the adult-to-child ratio weighs in our favor. At least until my phone is operational again?"

Connor and Ben were tossing one of Harvey's stuffed animals back and forth, attempting to engage the dog. Olivia crouched on all fours, nuzzling Harvey's neck.

"Absolutely. A wise woman told me once that moms—and grandmas—have to stick together. Please, sit. May I offer you coffee or tea?"

"Decaf," Carlos said through a cough.

Emmaline waived Dana off. "I've had plenty this morning. If I hadn't made that second cup, I might've paid more attention to the children's shenanigans. Please, don't let me keep you from whatever you were doing. You don't need to entertain me."

Carlos leaned back in his chair. "Let me ask you, Emmaline, would you read a romance with 'she sucked in a breath as his thumb traced the corner of her mouth?'" Without waiting for an answer, he picked up the paper and turned toward her. "Or what about a novel based on the premise two coworkers who hate each other and are vying for the same promotion at work get stuck in an elevator together and end up falling in love?"

Beverly cut him with a withering glare.

"That sounds exactly like the kind of book I would like to read, actually," said Emmaline. "I'm always a sucker for a sappy love story. Is that what you're writing?"

Dana cut in before he could say something that might make Bev react in ways requiring Dana to give a witness statement later. "That's Beverly's manuscript. She writes fun and touching love stories, while Cynical Steve over here writes suspense."

"Thrillers, actually," Carlos corrected.

His fourth novel had stayed on the bestseller list for several months, and he was already a breakout sensation when Dana and Bev met him as their creative writing professor at the local community college four years ago. She could've bragged on him, but she didn't. Punishment for his exasperating take on their friend's work lately.

"You'll want to keep an eye out for Beverly's debut novel this spring. I've read all her work, and every story is terrific," Dana gushed.

"Thank you, dear. That's why your name is front and center in the acknowledgments while Carlos is recognized by his honorary title—Professor Sourpuss." She pretended to make a note in her spiral notebook. "Although Cynical Steve does have a nice ring to it."

The phone buzzed, Josie and the triplets' photo appearing on the screen. "I'm sure this is for you." Dana held it out to Emmaline.

"Hey, sugar. Any luck?" Emmaline waited with bated breath, then blew it out, the tension melting from her shoulders. "You're an angel. An absolute saint of a daughter-in-law. Thank you." She gave the phone back to Dana. "Her friend Elisa is going to fit me in if I can get there right now." She pointed to the children. "I don't suppose—"

"Say no more." Dana waved her hand. "I'll watch the kids while you get…repaired. Leave them, and as soon as we finish up here, I'll take them home and make their lunch."

Emmaline stood and pressed her hands together under her chin. "I can't even begin to thank you." She turned to leave. "Don't let them near scissors. Or your phones."

Harvey lifted an eyebrow as if to say, "What about me?"

Dana closed the door behind her and picked up the remote. She selected an age-appropriate TV show and returned to her chair at the dining table. "This'll keep them busy for about fifteen minutes, so let's pick up the pace."

"Man, I'm sure glad my sons came one at a time," Carlos whispered.

Bev shook her head. "I just can't believe they don't keep all the dangerous stuff under lock and key over there."

"Give them some grace," Dana said. "You and I both know that kids don't behave the same for grandparents as they do for their parents."

"Yeah, and sometimes you can do everything right, and they still get into stuff because they're shifty little buggers." Carlos put down his pen and laughed. "My youngest worked his fingers into a drawer, *with* the child lock still on it, and got ahold of superglue. By the time we found him, the tube of glue was stuck to one hand, and the other was fused to the tile floor."

"Just picture *three* kids getting into superglue." Beverly clutched imaginary pearls.

Mesmerized by the dog sprawled in the middle of the floor and by the animated characters on the screen, the triplets were currently quite angelic. Hard to believe the havoc they could cause. But Dana knew firsthand how quickly their attention could shift. Her house hadn't been toddler-proofed in many years, and the Caraway kids had on occasion gotten into enough mischief over here to remind Dana why she preferred to babysit them at their own house. "Let's wrap this up before we have a chance to find out what that would be like."

The critique group finished their chapter exchanges and were packing up when Dana's phone rang. She reached to decline the unknown number, but its origin, Oklahoma City, gave her pause. "Hello?" she asked flatly.

"Thank goodness you answered. Dana, it's Emmaline. I was in such a rush to get to the salon that I left my purse. I have no way to pay Elisa for whatever magic she can work on my hair."

Dana repeated her dilemma aloud. "You forgot your purse?" She could bring it to Emmaline, but without booster seats, the triplets would be riding illegally in her Tahoe. "Do you think it's okay for me to buckle the kids into regular seats?"

Carlos nudged her arm. "Where's she at? I can drop it by."

She mouthed a thank you and lifted the phone. "Emmaline, my friend Carlos is going to run it by in a few minutes, okay?" She pulled a face at Emmaline's request to give him a giant hug. "You can thank him yourself when he gets there."

Eventually Dana got her to stop gushing and hung up. She gave Carlos a hopeful smile. "You sure you don't mind?"

"I don't teach on Fridays, and I've got nothing until school pickup." He scratched his head. "Plus, I saw that lady's hair. Getting her purse to her is the least I can do, next to hosting a telethon or starting a fundraiser for grandmas who've been victimized by their descendants. Yikes."

Dana smirked. "Well, come on, Jerry Lewis. Let's go be heroes."

His blank stare told her the joke was lost on him. "Who?"

Beverly groaned. "The Muscular Dystrophy Labor Day telethon? What are you, twelve?"

"Rather than bemoaning our age gap, how about we get the kids across the street and find Emmaline's purse?" Dana closed her laptop and stood. "Who's ready for lunch?"

Three little hands flew up. "Me!"

"How can I help?" asked Bev.

"Want to walk over with us and make sure Carlos finds the purse?" Dana was an old pro at herding the triple threat across the street but far be it from her to turn down extra help.

The purple leather handbag was on the guest room dresser, just as Emmaline said it was. Carlos slipped it over his arm and sashayed across the living room. "Well, I'm off. Ciao, ladies."

Bev chuckled. "I don't know what to make of that man half the time, but he sure does need to find a special lady. ASAP."

"I've been trying to set him up with someone. It's not as easy as I had hoped to get them in the same place at the same time."

"It's not that itty bitty thing who fell off her high heels at your block party, is it?"

Dana stiffened. "What's wrong with Zola?"

"Nothing." Bev shrugged. "She strikes me as a bit high maintenance, and two fussy people together is more like a reality show than a relationship."

Was she right? Had Dana and Josie been misguided in their attempt to set up their friends? After all, their motives weren't exactly pure. Shoving two unwitting red-flag magnets into a relationship to get them out of everyone else's hair seemed like a great plan originally, but maybe playing Cupid was best left to God. And Hallmark.

Chapter 28
Josie

Josie's fellow viola player in the high school orchestra stood in the corridor of Tía Clara's house. Conversation and mock organizing ground to a halt as everyone swiveled toward the unfamiliar face.

"This is my old friend Celeste." Josie drew in a steadying breath and powered on. "I thought she might be able to help Clara and Silvio get ready for the next phase of the renovation."

Clara shifted, smoothing her features into a polite welcome. "Well, more hands make light work, I suppose."

Celeste's gaze swept the maze of photo frames and stepped around them with precision. "I'm here to help in a different way."

"I don't understand." Clara shook her head. "We had a flood, and we need to clear the house so the floors and damaged drywall can be redone. But we've got to get everything sorted first. That's the kind of help we need."

Tino pushed up from the sofa, dislodging a mountain of papers and a box that probably outweighed him. "Clara, we've been at this for two weeks. Can you honestly say we've made a lick of progress?"

"Of course. You see how full that storage unit is getting." Clara gestured, chin lifted with pride.

"Not full enough. At this pace, we'll still be digging through this same room at Easter." Tino scrubbed both hands over his hair. "In two weeks, we should've emptied the house. But it looks exactly the same as on day one. And some of us need to get back to our lives."

"Aye!" Marie's cry floated from the guest bathroom.

Josie had been so absorbed in her uncle's monologue she completely forgot about the hidden tablecloth.

Marie reappeared with the paper-wrapped bundle raised in triumphant. "Clara, you have a problem. I've been searching everywhere for this for thirty years, and all this time, you've been keeping it from me because you are a *hoarder.*" She spit out the last word as if it meant something much more scandalous than trash collecting.

"*Ladrona!*" Clara shouted.

"I am *not* a thief. You're the one who stole from *me.*" Marie clutched the tablecloth to her chest and narrowed her eyes as though readying herself for battle.

With hands clasped and head dipped in reverence, Tino stepped between the sisters and declared, "Silvio, Clara, this is an intervention. You are not stewarding the blessings God has given you by keeping everything and hiding sentimental treasures that belong to others. Holding Marie's tablecloth hostage was unkind."

Clara jammed her index finger at Marie. "She snooped through my personal things to find it."

Josie hurried to her mother's side and opened her mouth to confess her role in the tablecloth heist, but Tino raised his hand to stop her.

"Not now, Josefina," he murmured. He turned back to the homeowners. "Guys, we aren't judging you. We're all family here, and we love you. But we also can't help you until you accept how you're hurting yourselves and the people who care about you."

Silvio squared his shoulders and poked his brother-in-law's chest. "Care about us? You only came here to take what's ours so you can profit from it."

"Gentlemen, I think I can help if you'll hear me out." Celeste took over and gave her professional spiel.

Marie inched her way around Josie until she was next to the console television. She raised onto her tiptoes, and her eyes widened as they landed on the candlesticks.

Josie tugged her out the door. "Mom, you got what you came for, so let's leave this to Celeste and not start an all-out war between your sisters."

Outside, her mother tucked the wrapped tablecloth under her arm and pulled out her phone. "Flor and Mirabel should stop blaming one another for Mamá's missing candlesticks. I think they deserve to know who had them all these years, don't you?" She was already typing, obviously unconcerned about Josie's opinion on keeping peace.

"Mom, can we please go back to Lubbock? I need to get home to my kids before they scalp their Gramma completely."

Her mother's shoulders drooped. "Yes, mija. I'm ready to go home."

Josie wrapped her arm around her mother. "Should we go back in and say goodbye first?"

"Not after the text I just sent Flor and Mirabel. It'll be a bloodbath any minute now." The corners of her mouth curled smugly. "Besides, I just wrote a nice fat check to your violist friend, so let's let her earn her keep."

"She's a therapist, Mom. You didn't hire her to serenade them while they sort junk."

"I bet she could though. Unlike you, some musicians stick with it."

Josie jerked a thumb over her shoulder toward the house. "Want to go back in and take your turn with the shrink? I don't mind waiting."

Her mother pursed her lips. "Very funny."

Marie dropped Josie at her curb around nine that night with a pat on her cheek. "Te amo, mija. I will come see my babies tomorrow. Sleep well."

"I love you, too, Mom."

Home at last. The blue flicker through the living room window let her know Hunter was watching television as he waited up. She entered to find him and Emmaline engrossed in a true-crime documentary.

"Nothing says family bonding like murder at bedtime," Josie said.

Hunter kicked down his recliner's footrest, jumped up, and threw his arms around her. "Welcome home, babe. The kids wanted to stay up to see you, but they sacked out a while ago."

Josie rested her head on his shoulder, weary and unwilling to let go as if she hadn't seen him in weeks. Had it really been only four days? "That's okay. I'll sneak in and kiss them anyway."

Emmaline hugged Josie. "I didn't get to say hi to your mom."

"You're staying through the weekend, right? She said she'd stop by and see the kids tomorrow." Heaven help Emmaline through that meeting. They'd been great co-grandmothers so far, but then again, they typically stayed out of one another's lanes.

Thankfully, Josie wouldn't be around to worry about how the two got along as tomorrow was the big day at Agape House. Josie had already texted Zola to let her know she was on her way to town and ready to step up to the salon chair, but her fellow hairdresser hadn't replied. Ah, the silent treatment, every passive aggressive's punishment of choice.

"Did you and your mama get everything worked out in Albuquerque?" asked Emmaline.

"Hardly." Josie snorted. "We kicked up a hornet's nest and bolted."

"What do you mean?"

Hunter led Josie to the sofa. "I haven't filled Mom in on your family saga."

"Here's the Cliff's Notes version," Josie said. "After days of trying to clear out the house and getting nowhere because my aunt and uncle wouldn't let anyone get rid of anything, we gave up. Called in a therapist who specializes in their form of chronic and compulsive accumulation."

Emmaline nodded gravely. "That's all you can do."

"Yeah, but it's discouraging to know there's a good chance the house will never be repaired properly because Silvio and Clara can't let go. It doesn't make any sense."

"We live in a fallen world, sweetheart, and some things are beyond our understanding." Emmaline touched Josie's cheek in a maternal show of affection.

"Why can't they see how much they're hurting the entire family?" Josie fisted her hands on her lap.

"Other people's brokenness is so much easier to see than our own. But God can heal anyone. Remember that."

Hunter kept his arm around Josie throughout the exchange, silent but steady. Now he squeezed her shoulder and offered a small, reassuring smile.

"Em, what if He doesn't heal my aunt and uncle? What if my grandparents' home falls to ruin?"

"Everything this side of heaven will fall to ruin eventually. Nothing lasts except faith, hope, and love. And you have a family that genuinely loves one another." She pointed toward the hall. "The legacy your grandparents handed down to you is alive in this home with the absolute cutest kids God ever created."

Josie turned to study her mother-in-law's hair. "Speaking of the cutest and world's youngest hairdresser, what's the damage? I halfway expected to see you with a shaved head or a wig."

Emmaline lifted the hair on her left side, revealing a section of extensions. "Elisa hid Olivia's work masterfully."

"And I've zip-tied the handles of all the scissors together, so there's no chance of a copycat offense," added Hunter.

"Nice." Josie pressed her lips together. How did he suppose she would cut the ties so she could use the scissors herself? "Wouldn't it have made more sense to lay down the law to all three kids and make them understand they may not cut hair?"

"You solve problems your way, and I'll solve them mine."

"I'm just glad to be home, and if it means I can't cut anything in my own house, so be it." Josie kissed him.

"I'm going to go call Peter and turn in." Emmaline gave them each a side hug and stood. "Good night, you two."

As Emmaline's door closed, Josie turned to Hunter. "How did the parent-teacher conferences go?"

He brightened. "Better than I expected, to be honest. Both teachers mentioned the boys need to work on impulse control, but they're on target for their age."

Josie groaned. "Meaning they're the youngest in their classes, and we should've waited another year to put them in school?" Her mom's words echoed in her mind.

"No one said that. In fact, Ben's teacher said she's been giving him more challenging assignments when possible because part of his restlessness is boredom." He nudged her. "He's smart, Jos. And all this time we thought he might be…you know."

She arched a brow at Hunter. "We did not." She huffed outwardly as she reconsidered her stance. "Okay, maybe a little, but can you blame us? He's never still." She settled back against Hunter.

"And he only talks about one thing."

"Playing outside," they said together.

"And Connor?" She held her breath. Connor didn't hyper-fixate on the outdoors to the extent his brother did, but he had the same obstinate streak and tested every boundary as if it were his God-given duty.

"Right where he's supposed to be. Miss Piper didn't mention him being extra smart and needing to be challenged, but I took it as a good sign she also said nothing about him starting a preschool fight club."

"What did she say about Livvie?" Josie asked.

"She's a bit timid. Watches everything before she jumps in, but she's kind and follows the rules."

"I wish we could transplant some of Connor and Ben's boldness into her." She held her thumb and forefinger a breath apart. "Just a touch."

Hunter gently pushed her hand down and closed his fingers over hers. "Now, why would you wish such a thing?"

"I don't want her getting swallowed up by their big personalities." The worry crept in before she could help it.

Hunter tipped her chin up. "Jos, she's still finding her footing in pre-K. And our girl has *zero* trouble making herself heard when she wants to."

This was true. Olivia might be timid at school, but last week she'd ordered Connor into timeout for picking her doll up by its leg. "He's not being uh-spectful to Josefina," she'd announced, stomping her foot.

Josie chuckled to herself at the thought of Connor trudging to the timeout spot as if his sister had any authority over him. "You're right. We should be thankful she's not making her teacher's life more difficult and leave it alone for now." Soon enough, Olivia would grow into her self-assurance. But if they pushed too hard, she might end up on the wrong side of the fine line between bold and brazen, and the world didn't need another version of Zola.

The cramped salon at Agape House had buzzed with a steady stream of clients all afternoon. Josie handed the lady in the chair a mirror to inspect the back of her new layers and watched her confidence bloom.

"I love it. Thank you so much." The lady jumped out of the chair and hugged Josie, the cape still fastened around her neck.

Even Zola radiated joy as she shampooed, cut, and curled with her usual precision.

Josie grabbed the broom from behind the door and swept blonde locks into a pile. "You're in a good mood."

"Why wouldn't I be? My regular Sanctuary clients don't get this excited about their makeovers. I enjoy helping these ladies see themselves in a whole new light." Zola drew a shoulder to her cheek. "And I have a date tonight. I think there could really be something with this guy."

Because the dating apps had been so productive thus far. "Please tell me this one doesn't live with his mother."

"It was the first question I asked. You'll also be happy to know he's in his thirties, and my friend who works for the county assured me he doesn't have an arrest record or outstanding warrants." Zola's enthusiasm for those basic traits was both promising and concerning.

If only Josie had let Dana introduce Zola to Carlos sooner. Instead, she'd overcomplicated the entire process, leading to Zola dating a slew of duds. Perhaps he hadn't had his license revoked like leather-coat-wearing Royce, but who knew what issues this new guy would have?

Josie lifted the waiting list clipboard from its hook by the door. All the names on it had been crossed off. "Looks like we're done for the day."

"That went by fast. I guess now I have time to get my nails done before tonight." Zola hummed as she cleaned her station.

"I'm ready to get home to my kids. This week was the longest I've ever been away, and I only got to see them for a few hours this morning." Josie stepped into the hall. The bustle had tapered off, the building settling into an end-of-the-day hush. She and Dana had carpooled, so she hoped her neighbor was close to wrapping up too.

She poked her head back into the salon. "Good luck on your date. Call me if you need an escape."

Dana sat at a folding table in the lobby, typing on a laptop as a woman with a baby on her lap looked on. "How about we write 'childcare specialist'?"

Josie took a seat in the corner and thumbed through a women's magazine while she waited.

The program director of Agape House drooped onto the chair beside Josie. "We sure appreciate y'all coming today. I can't remember the last time I've seen so many smiling faces around here."

"I'm glad we could help." Josie shifted in her chair. "Why are so many residents looking for work at once, though? Is that normal?"

Yolanda chuckled and folded her hands on her lap. "We've got a wide range of situations here. Many residents have struggled to keep steady employment. Sometimes because of addiction or unreliable daycare. Others had to leave their jobs so abusive partners couldn't track them down." She gave a small, knowing sigh. "But every woman is here because she wants to build a better life for herself and her children, and that begins with a steady income. Even those who are already working need resources to find higher-paying positions with room to grow."

Her face glowed. "That's why it's been such a busy day. Your group gave our ladies hope for a brighter future. I even overheard a few asking how they could get into cosmetology school and become hairdressers themselves."

Goosebumps prickled on Josie's arms. She'd never thought of herself as inspiring or even as someone who made much of a difference. She'd always been on the receiving end of positive role models, people who believed in her even when she barely believed in herself. Hunter's parents had even paid her way through cosmetology school. With so many faith-filled people showing up for her, how could she not land on her feet? Without them, might she have ended up at Agape House as a resident instead of a volunteer?

At Dana's table, the woman stood and settled her baby on her hip. Dana reached out and shook her hand. "I'll keep you in my prayers. I know God has the right position for you that lets you be the best mom to this little guy." She closed her laptop and tipped her chin at Josie. "Ready?"

"We hope to see you again," Yolanda said as Josie and Dana waved goodbye and headed for the parking lot.

Neither spoke until Dana steered the Tahoe onto the street.

"How'd it go in the salon today?"

Josie's cheeks ached from grinning so much, but she couldn't help it. "Fantastic. The best part was seeing women get excited when they looked in the mirror. Everyone this afternoon had such an ecstatic reaction. What about you?"

"It was fine." Dana's voice ticked up just enough to suggest her day had been anything but fine.

"That's it? No warm, fuzzy feelings from transforming mankind?" Josie's head bobbled. "Or womankind."

Dana's hands tightened on the steering wheel. "It made me realize how easy my life has been compared to most people's. I mean, I lost my mom, and we went through a lot when Will's parents died, but the total upheaval those ladies have survived overwhelmed me. Half the time, I didn't even know what to say to them." She flicked a look at Josie. "I thought hairstylists were supposed to double as therapists. Nobody shared their tragic life story with you today?"

Josie shrugged. "We mostly talked about our kids. Once they found out I had triplets, that's where the conversation stalled. Also, Zola was particularly chatty, and she dominated the small talk."

"Which is another reason she and Carlos would be such a brilliant match. As long as she's talking, there's no chance for him to say something snarky."

"About that." Josie pressed her fingertips to the space between her brows. "She has another date tonight."

Dana's head swiveled. "Oh no. Do you think we've lost our window?"

"No. Something tells me he's the same brand of third-rate 'single for a reason' kind of guy as the last one. She attracts that type like seagulls to a French fry. By Monday, she'll be on the prowl again. I'm on such a high from helping at Agape House I can't wait to introduce our friends to one another. This could change their lives." If she'd known serving others released so many endorphins, she'd have done it sooner.

"Maybe this time we should take a more direct approach and avoid near misses and scheduling snafus."

"Agreed." Josie held up a finger. "No more parties. I'm not cleaning house again." A picture of Tía Clara's house flashed in her mind, and she amended her declaration. "At least not for my colleague's love life." To avoid being buried alive or perpetuating the family affliction, she would clean everything. And become a minimalist.

"When we see them this week, we'll just outright ask them when they're free to meet one another," Dana said.

"Absolutely. Blessing two people with the gift of one another's companionship must be done as soon as possible." Josie hammered her fist against her open palm to drive home her point.

"That was a weird way to phrase it, but I like your enthusiasm." Dana tapped her horn to alert the driver in front of them, engrossed in his phone, that the light was green. "You seem to have forgotten, though, how aggravating Zola and Carlos have been lately. Blessing them with the gift of each other's company feels like a stretch."

"Look, if they hit it off, we'll be blessing everyone who has to deal with them."

"In that case," said Dana. "God bless us, everyone."

Chapter 29
Dana

Dana pulled into the garage and killed the engine, but she remained in the driver's seat, processing the battles Agape House's resilient warriors had overcome. Stories that cracked her heart and stitched it back together all at once. She'd helped polish their resumes, offering hope in a small way where heartache had stolen so much from these women, but there had to be more she could do to propel them forward.

A tap on her window pulled her back to the present.

"Are you coming in, or shall I bring your dinner out here?" Will's question was muffled by the glass separating them.

She opened the car door. "I just needed a minute to leave Agape House behind before I stepped into our comfy world where everything makes sense."

"Everything? You've solved the mystery of what happens to the missing socks that never make it out of the dryer?" he asked. "Because I'd love to hear that secret."

He took her purse from her and looped an arm around her waist. A faint tang of smoke clung to his shirt. She sniffed, nose wrinkling. Maybe he and the boys had lit the firepit.

She wrinkled her nose. "Okay, not everything, but it's not like we're facing eviction, addiction, or something else life-altering. My head is spinning from the unimaginable circumstances I learned about today. Right now, all I want to do is watch silly sitcoms and eat carbs."

He led her into the house and handed her a glass of wine already poured and waiting on the counter. "Then you're in luck. I made tomato bisque and grilled cheese sandwiches."

"How did you know?"

Will bit his lip and busied himself with stirring the pot on the stove.

The powder room door opened, and out stepped Dana's father. "Welcome home, daughter." He pointed to her glass. "I guess if you're drinking, Will already broke the news to you."

Will hadn't anticipated she'd come home reeling from her afternoon of volunteering after all. He was simply plying her with culinary therapy to soften the blow of the trouble afoot, whatever it may be.

She looked between Dad and Will, but neither gave anything away. "What's going on?"

Will placed the lid on the pot and turned off the burner. "Edward had an accident today."

Dana crumpled onto a barstool and studied her father with a practiced eye. "What kind of accident? Are you hurt?"

"I'm fine." He dismissed her concern with a flick of his wrist. "But if there were a blooper show called *Kitchen Calamities*, I'd be famous."

Such a promising way to open the story. Dana took a

generous gulp and set the glass down a little harder than intended. She crooked her fingers, beckoning him to spill the details. "Lay it on me. What kind of kitchen calamity did you have?"

"A minor oven fire. Didn't even have to call 9-1-1," Dad said.

Toenails, much smaller than Harvey's, clicked across the tile. Patch Johnson trotted across the room and dropped onto his haunches at Dana's feet. The wine turned sour in her throat. Patch's presence meant Dad had downplayed the severity of the fire. "Your furry little tattletale says you're lying."

Will came around the breakfast bar and rested his hands on her shoulders. "Honey, it's not that bad. We opened the windows and set up a couple of air purifiers." He straightened and stretched his lips into a toothy grin that had all the enthusiasm of a driver's license photo. "They'll stay here tonight, and after church tomorrow, Edward's place should be aired out and good as new."

"Like your shirt, right?" She raised an eyebrow and took a sip.

Will pulled his collar up to his nose.

Dana buoyed herself to ask the obvious question she wasn't sure she wanted the answer to. "How did the oven catch on fire?"

"Could've happened to anyone," Edward said, spreading his hands in mock innocence. "Turns out, parchment paper's great for baking but not so much for broiling. And crusty bread drizzled in olive oil? Flames up real pretty if you turn your back for thirty seconds." He gave a sheepish chuckle. "Maggie's gonna have my hide for that one."

"Do you think almost setting your house on fire is funny?"

He'd joked the same way after the police brought him home for trying to break into the wrong house, convinced it was his. Humor was his shield, his answer for everything serious.

"*Almost* doing it is a lot funnier than actually setting one's house ablaze."

When she didn't even crack a smile, Edward moved to put a hand on Dana's arm. "Sweetheart, it was an honest mistake by an old guy learning to bake for the first time in his life." His tone softened. "I made bread this morning. *Bread*, can you believe it? And I was so excited to toast it with roasted garlic and that fancy Greek olive oil from the import market your mom loved."

The knot in Dana's stomach, the one that had clenched the instant Will said 'accident,' finally eased. She leaned into her dad's touch. "Mom went through a whole phase with herb-infused oils, didn't she?"

"And baking." Edward laughed again. "When you were little, you cried because you just wanted a *normal* sandwich like all the other kids."

She sniffled through a chuckle. "If I'd only known then that PB&Js on homemade bread were so much more special than those on store-bought."

The scent of yeast and fresh-baked bread drifted through Dana's memory, and for a moment, she was ten years old again. Her mom's kitchen, sunlight on cooling racks, and laughter that always rose with the dough were so commonplace, she hadn't thought to savor them until they were gone. What she'd give for one more loaf of that honey wheat.

Edward pressed his palms to the counter, his expression teetering between smug and hopeful. "So, we're all in agreement I don't need to be shipped off to assisted living just yet?"

Dana huffed a laugh. "Hilarious. How'd you put the fire out, anyway?"

"Fire extinguisher, of course. Maggie brought me one the day she signed me up for baking lessons. Thought she was clever, I'm sure." His grin flickered, and for a heartbeat, the humor faltered. He turned to Will instead. "We about ready to eat?"

Will cleared his throat. Maybe reminiscing had stirred an ache in him as well. "Soup's ready. I'll fire up the griddle. We're eating store-bought bread tonight, but I did spring for the Texas toast."

The weight of Agape House's residents' stories melted as Dana's own familiar chaos enveloped her. She lifted a silent prayer of thanks for the beautiful way her life had turned out, called Nate and Adam to the table, and helped Will serve the soup and sandwiches.

Around the table, the boys greedily slurped their bisque and devoured grilled cheese. Will had been a chef when Dana met him, but for all his cooking prowess, the family appreciated his simple meals the most.

"This was just what I needed tonight. Thanks, honey," Dana bit into the buttery toast and let the gooey cheddar and Monterey jack melt away the remaining tension in her body.

Nate flashed a thumbs-up. "Yeah, Dad. Good stuff."

Out of nowhere, Adam dropped his spoon with a clatter

and sat up straight. "What are we going to do about Leah?"

Dana paused mid-bite. "What do you mean?"

"I asked how she was doing after the breakup, and she texted back *'Never better'* with a picture of herself eating an entire pizza in bed." He held out his phone like it was evidence in court. "Does that look like someone who's fine to you?"

Leah, the health-conscious athlete, had never eaten more than a couple of slices of pizza in one sitting. And during soccer season, she hadn't even done that.

Will lingered over the pic for a beat before handing it back to Adam. "Let's invite her to spend a few days here."

"That's a good idea," said Adam. "We can keep her busy playing games and stuff."

Edward pointed a grilled cheese triangle at Will. "Since I'm commandeering her room tonight, maybe hold off until Patch and I have somewhere else to sleep."

"I'll call her after dinner and see how she's really doing." Dana already dreaded it, like the sting of ripping off a Band-Aid, but confronting Leah head-on would save time and take the guesswork out of interpreting her state of mind.

"Seriously, Mom. Do you really think I ate an entire pizza on my own?"

Will and her dad erupted at whatever play unfolded in the game on TV. Dana glanced at the score as the Texas Tech fight song overpowered Leah's scorn crackling through the phone. If only Dana could teleport to the game in Kansas instead of having this awkward conversation.

She slipped into the laundry room office and shut the door. "Sweetie, why would you send your brother that photo unless you wanted him to think you were having a pity party alone?"

"There were three of us hanging out in the room. I was sitting *on* the bed, not lying *in* it. Adam needs to learn how words work."

Dana pinched the bridge of her nose. Talking to Leah was turning out to be so much worse than ripping off a Band-Aid. "And the pizza was *on* your bed?"

Leah huffed. "There's nowhere else to put the box except on the desks where our computers and books are or on the floor. Gross. I sent Adam a proof of life selfie. Didn't think I needed to tell Skylar and Mae to huddle up or else my family would assume I was depressed."

If eye rolls had a sound, Dana was sure she'd have heard it just now. "There's no need to get snippy. It's natural for the people who love you to be concerned about how you're doing after a breakup." She rolled a tube of Chapstick back and forth on the desk, willing herself not to bring up how Leah hadn't even mentioned the breakup to anyone besides her little brother.

"I'm fine," Leah snapped. "I never should've told Adam about Jordan and me, but I didn't want to make up an excuse about why we couldn't go to the ranch." She sighed, her former bite gone. "Uncle Kenny and Delia were so sweet to me. I wish I could've at least said goodbye to them."

Dana's fingers stilled on the lip balm. "Do you want to talk about it?"

The line went quiet for a few seconds. "There's not much to tell. Jordan was too possessive and didn't like me hanging out with anyone else. Once I moved into the dorm, he got really jealous. I couldn't even go to ministry events without him, and he made hurtful comments about me acting like I was better than him since I was going to college."

One of Nate's football games flashed in Dana's mind. Leah's defensiveness at being asked about her classes must've come from Jordan's insecurities. Dana remained silent even as she seethed. She picked up a pencil and doodled flowers on the edge of her grocery list to still her reeling thoughts.

"We fought a lot, and some friends at church helped me see the relationship was toxic. I finally got tired of trying to placate his fragile ego all the time and told him it was over."

Had Dana even known what a toxic relationship was at eighteen? "I'm proud of you for recognizing the warning signs and protecting yourself."

"I just wish I hadn't let him ruin half my summer." Leah sniffed. "Did you know he tracked my location when I went to dinner with Kate and Kaitlyn and showed up to confirm there weren't any guys with us?"

The pencil lead snapped. "He did what?"

"Yeah. Super insecure."

Dana planted her elbow on the desk and propped her head in her hand. "I'm guessing he didn't show his true colors until *after* church camp."

"We were never alone at camp. The thing was, Jordan could be super sweet and fun, which camouflaged his red flags."

"At least you caught on after a short time. I know women who've spent years married to men like that. And they don't improve with age, that's for sure."

"I want to marry someone who treats me like Dad does you. I mean, I know y'all fight and stuff, but he doesn't act like he owns you. He's affectionate, caring, and your biggest fan. He's so proud of your accomplishments as a writer because he genuinely has your best interests at heart, not like Jordan, who's threatened by a woman with big dreams."

Warm tingles ran down Dana's arms. "I didn't realize you paid attention to details like that."

"Whatever. I don't always have my nose in my phone, Mom."

There she was—the cheeky teen who'd lose her mind if she knew her grandfather would be sleeping in her room later. The tender moment between them evaporated like dry ice. Or was it sublimated? Dana could never remember. Either way, it was gone.

"I'll let you get back to studying, and I'll make sure Adam knows you haven't taken to binge eating in bed. And Leah, I mean it. I'm so very proud of who you are and how you live your life."

"Don't make it weird, Mom. I love you, too."

They hung up, and Dana stared at the landscape painting above her desk without really seeing it. The hum of the extra fridge filled the cramped space while she weighed how much she could tell Will without him plotting Jordan's demise. How many stories at Agape House had begun with controlling men whose threatening behavior escalated over time? If only those women had left early on as Leah had.

A cold shudder gripped Dana, and she knelt on the floor, hands folded on her leather chair. She bowed her head and prayed. *Thank you, Lord Jesus, for protecting my daughter. Thank you for giving her the wisdom to get out before her bad relationship turned dangerous. Thank you for Agape House and for the new beginnings You're offering there. Thank you for letting me share in a portion of that labor of love.*

"What are you doing?"

Dana bolted upright, bumping her funny bone on the leg of the desk. She cradled her elbow as Will crossed to her, amusement tugging the corner of his mouth. "Praying."

"Your conversation with Leah went that well, huh?" He grasped her forearm and placed a hand on her back, lifting her off the floor.

"It did, actually. She broke up with Jordan because he was domineering."

Will plunked into the chair. "I knew it."

"You did not. You were Team Jordan from the night we met him." Dana's first impression of the kid, leaning on the sports car with his hands on Leah's hips, left much to be desired, but even she hadn't suspected he was a problem of this magnitude. "We raised a wise young woman who saw him for what he was before they got more serious."

His brow furrowed. "Do I need to go to his house and confront his dad?"

She lowered herself onto his lap and wrapped her hands around his neck. "I don't think that'll be necessary. But you should've heard what Leah said about you."

"Yeah?"

"She hopes to marry someone who treats her as well as you treat me."

"I do treat you pretty good, don't I?" He nuzzled her cheek. "How ever will you repay me, Mrs. Harding?"

"Oh, I don't know." Her voice turned sultry. "I was

thinking after we put the kids to bed, we might let both dogs out and put clean sheets on Leah's bed for my dad."

"Way to kill the mood." He sighed. "I guess the gift of having you as my wife is repayment enough."

She rose from his lap and tugged him up. "At least for tonight. When Dad's not starting kitchen fires, we can revisit your proper reward."

Chapter 30
Josie

Josie crouched to eye level with her client, Paloma, and grasped a section of hair from each side of her head. She snipped a little off the left and examined it again as her phone dinged. The consummate professional, she ignored it.

"Don't you need to check that?" asked Paloma.

"That's okay. I'm sure it's not important."

"What if it's about your kids?"

"I don't think the school would text." Even so, Josie grabbed her phone off her supply cabinet and clicked on the new message sent by her uncle Tino. He'd snapped a photo of the inside of the roll-off dumpster, significantly fuller than when she'd climbed on it. The floor was no longer visible, and boxes and magazines now covered the ruined drywall.

Baby Steps.

She smiled as she typed. **I guess you really can teach old dogs new tricks.**

Tino: **Your therapist buddy is giving us the friends and family discount, right?**

Celeste had graciously offered to meet with Josie's relatives at a cut rate, but the amount of therapy necessary to get that house cleaned out would still out price the home insurance deductible for the water damage.

"Everything okay?" asked Paloma.

"Just my uncle." Josie set the phone down and went back to trimming.

Zola breezed by and waved, her good mood from Saturday still in full effect. "Hey, girl," she practically sang.

"Hello," Josie said.

Zola had given her the cold shoulder for leaving town to help her mom, and she'd only defrosted at Agape House because of her impending date. If this mystery guy was behind her landlady's new attitude, Josie and Dana might need to rethink their matchmaking. After all, the goal was to make their colleagues more tolerable, and so far, Zola was. Maybe they should find a new candidate for Carlos.

Paloma fit the age range, and she wasn't married. Josie didn't know her well, but she seemed nice and had a lovely smile.

"Are you seeing anyone?" Josie asked over the whir of the blow-dryer.

Paloma worked her arm from beneath the cape and wiggled her fingers. A shiny diamond glinted in the fluorescent light. "I guess you could say that."

"Congratulations!" Josie grabbed her hand for a closer look at the engagement ring. Was that a three-carat solitaire? "How'd you meet him?"

"I was his mom's home health nurse. She got better, and we realized how much we liked one another."

"Ooh, did someone get engaged?" Zola popped in and ogled the ring. "So amazing! I just love love."

Yep, Carlos wouldn't garner a second look from Zola while she was goo-goo eyed over this new man.

"I might get some new bling of my own in the next few months." Zola hugged herself, practically bouncing on her toes like the triplets when they got excited.

"Haven't you just been on one date?" Josie wrapped a section of hair on a round brush and aimed the dryer on it.

"Two. Saturday night was so great we ended up spending all day together yesterday, too. I can't remember the last time I've had such a connection with someone. And I've never laughed that much." Stars lit in Zola's eyes as she talked about this guy.

"You didn't spend Saturday night with him, did you?" Ugh. The words scraped out before Josie could stop them. That leather-sport-coat guy with the fancy car name had set off every internal alarm she had, and the feeling hadn't shaken loose since. Zola would be livid at Josie's protective instinct toward her, but it couldn't be helped. Zola's taste in men made her a danger to herself.

"Ew, no. Get your mind out of the gutter," Zola balked. "He was a perfect gentleman. We couldn't get enough of each other and decided to meet for Sunday brunch. Then we ended up hanging out until it was time for me to pick up Beckett from his dad."

Josie set the dryer in its holster and reached for the straightener. "So, who is this mystery man?" She steeled for another dating app story, though Zola's excitement was a departure from her typical disastrous romantic history.

"It's so weird. I just met him Friday morning."

The receptionist poked her head in. "Zo, your eleven o'clock is waiting."

"Thanks." Zola turned to go. "I'll catch you up later."

"Looks like love is in the air around here." Paloma gave

her hand a lingering look before tucking it back under the cape.

Something sure was in the air, but it smelled a little too fishy to be love. Falling head over heels after meeting a man less than three days ago was a terrible sign. If Zola's past was any indication, this guy had a good chance of turning out to be too good to be true.

Emmaline rolled her suitcase to the front door. "That's it then. I guess I'm ready."

Olivia clung to her leg. "No, Gramma. Stay."

She bent and patted Olivia's back. "I wish I could, sweet girl, but Grandpa Peter's taking care of Great Gran and Grandpa George all by himself. I better get home and help him."

"Grandpa Peter can just bring them here," said Ben.

Josie and Hunter's eyes met, and they grinned.

"Great Gran would have a hard time traveling this far." Emmaline opened her arms and drew Connor and Ben to her. "But you're going to visit us in Oklahoma for Thanksgiving, and your Abuelita Marie will come, too."

"She will?" Hunter and Josie asked in unison. Not that Josie had a problem with her mother joining them. But with Hunter's brothers, the house would be crowded and loud, which wouldn't suit Marie Saldana at all.

"I invited her at church yesterday." Emmaline stood straight and hiked her purse higher on her shoulder. "Your sister will be with her in-laws, and after the fiasco with the house in Albuquerque, Marie won't be up for another extensive cleanout with *her* sisters so soon. Families should be together for the holidays, and Marie is family."

What kind of a daughter was Josie that it hadn't even occurred to her they would be leaving her mother alone for Thanksgiving? Shame masquerading as heat flamed her cheeks. "You're sweet to include her. I guess I hadn't thought about her not having plans. I should've though."

"Babe, don't beat yourself up." Hunter gave her shoulder a light squeeze. "We would've realized soon enough and invited her. Mom just beat us to the punch."

"That's right," said Emmaline. "That pesky flood was the real wrench in her original plans."

"Let me put that in your trunk." Hunter took the suitcase outside while Josie pried the triplets off their grandmother.

Emmaline wrapped Josie in a hug. "You don't know how special it was for me to get to pinch hit for you. I'm sorry you had to deal with that mess out west, but I loved getting to help here. Thank you."

"I'm the one who needs to thank *you*. Hunter wouldn't have done well on his own for that long. Neither would I, for that matter. This is a two-person job." Josie stepped back and held the door open for Emmaline and the kids to walk through. "I'll admit though, after how worn out you were at the end of our Labor Day trip, I was surprised you wanted to come."

Emmaline shot her a horrified look. "I always want to be with my grandbabies. The water park was a little more than I'd bargained for, it's true, but I don't want to miss a moment of it. These kids are getting big so quickly, and I'll be there for as much as I possibly can, even if it's in a giant, chlorine bubble full of wet strangers." She shuddered.

Josie laughed. "You know, every stage is likely to have a whole new set of challenges, and I can't promise they won't include more aquatic mayhem. Or something worse." Might be too soon to bring up the butchering Olivia had inflicted on her hair.

"You, Hunter, the kids—all of you are worth showing up for. No matter what." Em swallowed hard and hugged her again. "You're a terrific mother, and don't you ever forget that."

Josie nodded. If she tried to say anything, she'd only choke on her words. She stepped back as Connor, Olivia, and Ben crowded their grandmother for one more hug before she got in the car.

Water park trauma hadn't scared Emmaline off, just like a family of hoarders couldn't scare away Marie. That was love. Or madness. Probably a little of both.

Chapter 31
Dana

Dana entered the Wednesday MOMS meeting and surveyed the room with a renewed lightness. Before Agape House, she'd questioned what a crime novelist could offer women clawing their way out of crisis. But sitting across from them on Saturday—one tapping a nervous rhythm on the table, another with her chubby-cheeked infant on her lap—something had shifted. Dana gave encouragement and prayed with each of them as she typed resumes and set up emails. In one case, she even helped scrub a questionable social media account.

And the Agape House residents had responded. Shoulders straightened. As if someone opened a window in a dark room, eyes that had arrived dull and guarded soon glowed with hope. Dana left knowing she hadn't just shown up, she'd connected.

Josie sidled next to her at the snack table and looked over her shoulder like they were being watched. "Zola's seeing someone, and she's weirdly giddy and starry-eyed. Might not last though. This guy could easily slink back into the ooze her other dating app losers crawled from. But until he does, she's not likely to be open to meeting Carlos."

"Is she easier to work with?" Dana grabbed a water bottle, keeping her eyes peeled for the feisty hairdresser.

They headed to their assigned table.

"Yeah. This morning, she even stopped at every booth and asked if we needed anything." Her tone dropped to almost a whisper. "There's a possibility an alien has taken over her body, and the real Zola is no more. But until it tries to eat my face or whatever, I'm going to enjoy it."

Their friend Kathy approached the table and took the seat opposite Dana. "What's new?"

"You wouldn't know any single ladies who might be interested in a thirty-something grouchy professor who doesn't own a hairbrush, would you?" asked Josie.

Dana glared at her. Just because Josie had a better working relationship with Zola while Dana was still stuck with Carlos's eternal crankiness was no reason to involve other people. It was bad enough they were gossiping about their colleagues with one another, but dragging Kathy into the conversation was going to earn them a permanent spot on Anita Steen's prayer list.

"Grouchy with messy hair. Sounds like a real catch," said Kathy.

"He's also a best-selling author and a great dad." Dana couldn't help but feel a tad defensive on his behalf.

"Offhand, I can't think of anyone." Kathy craned her neck to scan the room. "But I'm sure there are a few single moms here."

The tinkling of Serena's bell silenced the chitchat. She stood at the podium with a smile that stretched from ear to ear. "Good evening, ladies. Wasn't Saturday such a blessing?" She paused while applause filled the air.

Serena pressed her hand to her heart. "Y'all, I just never imagined how much love a group of women could pour out in one day, but God took our small offering of our donations, time, and services and magnified it for His glory."

If Serena weren't one of the kindest women Dana had ever met, she might've rolled her eyes at her over-the-top effusiveness.

Someone shouted, "Amen" from across the room.

Serena smoothed a sheet of paper on the podium. "I got an email from Yolanda asking me to thank everyone who helped make Saturday possible. One resident had an interview yesterday and was hired on the spot. She wanted us to know that what the moms in this room did brought her one step closer to reuniting with her two children in foster care."

Another round of applause broke out.

Serena took off her reading glasses and wiped her cheek. "You sacrificed half your weekend for strangers, and it will have a lasting Kingdom impact. MOMS came about as a haven for mothers seeking mentorship and solidarity, but you ladies are so much more than moms. You're world changers."

Warmth settled in Dana's chest, and the tears she'd tried to keep in check spilled over. At least she wasn't the only one crying. Sniffles and under-eye swipes abounded throughout the room.

A hand went up next to Dana.

"What's next?" asked Anita Steen. "Jobs, housing, even sobriety matter little unless they give their lives to Christ. How can we help in the spiritual arena at Agape House?"

"Funny you should ask," said Serena. She slipped her

glasses back on and found her place on the paper in front of her. "Yolanda said one of the young mothers attended their Sunday service for the first time this weekend because she felt so loved on by everyone at the employment-readiness fair. She had to see what made the volunteers different. You *are* having an eternal impact, but there's more to come. Beginning in January, Yolanda and I are starting a Bible study group on Sunday evenings at Agape House, and I am hoping many of you will join us. We need faith mentors who will walk alongside the residents and help them grow in the Word."

"Sign me up." Anita pumped an excited praise-hand-fist hybrid.

Breathless, Zola dropped into the last empty seat at the table. "What'd I miss?"

Anita patted her hand. "Nothing yet, sweetie. You stick with me, and we're going to become missionaries together."

Zola's eyes grew round. "Missionaries?"

Bless her heart. If Dana knew Anita, she'd have the salon owner washed in the Blood before the new year and testifying on Sunday evenings at Agape House.

As the room buzzed with talk of mentoring and Bible study, Dana squirmed. The same longing that first nudged her after serving on Saturday returned with a persistence she couldn't ignore. Serena had asked her to consider teaching a writing class to help the residents process their trauma, and she'd shrunk from the idea. But now, it sparked a desire within her. If one day could make such a difference for the ladies, writing their stories and documenting God's provision would honor their journeys and help others hang onto hope.

Her foot twitched under the table as the meeting continued, urging Serena to wrap it up. Once she finally did, Dana burst out of her seat and made her way to the podium with a single-mindedness barring anyone from distracting her.

Serena stuffed her bell and papers into her bag. "Wasn't this weekend absolutely exhilarating? You'll help with the Bible study, won't you?"

"Maybe," said Dana. "But I was hoping we could revisit the creative writing class."

The pastor's wife's eyes widened as a smile spread across her whole face. She grasped Dana's hand. "Does this mean you'll do it?"

Dana nodded. She had to get the words out before she lost her nerve again. "I will." *How* she would do it was another thing entirely. A problem for another day.

Friday morning, the critique group reclaimed its usual table in the coffee shop, like a turf war between the writers and pumpkin spice lushes. However, they hadn't accomplished their usual level of critiquing as they exchanged stories of their volunteer work last weekend.

"I really had to put my creative writing skills to the test. There was just no good way to spin why a sweetheart of a girl with a college degree had a ten-year employment gap," said Beverly. "Spoiler alert: She was living on the street with a methamphetamine addiction." She shook her head. "It's not something you expect from an elementary teacher."

Carlos harrumphed. "The way our system abuses

teachers, coupled with the lack of discipline in kids these days, I don't see how more teachers aren't hooked on ice."

"Oh, good." Bev leveled him with a sardonic look. "I was hoping Professor Sourpuss would make an appearance today."

Dana picked up a stapled set of papers. "I agree with our resident curmudgeon on this one. If I had to deal with the things public school teachers face, I might be right there at Agape House trying to piece my life back together, too. Oh, and you'll never guess what I came home to after the fair."

"Was it another neighbor with a bald spot?" Bev snickered.

"Close. My dad caught his oven on fire, so he and his little mutt had a sleepover at my house. Spent most of the next day scrubbing everything and lighting candles to get rid of the smoke smell."

"Candles sound like a good way to start another conflagration," said Carlos over his laptop.

"I'm aware. Thanks." Dana tried to imagine what had turned Carlos from the perfectly agreeable writing instructor who'd convinced her to pen her first novel into the grump who spouted doom and gloom at every turn. "What'd you do after your old man soccer game last weekend, Eeyore?"

Carlos pushed his glasses up at the nosepiece. "Old man? It would be rude to point out the age gap between us."

"You may be a toddler at this table, but there's a reason you don't see many professional athletes your age." Bev patted his arm. "I wouldn't want to see you get hurt out there."

"Thanks, but it's a thirty-five and up league. We aren't exactly going against young guys in their prime."

Dana grinned. "Is this your way of telling us you went home and iced your knee all evening?"

"If you must know, I went out. With a woman. And she didn't have any sort of creature in her purse or anything."

Bev's hand flew to her chest. "A date? Well, I'll be. Are you going to see her again?"

The corner of his mouth pulled into a crooked grin. "Already have. She's funny and smart, and I can't get enough of her."

"How'd you meet her?" Dana asked, already gearing up to tease him about jumping back into the—what had he called the dating pool? A festering pond of desperation? No, it was something with an animal. Snapping turtles. That was it! She was so preoccupied with crafting her comeback, she missed most of Carlos's explanation.

"Luckily, I always keep jumper cables in my trunk, so I gave her a boost. She insisted on taking me to dinner to repay me for helping her, and I agreed. And it's been the best week of my entire year."

"Wait, if you're so happy, why are we still getting Crabby Carlos?" Dana pointed between herself and Beverly.

He shook the paper in his hand. "You want a happier Carlos? Bring better chapters to crit group."

If his current mood while in the swoony phase of dating was identical to his customary lonely and jaded default mode, then the return on investment from setting him up with Zola would've been negligible.

At least Zola's newfound happiness was giving Josie a temporary reprieve. Under the table, she texted her neighbor: **In a funny twist, Carlos is also seeing someone. Sadly, he's still being a critical butt.**

Josie: **Lucky lady.**

Carlos and Zola didn't need help making a love connection after all. But to start a writing class at Agape House, Dana would need his help.

She cleared her throat. "The leader of my MOMS group asked me to lead a creative writing class for Agape House's residents." She picked at the sleeve of her coffee cup, not quite daring to meet Carlos's eye. One look of disbelief and her confidence would crumble like his croissant all over the table.

Beverly looked up from the pages in front of her. "You mean like the one we met in? Is there a big need for a class like that? I don't recall anyone I helped last week saying she wanted to be a writer."

"This would be more of a therapeutic writing class. A way of processing the difficulties the women have overcome. I'm not even sure anyone would sign up."

"Oh, Dana, what a wonderful idea. Let me know if you need any help," said Bev.

Professor Sourpuss nodded. "I can give you my lessons and help you build a curriculum that fits the goal of the class."

"Thank you, Carlos. I appreciate that," said Dana.

"Sure, I love a good redemption story. I'll email you the material I used for the last memoir course I taught."

"Why would the college invest in a memoir class?" Bev scratched her head. "Do students even have enough life experience to write about?"

"You'd be surprised how many nontraditional students take my classes." Carlos shot pointed looks at both women. "Good writers explore multiple avenues of writing, including memoir."

Dana had only explored the one—crime fiction. What purpose would studying memoir have served when her life was anything but fascinating, and she hadn't experienced a radical transformation worth reading about? She pushed the thought aside. This class was about helping others work through their own stories. The women would draw closer to the Lord or point others to Him in the process. She silently thanked God for her boring life story that kept her out of harm's way.

Chapter 32
Josie

Josie stepped into the house after work on Friday to the triplets in the middle of the living room floor playing a rowdy game of Hungry Hungry Hippo with toys scattered around them. Her mother was sprawled on the sofa with her arm overhead. That alone was cause for alarm. Marie Saldana never sprawled.

Her usual Friday afternoon ritual involved whisking the children far away from home—to the science museum, park, or another play place where their chaos wouldn't infringe on their surroundings and make more work for anyone. Since the start of school, not once had Josie returned home to this level of disarray.

"Hi, Mama." Olivia said without looking up from banging her hippo's lever.

"Hey, Livvie. Hi, boys." She set her purse on the entry table and inched into the room as if approaching a wild animal caught in a snare. "Mom, are you okay? Is it your back again?"

"I'm fine, mija. Just letting the children have a little fun, and it's a bit too chilly to play outside."

"It's just…I'm not used to…" Josie picked up a dump

truck and dropped it into a toy bin against the wall.

"Spit it out, Josefina."

"You're letting the kids make a mess." She raised her voice to be heard over the ruckus of smacking levers as hippos gulped marbles in the game.

Her mother sat upright and shrugged. "So?"

"You don't believe in messes. You're a devout practicer of 'play with one toy at a time and put it away before you get another one out.' That's been your mantra all my life."

"It finally occurred to me that in my effort to keep from turning into my mother or sister, I might've swung too far in the opposite direction. Cleanliness is good, but not when it hinders creativity." Marie gestured toward the kids, who were shaking marbles back into the center of the board for another round. "This is the best they've played together in ages. All this time I've been worried your poor housekeeping was a sign of our genetics seeping through, despite my many years of programming it out of you and your sister."

Josie crossed her arms, her jaw clenching. How had her mother managed to turn the conversation back to her shortcomings so quickly? "I'm sorry your best attempts to save me from myself were a total failure." A tiny part of her wanted to run to her room and slam her door. Not that she'd ever dared slam a door in her mother's house, and now, it would set a bad precedent for the children.

"No, my darling. After two weeks of wading through absolute disorder in my childhood home, I resolved to eliminate everything I haven't used in six months from my entire house. I've already donated quite a bit of stuff."

Marie had only moved in a few months ago. "Mom, how much junk could you possibly have accumulated so soon?" Josie eased into Hunter's recliner, still wary of her mother's sudden epiphany. Her feet, at least, offered no such skepticism and sighed in relief after a long day on them.

"I'd rather have nothing burdening you and Laurel when I leave this world than think about you two wading through a lifetime of rubbish." Marie put up her hand. "That's not my point. Anyway, when I was cleaning up from lunch, the kids were playing quietly. Too quietly. So, I snuck down the hall to see what they were up to, and it was beautiful. Livvie had her dolls and stuffed animals lined up with books and crayons in front of each. They were pupils in her make-believe classroom. I peeked into the boys' room just in time to hear them count to three and demolish a massive block tower with trucks. They cracked up and started building it all over again."

So far, her mother had offered nothing earth shattering. Josie listened with what she hoped was a pleasant look on her face.

"My first thought was, 'what a mess. These kids need to pick up after themselves,' but they radiated pure, childlike happiness. I stood at the door and watched. This time, Ben added little figures and animals, and they made up a story about the whole thing. Josefina, they're so smart. They have wonderful imaginations, and I realized all this time I've been stifling them by prioritizing cleanup over play. And maybe that's just as bad as hoarding. Well, nothing is that bad, but you know what I mean."

The kids abandoned their game and moved on to other pursuits. Olivia shot a glance at her grandmother, returned to pick up Hungry Hungry Hippo, and deposited it on the shelf where it belonged.

What was happening? Had Josie gone through a portal to an alternate universe where her anal-retentive mother was now a freewheeling slob, and her children, a mini demolition crew in her world, played nicely and put toys away without even being asked in this one? And by 'asked,' she meant cajoled and mildly threatened into obedience.

She rubbed her temples. "I'm so confused right now."

Her mother leaned forward and placed a hand on her leg. "Sweetheart, I've been way too hard on you, and I'm sorry. Your method is not wrong. It's never been wrong. I should've realized it sooner."

Not an alternate universe where up was down. No, this was worse. An alien had invaded Marie's body. The same breed of skinwalker that had taken over Zola's form must've infiltrated the Caraway home. How could she test her theory? If only they had a family safe word only the real Marie would know.

Josie had been so caught up in speculating what might've happened to her mom that she didn't hear the garage door when Hunter got home.

He walked into the living room, and his smiled faded as he spied Josie. "Babe, what's wrong?"

She reached for his hand, eyes locked on Marie. "I think this woman is an imposter. The kids might be too," she whispered.

Her mother swiped her suggestion away. "Don't be silly, mija. Everyone is fine."

Hunter looked around the room and studied Marie with a tilted head. "You feeling okay, Marie?"

"I *just* told you everyone is fine," she snapped. "Why did you ask me that?"

He shoved one hand in his pocket and waved the other over the floor, still littered with toys. "The house is usually a bit more picked up on Fridays. And I'm not saying it should be, but I've also never seen you look so…" He rose onto the balls of his feet with all the self-assurance of a fourteen-year-old boy.

Un-pinched. Body snatched. Like a shapeshifter. Josie mentally filled in the words he couldn't spit out.

"Relaxed while there's disorder within your sightline." Hunter's wording was the more magnanimous way to go.

Marie smiled. "I'm trying something new. I realized today that my obsessive tidiness is like Clara and Silvio's problem. It idolizes an unattainable standard of keeping everything in its place, while hoarding is just keeping everything. They both stem from a need for control, and by hanging onto it, I'm not giving God lordship over my life and the material things in it."

Hunter's cheeks puffed out as he exhaled a heavy breath. "Wow, Marie. That's a very wise perspective. How did you land on that?"

"I'm still haunted by the state of my parents' home. I guess I always have been. In contrast, I saw how much happier and more imaginative the kids were today with fewer restrictions on their play."

"So, you're not dying just a little inside with these toys haphazardly strewn about?" Hunter raised an eyebrow at Marie.

She swept the room with her gaze and pressed her hands to her temples. "I had to lie down and do breathing exercises."

Josie knew it!

"It's going to be an adjustment, but it's what's best for the children," said her mother.

Maybe that shift would keep her own kids from having anxiety attacks or postponing fulfilling their dreams like Josie had. Good for them. The triplets deserved this better version of Marie than Josie and her sister had gotten, but why couldn't she have had this epiphany forty years sooner?

The usual flurry of clients at Sanctuary Salon had dulled in the past few days to only a handful of appointments. While the breathing room was a pleasant change, Josie couldn't help worrying she'd caused the drop-off by canceling when Ben was sick and then dashing off to New Mexico.

Her booth neighbor, Elisa, assured her it wasn't her fault. "Embrace it because a week before Thanksgiving, you'll be slammed. Everyone wants to come in right before they go to office Christmas parties or sit next to their sisters at family gatherings." She filed her nails as she chatted, and Josie flexed her jaw, trying to pretend the sound didn't grate on her nerves.

"I get that," said Josie. "I watched one of my aunts reach over and yank a gray hair right off my mother's head last week. And Mom *thanked* her. Made me glad I'm taller than all of them so no one could get a good look at my roots."

"You mean your mom doesn't embrace her grays like your mother-in-law does?"

"Nope. Quite the opposite. She's been dyeing it religiously since I was a kid. By the way, great job covering Emmaline's bald spot. I appreciate you squeezing her in without notice."

"No problem. It gave me a chance to hone some skills we rarely get to use. I like emergency hair management."

Zola floated in with the same dreamy expression she'd had since Agape House. "What are y'all talking about?"

"How Elisa saved the day when my daughter channeled her inner Edward Scissorhands and cut a massive chunk out of her grandmother's hair."

"Why on earth would she let a child anywhere near her head with scissors?" Zola asked.

"The simple answer is triplets." Josie nodded at Elisa. "But this one here covered it with extensions so masterfully no one will ever know."

"I didn't know your in-laws were local." Zola leaned a hip against the doorframe.

Josie blinked. Usually, Zola offloaded any information—like the whereabouts of her colleagues' relatives—that wasn't about her. Beckett's dad's less charitable assessment about Zola being a narcissist flickered through her mind. His name-calling had been mean-spirited but less off base than Josie had realized back then.

She'd been different lately, though. Whether it was Agape House, the MOMS group, or the new man orbiting her life, Zola had softened. Maybe it was a combination of the three.

"They're not," Josie said. "My mother-in-law came to help Hunter while I was in Albuquerque with my mom."

"I think I did her hair the morning your car wouldn't start, Zoe," said Elisa.

The faraway look in Zola's eyes returned, and she smiled. "You mean the day I met my knight in shining armor. Or in a silver Honda, anyway."

Josie sat in the styling chair and spun it to face Zola. "Wait, so you *didn't* meet Prince Charming on a dating app?" Not that it changed anything. Zola's magnetism of the wrong type extended far beyond online matchups.

Zola shook her head. "Nope. Right here in the parking lot. I had to get a jump from my neighbor to take Beck to school, and then I drove around long enough to charge the battery before I got here. Didn't work though because when I tried to leave for lunch, it was dead again."

She'd shared a lot of information about the car battery and very little about the new man in her life. Josie circled her hand. "Skip to the part about the guy."

"That's just it. My car wouldn't start, so I came inside asking if anyone could give me a jump, and this beautiful man appeared out of nowhere." She sighed much the way she probably had twenty years ago at the mention of Zac Ephron or some other teen heartthrob. "He got my car started and then followed me to the parts store to make sure they installed the new battery without issues, and I could be safely on my way."

"That's when he asked you out?" Elisa inspected her nails.

"I asked *him*, actually, as repayment for all his trouble. But being the gentleman that he is, he wouldn't let me buy dinner. He's so chivalrous." Zola clasped her hands like a Disney princess. "He's been treating me like a queen ever since."

Any second now, woodland creatures would circle around Zola and harmonize a tune. At a minimum, a group of mice were probably already stitching her wedding gown.

Corny though it was, Zola's fairytale-level happiness and whirlwind romance warmed Josie. "That's great. You deserve to be treated like royalty."

Zola sagged against the doorframe. "He's amazing, but I'm still nervous about introducing him to Beckett. Which reminds me why I walked in here. Is there any way you could watch him until eight o'clock Saturday evening? My guy's taking me to a play."

"I guess so. Does he at least *know* you have a kid?" Josie shifted in her seat. Zola had burned through a handful of men who weren't looking for instant families, and if Mr. Jumper Cables was another one of those, she'd be crushed.

"Of course. We tell each other everything. He has two boys of his own. But we agreed to take things slow and wait awhile before we involve the kids."

Such wise decision-making was so…un-Zola-like.

"That's smart," said Elisa. "My sister fell hard for a single dad and his little girl. Then they broke up, and the girl took it even harder than my sister did."

"That's not going to happen to us," Zola snapped. "Just because your sister got dumped doesn't mean I will."

If this were a movie, ominous music would've swelled, scattering the woodland creatures and leaving Zola framed in shadows reserved for villains.

Elisa checked the imaginary watch on her wrist. "Ope. I have a client." She squeezed past Zola. Once safely behind her, she shot Josie a wild-eyed look and twirled a finger near her temple before ducking behind the partition separating their booths.

Their landlady wasn't unhinged, as Elisa's gesture implied, only insecure and self-centered. Not exactly a catch for her Prince Charming.

"You okay there? That took a dark turn," said Josie.

"Fine. I just don't need anyone jinxing my relationship before it even gets off the ground."

Josie stood and idly rearranged her supply drawer, putting distance between herself and Zola's intensity. "That's not a real thing. And Elisa was affirming your decision to delay involving the kids." Which hadn't merited the reaction of a Chihuahua in attack mode.

Zola dropped her head and huffed. "I should apologize to her, shouldn't I?"

Obviously. Instead of saying as much, Josie pursed her lips and raised her chin.

"Fine, I'm going." Zola flopped her arms to her sides and slumped away like a teenager with a Saturday chore list.

She still had a ways to go in her journey to becoming a better person.

Chapter 33
Dana

Stiff from too many hours hunched over her keyboard, Dana leaned back in her chair and stretched. She'd been tailoring Carlos's detailed course notes on memoir writing into a more manageable format for Agape's residents. Serena and the director, Yolanda, were eager to get started with the class as soon as possible rather than waiting until the new year.

"Strike while the iron is hot," Serena had said. "The residents have a fresh fire after the toy drive and job-readiness fair. And there are many more former residents who have moved into permanent housing and are in the next phases of their new lives. They're ready to share their stories of recovery and hope."

Dana's stomach growled. She pushed back from the desk and stood. After the mental aerobics it took to slog through hundreds of pages of curriculum, she'd earned an afternoon snack. Soft laughter filtered through the laundry room door. She made her way into the kitchen where Will stood, arms folded, smiling at something beyond her sightline.

He turned and caught her in his arms. "Come look at

this," he murmured in her ear. "But don't make any sudden movements."

She shot him a dubious look. Were there rhinos in the living room? And why would they be laughing? She peered around the doorway where Adam, Nate, and Leah sat cross-legged on the floor, tossing cards onto a pile between them. Uno. The kids were playing Uno just like the old days.

A reflexive impulse beckoned Dana to go to them and offer snacks, hugs, compliment them for getting along so well. Will must've felt her lurch because he pulled her back by the arm and led her into the kitchen. "Don't interfere, or the magic will fade like that blasted Elf on a Shelf. Leave them alone, and I'll bet you she stays for dinner."

He was onto something. Let Leah think her parents could take or leave her being home, and she'd be more likely to stick around than if she knew that's exactly what they were hoping for.

"Why didn't you tell me when she got here?" Dana asked as she pulled a foil bag of Pop-Tarts out of a box in the pantry.

"I don't even know when that was. I walked out of our room, and her door was open. There she was, lying across the bed with the dog at her side like she'd never left."

Dana had her mouth open, poised to take a bite, and stopped. "Did you talk to her at least?"

Will cocked his head and pursed his lips. "What do you think?"

She bit off the corner of the Pop-Tart and waited him out. He had to know it wasn't really a yes or no question. The details were the part she cared about.

"Of course I talked to her. She said she came home to

look for her fur-lined boots for walking to class now that it's getting colder. But I guess the comfort of home enticed her to settle in. Then Adam did what he does best and made his big sister play a game with him."

"And she's not just killing time over here before she babysits across the street?" Dana would gladly take a visit from Leah any way she could get it, but there was something more special about believing their home, the family, was more than an afterthought to the teen.

Will shrugged. "She hasn't said anything."

Cards rasped and hissed as someone shuffled them.

"Hey, Mom." Leah breezed in and grabbed a bottle of water from the fridge.

Dana told herself to chill out before she came off like an over-excited puppy. "Hi, sweetie." She gave Leah a peck on the temple. "I would have said hello sooner, but I've been holed up in the laundry room and didn't know you were here."

"That's okay. Nate said we should let you work because you were putting together material for a class you'll be teaching."

"Yes, it's a memoir-writing class at a women's shelter." Dana held out the second Pop-Tart in the silver package to Leah.

She took it with a smile. "Memoir. Is that like an autobiography?"

"Exactly. But it usually covers a smaller snippet of time rather than a narrative spanning a person's entire life."

"That's cool. It's like you're helping them share their testimonies."

Dana ducked her head. Her daughter just called her

cool. Technically, she'd said it about the class, but close enough. "That's the plan."

"You're going to do great," Leah said. "What are we having for dinner?"

It wasn't yet four o'clock, and they were both eating Pop-Tarts. Ordinarily, Dana would've pointed this out, but in keeping with Will's advice not to spook Leah, she simply shrugged. "What sounds good to you?"

"Leah, hurry up," yelled Adam. "It's your turn."

"We can figure it out later," said Leah. "I'm not even hungry yet." She skipped back into the living room.

Will's eyes were wide when he whispered, "Did we just have our first unicorn sighting?"

Leah's lightness returning was more evidence that Hirschfield kid had been nothing but trouble.

A soft tap at the front door was barely audible over the kids' card game. Harvey gave a whimper and crammed his hundred-pound body under the coffee table.

Dana opened the door to the triplets and Josie.

"Can we see Leah, please?" Olivia asked with her hands clasped under her chin. Connor and Ben flanked her, bouncing on their toes with all the patience of a boiling teakettle.

"Sure." Dana stepped back, pulling the door wider. The kids ran past her and tackled Leah. Nate grabbed the stack of cards out of the way in the nick of time, Uno postponed for now.

"I'm so sorry to barge in," said Josie. "We were about to go for a walk, and they spotted Leah's car."

"I get it. She's pretty popular around here." Dana motioned Josie inside.

"You never play with us anymore," said Ben.

Leah struggled to sit up under the triplets' weight. "Blame your parents. They haven't asked me to babysit in a while."

Josie plopped onto the sofa. "It's been hectic at our house. I went out of town, and my mother-in-law stayed with the kids and Hunter. We need a date night soon, though." She twisted to face Dana, who'd taken a seat in the club chair across the way. "Get this, my mom has decided to turn over a new leaf and become more laid back about the children's tidiness."

"Your mom. Laid back?" First, a kind, complimentary Leah. Now, a Marie Saldana who tolerated messes. Unicorns were frolicking all over the cul-de-sac.

"We'll see how long it lasts, but she said her obsessive cleanliness stemmed from the same place as my aunt's hoarding issues, and she's afraid it's warping the you-know-who." Josie pointed at her kids as they tussled with the three Harding children. "Too bad she didn't figure that out before she warped my sister and me, but better late than never, I guess."

"Wow. Feels like all kinds of tides are shifting around here." Dana stiffened as soon as the words were out of her mouth. How would she explain the changes in Leah right in front of her? If only Dana could suck the words back in.

"What do you mean?" asked Josie.

Think! "Carlos. He…uh. Well." Dana scratched her head. "He's seeing someone, and we thought it would improve his crankiness, but no. He says he's happier than he's ever been with this woman with the dead battery, but he's still cranky. However, he gave me all the notes from his college memoir course to incorporate into the new class at Agape House, so maybe he's turning the corner after all. Another shifting tide." She took a breath. That was quick thinking. All true. All believable.

"What did you say about a dead battery?" Josie leaned forward.

"I wasn't paying attention to his story as well as I should've been, but he definitely said something about how he had jumper cables in his car, and the lady asked him to dinner to repay his kindness."

Josie jumped out of her seat, hands clasped over her head. "When? When did this happen?"

"I think they had dinner last Saturday."

"What are the odds?" Josie paced in front of the sofa.

"Mama, are you okay?" asked Olivia.

That child had the emotional intelligence of a much older person. She'd make a good therapist someday.

"I'm great, Livvie." Josie dropped her arms. "Dana, a guy came into the salon last Friday when Zola's car battery died. He jumped it for her, and she asked him out for the next night."

Now Dana was on her feet, too. "Carlos went to Sanctuary to deliver Emmaline's purse to her after the unfortunate home haircut."

"All that brainstorming. The party. Our hard work, and it turns out, Emmaline was the true matchmaker, and she didn't even know it," Josie said. "I can't believe it."

"She had Livvie's help," said Dana.

Olivia sat up and thumped her chest. "I'm a good helper."

Josie lowered herself back onto the sofa. "Are we sure

Zola and Carlos are dating, and this isn't a cosmic coincidence? Has he ever said the name of his new lady?"

Dana had already admitted to her poor listening skills, but surely her ears would've pricked at the mention of Zola's name. "I don't think so." An idea took shape, and a smirk played on her lips. "How can we use this to mess with them? We *are* going to mess with them, right?"

"Do you want them to go back to being the grumpy meanies we've been dealing with for months?"

"Meh." Dana shrugged. Carlos hadn't changed, so what difference would it make?

"I'll think on it. Wouldn't hurt for them to have a little payback for what they put us through." Josie rose again. "Kids, say goodbye. We have a walk to get to before it gets too cold."

The triplets took turns hugging Leah, Nate, and Adam and trudged to the door.

"Bye, Dana." Ben waved. "Love you."

"Love you too, Benny. Bye, guys." Dana held the door for the neighbors. Life was so weird in the most wonderful way. If Leah hadn't come by for boots and gotten pulled into a card game with her brothers, the triplets wouldn't have seen her car and insisted on stopping by. Then Dana and Josie would still have no idea that their setup had worked in its own timing. In God's timing, perhaps. She closed the door and crossed the room where her half-eaten toaster pastry waited on the breakfast bar, no longer holding any appeal.

Will traipsed through the room, jiggling his car keys.

"Where were you hiding while the Caraways were here?" Dana asked.

"Wasn't hiding. At least not on purpose. Your dad called."

Her knees went weak, and she gripped the counter for support. Will must've seen the color drain from her face because he rushed to her and took her hands in his.

"Everything is fine, I promise."

"Dad calls you instead of me when something's wrong. Like a kitchen fire or when he's fallen and doesn't want to worry me."

"Dana, it was just about his car. Since he doesn't drive anymore, he wanted to talk with me about options."

She studied his face. He was telling her the truth. No disasters.

"I'm worried if he sells it online, someone will try to take advantage of him," she said.

He leaned close and whispered in her ear. "He wants to give it to Nate for a birthday present. Let's talk about it later, okay?"

"Okay." She and Will had looked at used cars for Nate a few times, but with university tuition payments and the unreal cost of insurance for teenagers, they hadn't found anything that fit their budget.

After getting lost driving to church, Edward had finally made the decision on his own last spring to give up driving. Between the Hardings, his housekeeper Maggie, and rideshare apps, he'd had no trouble getting around. His Buick probably wasn't what Nate had in mind, but a low mileage, well-maintained grandpa car was better than no car at all.

"I'm going to get Edward and bring him here for a family dinner. Nate, you want to drive to pick up your

Pops?" Will asked.

"We're in the middle of something," Nate called as he slapped a card on the pile, the Uno game back in full swing. "Next time."

There may not be a disaster at her dad's house, but what if there was one brewing over here instead? Nate never turned down a chance to drive. "You feeling alright, Nate?"

"I'm fine, Mom. But I'm beating Leah for a change, and if I leave, she'll have the winning record. Draw two, sucka!"

"Well, okay then." Will gave Dana a wink and left through the garage.

She eased onto the barstool and swiveled to watch the kids. Countless times over the years, she'd had to step in and break up sibling fights over friendly competitions that escalated into warfare. Today though, their easy banter gave her all the warm fuzzies, and she savored it. This was heaven.

"Uno!" Leah clutched her last card to her chest and flicked a glance at Dana. "We could deal you in, Mom. No need to sit there staring at us like a weirdo."

Almost heaven anyway, with a side helping of humiliation. "I'm in."

The four of them played until Will returned with Dana's dad in tow.

"I fold." Dana squared up the thick stack of cards she'd struggled to hold and tucked them under the pile. "Hello, Dad." She held onto the coffee table and pulled herself upright.

"Hey, Pops," said Leah as she tossed down her stack and jumped up to hug him. "Remember when you taught me how to change a tire?"

"I know I'm forgetful, but of course I remember that. You were so mad you didn't talk to me for a week afterward." Pops chuckled as he dropped into the club chair.

The spring before she turned sixteen, Leah had gone to her grandfather's house for a brief lesson in car maintenance. Instead, she'd spent the afternoon rotating the Buick's tires and changing the oil. Dana had found her fuming daughter on the front porch, too filthy to wait inside.

"Well, thank you."

Dana almost snapped a vertebra jerking her head so hard. Had she heard her daughter correctly?

"Your gratitude is about three years overdue, but you're welcome, granddaughter."

Will folded his arms and perched on the arm of the sofa. "What brought that up? Did you have to change a tire?"

"Yep. A girl in the parking lot of the dorm had a flat, and these two guys were watching a video online and trying to figure out how to get her jack out of the trunk. I took over and had it changed in ten minutes. Those guys are probably still trying to pick their jaws up off the ground."

"That's my girl," said Pops.

"Why wasn't campus security able to help her? Isn't that one of their jobs?" Dana was all for helping others, but where were the adults when students needed them?

"They said it would be an hour or more before they could get to her. But I saved the day, and we didn't have to wait on a man, or as Pops said, a creeper, to come to our rescue." She straightened at least six inches taller. "And I got to be the one to teach the people standing around how to work a jack and loosen lug nuts. So, I'm basically a rock star at the dorm."

Dana smiled. "I'm proud of you. That's a useful skill to have." She looked over at Nate, who was stuffing Uno cards into their box. "How are your tire-changing skills?"

He shrugged. "Dad said he'd teach me after Thanksgiving."

His Pops shook a finger at him. "You come over, and I'll have you ready to work on a pit crew in one afternoon."

Leah scoffed. "Just make sure you wear grubby clothes because he's also going to make you change the oil and rotate all four tires."

"Why would you rotate less than four?" asked Nate with a surly huff.

Dana drank in the moment, committing it to memory. These were the little things too often taken for granted until they were gone. Three kids at home, a little good-natured ribbing, and her dad firing on all cylinders. What more could she ask for?

Chapter 34
Josie

Josie and the triplets walked several blocks to the park, but their playtime was cut short by a sudden north wind that turned the autumn afternoon blustery.

"Mama, it's too cold." Connor tugged his arms into his shirt, the sleeves dangling limp.

"I agree." Josie pulled him close and wrapped him in a hug to infuse warmth into his little body. "Olivia, Ben, let's go home."

Ben appeared at the bottom of the tube slide. "How 'bout you get the van to pick us up?"

She scooped him up and stood him beside Connor. "How 'bout no."

Olivia hopped off the swing, teeth chattering. "Can you call Daddy?"

Hunter had been at the store when they left. Even if he'd made it home by now, they could run home almost as quickly as he could get to them.

"The exercise will be good for us. Come on." Josie challenged her kids to a race to the corner. They repeated the game all the way back to their cul-de-sac. She punched in the code to unlock the front door and caught a whiff of garlic mixed with the smoky warmth of cumin and chili powder.

Connor stomped inside with more fury than a four-year-old had the right to possess. "Dad, why didn't you pick us up? We almost freezed to death."

"Froze. And no, you didn't." Hunter motioned Josie to him with a sideways nod. "Taste this." He pulled a large wooden spoon out of the stockpot, blew over the top of it, and held it out to her.

Josie's eyes rolled back as she savored the faint bite of peppers and the sweetness of onion. "This is delicious, babe. How did you make chili so fast?"

"Y'all were gone for a while, but it's a simple recipe. The hardest part was browning the meat."

She pressed her icy fingers to his neck. "Thank you for making dinner, but what makes you think the kids will eat chili?" They rarely tried new foods, and if it had even a hint of spice, they turned up their noses at it.

"Mom made chili while you were in Albuquerque. Turns out if you put chips in it and sprinkle cheese on top, they'll try just about anything." Hunter lowered his voice and shot her a sly smile. "Don't call it Frito pie, though. They don't like that. It's 'cheesy chip dip'."

"Whatever works." She laughed. "Kids, go wash up. Dad made cheesy chip dip like Gramma."

"Oh, yum!" Ben ran to the bathroom, his siblings hot on his heels.

Josie snagged a Frito from the open bag and dragged it through the chili. "Speaking of your mom, guess what I found out." She regaled him with the story she and Dana pieced together about how Carlos and Zola had met because of Emmaline's impromptu trip to the salon. "Maybe Dana and I should start our own matchmaking service. We clearly have better instincts than the dating apps."

"Or maybe since they met on their own without your meddling, it's God's way of telling you to stay out of other people's personal lives." Hunter winked.

"Shush. Everything worked out exactly how we hoped it would." Except for the part where Carlos was supposed to get happy and stop being mean about their group's romance novels.

"Speaking of my mom, I called her to find out what to buy for the chili, and I told her about Marie's transformation."

"It's a bit soon to call it that. She had one day of not harping on the kids for their messes," Josie huffed. "Let's see how long that lasts."

"I think she's sincere. Your aunt's flood opened her eyes to her own issues." He ladled chili into bowls. "The timing of her philosophical makeover is perfect since she's going to experience the full Caraway effect in Oklahoma at Thanksgiving."

"Or she'll revert back to her old fastidious ways as a result."

Hunter chuckled and nodded in agreement. "Mom said really nice things about you and how proud she is that you broke the cycle of generational affliction."

Her brows shot up. "Is that her way of calling my housekeeping lax? Or saying my parenting style is a bit too free-range for my mom's liking?" It was. Marie Saldana had said as much on plenty of occasions, but she couldn't bear the thought of Emmaline saying so, too. It conjured thoughts of her difficult client, Mrs. Pierce, who relentlessly criticized her own daughter-in-law.

"No, Josie. She's thankful for you."

Heat flooded Josie's cheeks. She busied herself adding chips and shredded cheese to the bowls to avoid meeting Hunter's eye. "That was sweet of her. A little random, but sweet." She said a silent prayer for the Pierce family, that they might experience a transformation of their own that led to deeper mutual respect.

The doorbell rang. Josie and Hunter exchanged questioning glances. Thinking maybe Leah hadn't gotten enough of the triplets earlier, Josie opened the door without checking the peephole first. Her gut clenched at the sight of Zola standing on the porch with her hand on Beckett's shoulder. Babysitting had slipped Josie's mind as soon as she'd agreed to it, but she quickly fixed her face to mask her shock.

"Hey, I was just wondering where y'all were." Josie beckoned them inside.

Zola pulled her knee-length houndstooth coat closed and urged a hesitant Beckett ahead of her. "I texted you like an hour ago."

Josie patted her back pocket. Empty again. Why did she even bother having a phone when it wasn't with her half the time? No matter. At least she was home, and Zola never needed to know about her slip. "Beckett, Hunter made Frito pie, but if you aren't a fan of chili, we can make you a sandwich."

The boy drifted toward the kitchen.

"He eats just about everything. My mom will be by to pick him up as soon as she and my grandma get out of BINGO," said Zola.

"What play are you and Carlos going to see?" Josie bit the inside of her cheek to tame her amusement.

"It's a community college production of *My Fair Lady.*"

"Are some of his students performing?" Dana probably had a better idea in mind when she suggested messing with Zola and Carlos, but Josie couldn't resist.

"I'm not sure." Zola shifted on her black high-heeled boots. "Wait. I don't remember telling you his name, and I *know* we never talked about his career." She narrowed her eyes. "Are you stalking me?"

"Yes, with all my free time between juggling work and three kids."

"Then how do you know so much about the guy I'm seeing?"

"Lubbock isn't that big, and people talk." A knowing smile crossed Josie's face. "You met him at the salon when he jumped your dead battery on the same day Dana's writer friend brought my mother-in-law's purse to her at the salon and used his jumper cables to help a woman in need."

Realization dawned on Zola's face. "Oh wow! All this time you and Dana could've set me up with an amazing man, and neither of you thought to?" Her slight headshake said everything about her disappointment.

Take the high road, Josie. She flicked that whispering angel right off her shoulder. "If you'd shown up to our end-of-summer block party about ten minutes sooner, you and Carlos could've started your happily ever after a week earlier." She sucked air through her teeth and shrugged. "He's who I wanted you to meet that night, but his son had a minor mishap, and they had to leave before you arrived."

"Are you kidding?" Zola's jaw dropped.

"Nope. And did either of you know you missed meeting at Agape House by less than an hour?"

Zola narrowed her eyes. "What are you talking about?"

"Carlos volunteered for the morning shift writing resumes." Josie cocked her head. "It didn't come up on your first date that night?"

"We were getting to know each other, not bragging about our good deeds." Zola gave her another look that mirrored Marie Saldana's displeasure—before her newfound enlightenment, that is. Zola rearranged her features into their former jubilance and flicked her wrist. "No matter. We've found each other now, and that's the important part. I better run."

Josie walked her out and almost fell over when the tiny salon owner turned and gave her an unbidden hug. "Thank you. You're a good friend."

As Zola teetered on her heels, Josie stood motionless, too stunned to even wave. Finally, she closed the door and made a mad dash to the kitchen to give Hunter a full report. "You're not going to believe who Zola's—" She remembered her audience as four little pairs of eyes fixed on her.

"Do you know my mom's new boyfriend?" Beckett blew over his bowl of chili.

Josie's gaze met Hunter's. "Y'all heard all that, huh?"

Connor gave her a toothy grin and popped a chip with the tiniest amount of "dip" on it he could manage into his mouth.

Hunter was probably right. Minding her own business and letting God arrange other people's affairs was the wiser way to go, but life was so much sweeter when people showed up—messes and all—and got all up in each other's lives.

Chapter 35
Dana

Dana clicked off the projector and closed her laptop. The first memoir class at Agape House had five students, including Yolanda. They'd taken notes on legal pads Yolanda handed out at the start of class and scribbled furiously as Dana clicked through her PowerPoint presentation.

"Your assignment for next week is this: write one to three pages about an object. Any object you've owned, seen, imagined, or wished you could own. Describe it and write about what made it so special." She could practically see the wheels turning behind the ladies' eyes as each considered what she would write.

As they filed out, Dana thanked them individually for coming. Her whole body shook as Yolanda grasped Dana's hand between both of hers and pumped it.

"I can't thank you enough for what you're doing here. Being able to express feelings and put words to the experiences they've gone through is a real gift to the women here. And to get to learn at the feet of such a talented author is a real treat."

Dana's cheeks grew hot. "I don't know how talented I

am. My friend Carlos is the one you should be thanking. He teaches writing at the community college, and he's a true best-selling author. I'm borrowing from his course material for this class."

"Please pass along my gratitude to Mr. Carlos," said Yolanda. She nodded toward the door where a woman lingered, eying her notepad. "I think someone is waiting patiently to speak with you. I'll see you next week." Yolanda patted Dana's hand again and slipped out.

The loiterer stepped cautiously to the front table. Her shy smile was half hidden behind her hair draped over the side of her face. She tucked a strand behind her ear and hugged the notepad to her chest. "I don't think I quite know how to describe my object. How would you write about an old piano that hadn't been tuned or taken care of in so long that its notes came out flat and haunting, but somehow, it gave you dreams of becoming a concert musician?"

Dana closed her eyes for a moment, envisioning a little girl sitting on a worn piano bench. "I can't say how *I* would write about it, but the way you just described sounds perfect. It's your story to tell, and the way it impacted *you* is the right way to tell it." Dana tapped the edge of the notepad. "You should write down what you told me because I pictured the flat and haunting notes reverberating from a worn, neglected piano, and I'm excited to hear more about it in our next class."

The student heaved a sigh of relief. "Okay good. This is my first time writing anything since high school, and I want to get it right."

"All you have to do is try. We'll learn how to make our words have more impact with the way we use them, but you're already on the right track."

The woman straightened, confidence lifting her just as it had the ladies at the job-readiness fair as they bolstered their resumes and saw themselves in a new light. "I can't wait to get started." She turned to go and stopped. "If I finish this early, what else should I write about?"

"Hmm." Carlos's notes scrolled through Dana's mind as she fished for a prompt that would develop the student's awareness of sensory writing and not dismiss her request thoughtlessly. "The best meal you've ever eaten. Write about what it looked and smelled like. What sounds were around you when you were eating it? How did it taste, and how did eating it make you feel?"

The woman stooped over the table, her lips moving slightly as her pen scrawled across the page. When she finished, she stood, gave Dana a silent nod, and left.

The drive home gave Dana time to ponder what she would have to say in her own story. What object would she have chosen to write about if she were a student in the class? A pen, perhaps. Her writing career began with a simple ballpoint, and she'd journaled her life's most important moments with a pen. Or maybe the ring Will had given her with each of the children's birthstones. Motherhood had defined her for the better part of two decades, and it was still teaching lessons at every turn.

A sports car revved its engine in the lane beside her. She'd certainly wondered what it would be like to own a fancy two-seater rather than a jumbo SUV large enough to haul a basketball team. It usually smelled like it transported a basketball team, too. Or livestock. An image of Jordan Hirschfield leaning against a Camaro flashed in her mind.

That rotten little… She let the thought fade unfinished. He wasn't worth the aggravation.

She pulled into the garage and narrowly avoided knocking over Adam's bike opening her door. His laziness should have annoyed her but instead only made her thankful once again for a life filled with blessings.

"Hey, Adam," she called a moment before she spotted him hunched over a book at the breakfast bar, pencil in hand.

"Yes?"

The sight took her by surprise, the bike all but forgotten. "I can't remember the last time a kid in this house had homework from an actual textbook instead of on a computer."

"What's a textbook?" He lifted the tome, revealing a cartoon cover. "It's a graphic novel, and this isn't homework. I'm teaching myself how to draw Marvel characters."

Dana set her tote bag on the counter next to a leftover container filled with LEGO bricks. "Where did these come from?"

Adam returned to his sketching. "Nate and I found them when we were cleaning our rooms."

"You cleaned your rooms? Both of you?" Dana looked around for a hidden camera. Someone had to be pranking her.

"We got in trouble for fighting, so Dad made us clean our rooms and grounded us from screens."

That made much more sense. Dana picked up the container of bricks and shook it. The object she'd write about would be LEGOs. They'd defined this season in so many ways. They represented the intersection between order, chaos, creativity, and pain. She huffed a small laugh.

"What's so funny?" asked Adam.

"Just thinking about your brother and sister sorting all those LEGOs. Genius idea you had there."

"I don't get nearly enough credit for my bright ideas."

"That's the burden of being the baby of the family, kiddo. You're hardly a little boy anymore though." Another fact made obvious by his decision to donate the construction bricks.

"Mom, I haven't been little for a while." Adam's tone, which mirrored Leah's in edge and Nate's in timbre, was evidence of the truth in his words.

Dana could no more write her children's stories for them than she could write anyone else's. Not the ladies' in her class. Not Carlos and Zola's. If she could, she'd keep her kids young for a little longer and blot out every inkling of pain—for all of them. There'd be no disappointment and nary a controlling or abusive relationship on any page. She would never be able to do justice to their stories anyway. God alone was the Author, and His ways were higher and better than anything she could dream up to pen. Nonetheless, she was thankful for the front row seat to watch them play out, to cheer them on, and to remind them that hope was always within reach.

Acknowledgements

My deepest gratitude to Team Barnabus—Allison Nance, Paula Peckham, Mary Hamilton, and Douglas Brown. Your weekly feedback has made me a better writer and given me stronger stories to tell. I love that we also get to celebrate life together and pray over one another, like a little literary family.

I'm so thankful to Cynthia Hickey for giving the Frazzled Moms wings.

Thank you as well to my wonderful friends—Kristen Leonard, Christina Barritt, Shyla Wilson, and Gina Bridges—who patiently read excerpts, answered my endless questions, and offered their expert advice.

To my mom, Sharon Whorton: thank you for being my willing first reader, my best marketer, and my most enthusiastic sales representative. And special thanks to your friends, who have become such loyal readers.

I am especially thankful for Brent. You are exactly the husband I prayed for, and I love our life together. Thank you for bringing me food and drinks while I write, for feeding the dependents—human and four-legged—and for encouraging me again and again. Without you and our children, I would have no inspiration for the Frazzled Moms. Life would be tidier but completely boring and meaningless.

And finally, dear Jesus, thank you for inviting me on this journey with You. I can't write a single word without You, and I pray we get to write many more together.